THE SWORD AND THE DAMSEL

The De Veres, Book 2

Leslie Vollard

ARE YOU SIGNED UP FOR DRAGONBLADE'S BLOG?

You'll get the latest news and information on exclusive giveaways, exclusive excerpts, coming releases, sales, free books, cover reveals and more.

Check out our complete list of authors, too!

No spam, no junk. That's a promise!

Sign Up Here

www.dragonbladepublishing.com

Dearest Reader;

Thank you for your support of a small press. At Dragonblade Publishing, we strive to bring you the highest quality Historical Romance from some of the best authors in the business. Without your support, there is no 'us', so we sincerely hope you adore these stories and find some new favorite authors along the way.

Happy Reading!

CEO, Dragonblade Publishing

**Additional Dragonblade books by
Author Leslie Vollard**

The De Veres Series
The Skull and the Lute (Book 1)
The Sword and the Damsel (Book 2)
The Broken and the Bold (Book 3)

CHAPTER ONE

Winchelsea, 1176 AD

ALAIS HAD PROMISED she wouldn't sneak out to meet a man again, but no one would be the wiser if she didn't get caught. And why would she?

As a second daughter, Alais was strictly ornamental. She might as well have been a tapestry on the wall for all the attention they paid her. No one listened when she tried to speak up on topics of substance. No one cared what she thought about the running of the town or political intrigue with the local nobles. Her only purpose was to look pretty and attract men. Was it her fault if she was a little too successful for her family's liking?

Gilbert was waiting when she arrived in the forest clearing a mile outside of Winchelsea where they agreed to meet. She took a moment to appreciate the lazy ease of his form as he strummed his lute and hummed. His half-blue, half-green cotte draped sinuously around him, and fitted, brown hose clung to his shapely legs. He had perfected the sensitive poet look with his lithe body, only delicately muscled, and the mop of chestnut curls that hung rakishly in his face. There was a dimple in his cheek that made her melt, and long, thick lashes dripped over those sinful blue eyes filled with ardor.

"Alais, I was afraid you wouldn't come," he said, putting

down his lute and helping her down from her horse.

"I almost didn't." She glanced around cautiously. "If we're caught—"

He put a long, tapered finger on her lips. "Shh. We won't be caught." He let his finger trail down and trace the neckline of her low-cut, blue dress. She could hardly breathe as warmth curled all through her. Her whole body must have been blushing.

Pulling her into his arms, he touched his lips to hers. It was like being carried away with the tide, a blissful oblivion. Alais lost track of what was around her. His kiss was overpowering, delicious. This was so much more decadent than the furtive kisses she'd stolen with previous admirers.

Was it love? Was this the grand romance she dreamed of? Her parents would consider him completely unsuitable, not that it mattered to her. She would happily sacrifice everything for the right man. But the right man would be willing to do the same for her, and somehow she suspected Gilbert wasn't the self-sacrificing sort.

Oh well. He was good for a few stolen kisses, and then she would let him go.

They collapsed together onto the soft grass. He continued to kiss her, tantalizing her neck, then tasting the bare skin above her neckline. New sensations flooded her senses as she offered herself up, drawn in by his caresses. Gilbert loosened the ties of her dress and slid her shoulder free so that he could taste it too. Things were going too far. She knew she should stop, but she couldn't resist the heat coursing through her.

A twig cracked nearby. She froze.

"Is something wrong, my love?" Gilbert nuzzled her neck.

Drowning once again in the bliss of his caress, she shook it off. "I'm sure it's nothing. Probably some animal."

Kissing her again, he reached down to start pulling up the skirt of her dress. He was going too far. She was about to stop him when…

"Alais?"

Oh no.

"Carenza?" Alais said, her voice oddly squeaky as she rolled away from Gilbert and tugged her dress back into decency.

Her sister, Carenza Rossignol, Countess of Winchelsea, towered above her on a majestic black horse, looking every inch a noble huntress in her leathers and blood-red gown. Carenza's hooded peregrine falcon dug its talons into her thick leather glove, and a brace of bloody hares hung from her saddlebag. Her eyes bored into Alais.

"I didn't know you were hunting," Alais said faintly as she finished making herself presentable.

Gilbert started edging away, the coward. As she suspected, he wasn't willing to fight for her when it mattered.

Carenza pinned him to the spot with an imperious glare. "You," she said, pointing her finger at him as if it was a sword. "Don't move." He hunched and shrank away, as if attempting to make himself small. "Alais, get on Snow now," she ordered without sparing her sister a glance.

Alais obeyed, mounting her beloved Snow, and looking nervously at her lover.

"Uc," Carenza called out, never taking her eyes off Gilbert. The castle falconer appeared through the trees and rode toward them with a fearsome goshawk on his arm. "We're going back to the castle," she told him. "See that this man accompanies us. We have business to attend to."

"Yes, my lady," Uc said, bowing his head, then fixing Gilbert with a steely, hostile look.

Alais knew Uc was a soft touch. She'd had him wrapped around her finger from her earliest days, but Gilbert looked like he might pass out as the grizzled falconer narrowed his eyes and beckoned him to approach. It was disappointing, really, that he didn't have a bit more spine. But then he was just a troubadour. What did she expect?

"Come," Carenza ordered in a sharp voice. Alais obeyed, tearing her eyes away from Gilbert.

She hardly dared raise her head, let alone speak as they made their way back inside the city walls, past the raucous docks, and onto the worn cobblestones of Castle Street.

"Are you going to tell Mother?" Alais ventured to ask as they rode up the street past inns, taverns, and merchant stalls. The All Saints' Day mass must have just been let out. The streets were teeming with ostentatiously humble pilgrims, some of them sporting seashells from Santiago de Compostela as if they were fine jewels.

"I should, you know."

"But you won't?"

Carenza took a deep breath and let it out. "It depends."

"On what?"

I'll grovel. I'll spend a week in silent contemplation in the chapel. I'll bribe you with honey cakes.

"On him," Carenza said, looking ahead.

Jesus' fishes on toast. I am in so much trouble.

⇻⇻⇻✦⇺⇺⇺

AN HOUR LATER, Alais sat on her bed, knees tucked to her chest, staring at the tapestry on her wall. It depicted young ladies on their palfreys, prancing across a flowering field. They seemed to be mocking her with their carefree smiles. She knew she was in for it this time.

The door opened, and she scrambled to sit up straight. Carenza came in, sat beside her, and took her hand.

"He's gone. He won't be coming back. I'm sorry it had to be this way." Carenza gave Alais's hand a gentle squeeze.

Thank God! Carenza is feeling sympathetic.

"It's not fair, you know. You got to marry your troubadour. Why couldn't you let me have a little fun with mine?"

"Daniel turned out to be an earl. I'm afraid Gilbert was only a clever man with a silver tongue and no name or fortune to speak of. You are lucky I was the one who caught you."

"I know," Alais admitted, defeated, "but I still wish you hadn't."

"Of course," Carenza said with a weary sigh. "One thing this makes clear to me is that we need to find you a husband. We can't put it off anymore. I'll speak to Mother about it."

"A husband? Now?" Alais sat bolt upright and stared at Carenza. "I want to marry. You know I do, but not until I find the right man."

"Then you'll have to find the right man quickly. We can't risk this happening again."

"It won't! I swear to you I'll be good!"

Carenza narrowed her eyes. "No, you won't. I know you, Alais. You'll be kissing someone new by the end of the week, and I might not arrive in time to stop you from ruin next time. You're eighteen years old, and it's high time you were married."

"Oh, don't act so high and mighty. I remember how you ran away when you were told to wed. Besides, you're only three years older than me. I don't know what gives you the right to decide my future." It really was ridiculous how condescending Carenza acted, as if having a child entitled her to mother Alais.

"You've been caught kissing three times in the last six months, and each time it was a different man. And today, it looked like you were planning to go a lot further than kissing."

Only three times that you know of, sister. I'm sneakier than you give me credit for.

"Lord Peter was not my fault. He cornered me, and I couldn't escape." *He was handsy as they come, and a sloppy kisser too.*

"It certainly didn't look like you were trying very hard."

"I was about to stop Gilbert," Alais said, ignoring Carenza's snide little comment. "I wouldn't have let him—"

"That's not what it looked like to me." Carenza gave her a hard look. "You're getting married. We can't keep doing this."

Alais closed her eyes. This was what she'd been dreading all along—a forced choice between men who would almost certainly treat her just like her family did. She would become some boring lord's ornament, relegated to making babies and sewing tapestries, all dreams of a grand romance crushed and all hope of having her intelligence acknowledged lost. Tears prickled behind her eyes, and she took a deep breath to stifle them.

"Take some time," Carenza said, not unkindly. "Rest and compose yourself, and I'll see you at dinner. The ward Helisende, Countess of Hastings, is sending to us should arrive today. You should be there with the rest of us to greet him."

Alais groaned. "I don't particularly want to meet anyone the countess might send. I still haven't forgiven her for holding Mother, Iselda, and me prisoner last year. And I bet she's still angling to get me to marry that nasty nephew she kept mentioning as a match." The countess had been a relatively gracious captor, but Alais had never been happier to see someone than when her brother-in-law arrived to secure their release.

"I know how you feel," Carenza said. "I'm not looking forward to this either. But we must do our best not to hold the sins of the countess against the poor child who will probably be terrified. I'm told his name is Victor. Do your best to be welcoming, will you?"

Alais sighed. "I will. You know I'd never be mean to a child."

"I know. And thank you."

Carenza gave Alais's shoulder a gentle squeeze and left her alone with her thoughts. Upon her sister's departure, Alais indulged in a good, long wallow. She'd never asked to be born a noblewoman. If she weren't a baron's daughter, no one would be nearly so concerned with her virtue.

This was all Gilbert's fault. He'd definitely had no business reaching beneath her skirts. And she truly had been about to stop him, not that anyone believed her. They all believed the worst just because she liked kissing. Her own mother had called her "wanton" the last time she was caught. Not that her mother paid attention to her except when she misbehaved.

Carenza was probably right. She *should* marry. She strongly suspected that the pleasures of the marriage bed would do much to calm her body's voracious appetites. But she hadn't met anyone she liked nearly enough to marry, and she was terrified they'd force her into a match she didn't want. The men she'd met so far were fine for kissing, at least some of them, but she had yet to meet one who truly piqued her interest. They were all so dull and shallow. None of them bothered to get to know the real her. Gilbert was the best of the lot and look what a disappointment he'd turned out to be.

She got into bed and pulled the covers over her head, giving in to the urge to cry now that she was alone. This wasn't the way it was supposed to happen. She was supposed to find a love match. Her parents promised after Carenza's disastrous engagement to Raymond de Broase, Earl of Hawkhurst, the previous year. Wasn't her family supposed to stand by her instead of throwing her to the wolves? Or, more likely, to a sheep? Which would be boring and above all, disappointing. A wolf would at least be interesting. *Please, dear Lord, don't make me marry a sheep.*

CHAPTER TWO

THE SUN WAS low in the sky when Alais's maid, Dora, came in to help her get ready for dinner.

"What happened, my lady?" Dora asked, her green eyes twinkling in her wrinkled face, beneath her crown of white hair. She poured water into the wash basin and dipped a cloth in to bathe Alais's tear-stained face.

"It's nothing. I can't talk about it."

"Is it because Gilbert left? I only just heard." She gently washed Alais's cheeks. The cool water was so soothing.

Alais closed her eyes and took a deep breath. "It's nothing, Dora. I'll be fine."

"As you wish, my lady." She wrung out the cloth and went to the wardrobe to help Alais pick a dress. "I think you should wear your red dress tonight."

"Really? I don't really feel like I'm in a red-dress mood. Do I have anything gray?"

"Trust me, my lady. Wear a red dress. It's your battle armor. If they see you melancholy, they'll ask questions. Your red dress always makes you stand taller."

Alais had to admit to herself that Dora was right and acquiesced. The folds of the gown hugged her curves, and the gold trim around the square neck accentuated the swell of her breasts. A matching gold belt dangled in a V from her waist. The sleeves were fitted from shoulder to elbow and dripped down in generous gathers to reveal her pale, delicate forearms. Her thick chestnut hair cascaded down her back in waves with a subtle curl at the ends. She felt confident, regal, aloof. It was perfect.

"Thank you, Dora. You were right, as usual."

When she went down to dinner, she was determined not to give the family any hint of her inner turmoil. She managed to joke and laugh as if nothing was amiss, despite her feelings. She commented on her mother's change of tapestries in the great hall, replacing picnicking nobles in a floral field with autumnal hunting scenes. Carenza kept giving her glances across the table, which Alais ignored.

Toward the end of dinner, a servant announced, "Sir Victor of Guestling to see the Earl."

Alais had almost forgotten about the ward from Lady Helisende. *Sir Victor?* This ward was old enough to be a knight? That didn't bode well. She had hoped he would be someone young, innocent, and malleable, who could grow to be part of the family. An older youth might be resentful and make trouble.

"Send him in," said Daniel with a nod.

She gasped as a full-grown man walked through the door, and she was not the only one. Daniel stood up, his brow furrowed and his jaw tense. Carenza reached for his hand, a warning look on her face. Alais shivered as the man's glance traveled over each member of the assembled party and settled, last, on her.

He was tall and powerfully built and walked with deadly grace, but the first thing that drew her eye was a diagonal scar across his face. His right eye was covered by an eyepatch, and a line of scar tissue ran from the patch, across his nose, and down to the left corner of his mouth, giving him a permanent half smile. His one visible eye was deep twilight blue, and his sandy blond hair hung to his shoulders. He wore a brown leather tunic with cap sleeves and buckles down the front that conformed to the shape of his muscular chest, and the sinuous lines of his arms and legs were plain to see beneath the fine, black fabric of his fitted shirt and hose.

He must have once been devastatingly handsome, and Alais couldn't help whispering to Carenza, "What happened to his face?"

She hadn't meant to be overheard and immediately regretted saying anything at all.

He turned his piercing blue eye on her. The palpable tension in the room heightened. Daniel's hand strayed to his sword, and Alais's father gave subtle hand signals to the servants to summon armed guards.

"Cut myself shaving. Very clumsy," he said, deadpan, looking her in the eye.

For a long moment, no one reacted. Daniel's fingers twitched against his sword hilt.

Then Alais couldn't help herself and burst into loud, awkward laughter. "Oh, I like you! You're funny!"

He laughed with her, and the tension in the room broke. He had a marvelous laugh, rich, sonorous, and infectious. Soon everyone at the table was chuckling, though Carenza kicked Alais's foot beneath the table.

"Thank God he has a sense of humor. Now keep your mouth shut," Carenza whispered while everyone else was distracted.

She really hadn't meant to be rude. Or overheard. Everyone else must have been wondering the exact same thing. Could she help it if she said what they were all thinking?

"Lord Daniel and Lady Carenza Rossignol, I am at your service," he said with a bow to Daniel and Carenza. "My aunt sends her regards to you and the whole de Vere family." He bowed to Alais's parents, Lord Martin, and Lady Isabella de Vere. "From what she told me of her reasons for sending me, though, I don't imagine her regards are particularly welcome. Nonetheless, here I am as a peace offering. I know your agreement specified she should send a ward or someone to marry into your family. I'm a little old to be a ward. I think my aunt is hoping I'll marry, but I assure you I have no such expectation. Instead, if you'll have me,

I am prepared to swear fealty to you and enter your service. My aunt has released me from my oath to her so that I can join your household."

Daniel stroked his thick, black beard. "I asked for a ward, not a vassal. This violates the terms of our agreement. Why should I accept you instead of tying you up and taking my knights to Hastings to remind your aunt what she agreed to?"

Sir Victor knelt slowly and then drew his sword, presenting it hilt first to Daniel.

"I'm a skilled fighter and an experienced battle commander, and my sword is yours, my liege, even if you order me to use it against my aunt. This is what she asked of me, and it is what I offer. Please, accept my sword."

Daniel refrained from taking the sword, but he nodded slowly. "Tell me more. Of what value are you to me? I have swordsmen aplenty."

"With all due respect to your swordsmen, it is unlikely you have any with my skill and experience. I returned a year ago from leading my aunt's troops in Spain where we supported King Sancho II of Castilla and Leon against the Umayyads in the south."

"Mark," Daniel ordered one of the servants, "Go get Sir John and two wooden swords." Then he turned back to Sir Victor, who was still kneeling. "Tell me more."

"My aunt assigned me to lead Hastings's Watch upon my return, so I have experience tracking and apprehending criminals and scofflaws and thwarting their activities," Sir Victor continued. "I speak and read French, Spanish, and Latin. I have long familiarity with the traders and port business of Hastings and could be of assistance ensuring the smooth operations of your custom house."

Daniel nodded slowly. If Alais had to guess, he was softening toward this idea.

At that moment, Sir John came in with two wooden swords. The sinewy old man looked wary as he assessed the stranger before him.

"Sir John commands my soldiers," Daniel said. "He's as skilled a swordsman as any I've ever met. You will fight to the first touch with wooden swords. The hit must be on the torso. Limbs don't count. And you'll lose automatically if you strike above the shoulders. If you win, you stay. If Sir John wins, I tie you up and take you back to your aunt. Understood?"

"Yes, my lord," Sir Victor said, standing and sheathing his actual sword. With a perfunctory bow to John, he accepted the wooden sword. Sir John bowed back, and they took their positions.

"Begin," Daniel called out, and Alais could hardly breathe. This might well be the most interesting dinner she'd ever had. Sir John was a formidable opponent. She'd watched him fight on many occasions and rarely had anyone bested him. On the other hand, this newcomer looked every inch a fighter, his long powerful arms moving with deadly precision.

The wooden blades clacked again and again, their movement too swift to follow. At first, it seemed they were evenly matched, then Sir Victor gained ground, forcing Sir John back into the limited space at the end of the dining hall. John thrust. Sir Victor dodged. A loud thwack sounded as Sir Victor's blade smacked against Sir John's left side, just below his ribs.

Alais realized she had bitten her lower lip hard enough to bleed and promptly let it go, trying to ignore the general warmth she felt after watching such a display.

Sir John stood straight and turned to Daniel, panting. "He's a fine swordsman, my lord. He beat me cleanly, no tricks." Turning back to Sir Victor, Sir John bowed, and Sir Victor returned the gesture. The two of them seemed pleased with each other, as if delighted to have found a truly worthy opponent.

After handing back his wooden sword, Sir Victor turned to Daniel, unsheathing his real sword once more. "Will you accept my sword, my lord?"

Daniel gave him a long, assessing look. "I will."

Once again, Sir Victor knelt and held out his sword. "Upon my faith, I swear to be faithful to you, Daniel Rossignol, Earl of Winchelsea. I will never cause you harm, and I will observe my homage to you completely against all persons in good faith and without deceit."

Daniel accepted his blade and his vow and invited him to stand.

"I hear you are a troubadour, my lord," Sir Victor said, smiling as Daniel shook his hand. "I've made a hobby of learning every lewd troubadour song I can find, though I'm sure that won't endear me to the ladies present."

Intriguing.

Daniel laughed, returning to his chair. He was hooked. No doubt about it.

I guess this Sir Victor will be staying. She regretted her careless words even more now. No matter who he was, she didn't want yet another person in the castle to think she was thoughtless and shallow, though perhaps in this case, she deserved it.

"You know the one with the cat?" Daniel asked.

"And the man from Auvergne? Indeed, I do," he said. His crooked smile was infectious.

Oh my. I absolutely must hear this song.

"Ha! Well, I'm sure we'll find a way to put your various talents to use. Come join us. Have some dinner. Let me introduce you to the family. This is my wife, Carenza Rossignol, Countess of Winchelsea." She nodded her head politely. "Lord Martin and Lady Isabella de Vere are my vassals but also my in-laws." They inclined their heads in acknowledgment. "And these are their two youngest daughters, Lady Alais and Lady Iselda." When Alais looked up from her polite nod, a sharp shock ran through her as their gazes briefly met. She couldn't recall ever having such a strong reaction to a man. It must be her mistrust. Anyone sent by Lady Helisende was suspect, especially this entirely unexpected man.

Daniel offered the seat across from him, which happened to

be next to Alais. She kept quiet as he talked with Daniel and her father about the port's business, listening carefully. No one knew or cared that she took an interest in how Winchelsea was run. Why should a second daughter bother? Besides, they all thought she was a brainless flirt. And she *was* a flirt, just not a brainless one.

This Sir Victor was quite knowledgeable, easily keeping pace with her father. He'd be a great help to Daniel who was still so new to it all.

Funny, smart, competent, if still highly suspicious. And I had to insult him with the first words out of my mouth.

She kept quiet under Carenza's watchful gaze, only speaking to pass food.

"Oh, I'd skip the venison if I were you, my lord," she said as Sir Victor asked her to pass the dish. "It's a bit tough tonight, and the cooks over-spiced it. Try the snapper instead. It's delicious." She passed the platter with the snapper. Determined to do everything in her power to make up for her earlier blunder, she gave him her warmest and sweetest smile.

"Thank you, my lady," he said, serving himself some.

"Get some of the red wine sauce too. It's divine."

He complied and took a bite. "Mm, that is good. Thank you for saving me from mediocre venison. I am in your debt."

Carenza was momentarily distracted by a question from Daniel, and Alais decided to take full advantage.

"Then perhaps," she said in a conspiratorial whisper, "you'll explain about the song about the cat? I'm dying of curiosity."

Sir Victor nearly choked on his snapper. "I don't think your family would approve, my lady." He nodded at Carenza who turned to give them a suspicious look.

"Don't worry about her. She doesn't approve of anything." She said it loud enough for Carenza to hear, which earned her a kick under the table. "Well, you don't! Ow!" Another kick. "Do you have sisters?"

"No," said Sir Victor. "I was an only child. My mother died

when I was young."

"I'm sorry about your mother. Be grateful you don't have sisters, though. They ruin all your fun."

"When have I ever ruined your fun?" her younger sister Iselda interjected from her other side, her long brown braid draped over her shoulder.

"Not you. You're lovely." Alais gave Iselda a little side hug. "*She's* the one that ruins everything." She pointed her knife at Carenza.

"I know you're mad at me," Carenza said through gritted teeth, "but can you please try to behave with some civility in front of our guest?"

Alais laid a hand on Sir Victor's arm and batted her eyelashes at him. "Do you find my behavior objectionable, my lord?"

Sir Victor's brow furrowed, and he stared at her with undisguised disapproval. Obviously, his answer to her question was *yes*.

"I'm sorry, my lord." She released his hand and dropped the flirtatious look. "I didn't mean to make you uncomfortable."

Christ's eyebrows. He must still be mad about what I said.

Alais managed to behave herself for the rest of dinner, but barely. She stayed as quiet and demure as she could manage. Pretending boredom, she listened avidly while Daniel and her father quizzed Sir Victor about his work in Hastings and his time in Spain, but when the conversation turned away from Sir Victor, she found herself ruminating once again about the dismal prospect of a loveless marriage. If only she hadn't gotten caught with Gilbert...

At last, dinner was over, and she couldn't wait to retreat to the privacy of her room where she wouldn't have to pretend anymore. Sir Victor kissed the hands of each of the ladies present before taking his leave. When he came to Alais, she wondered what he was thinking as he took her hand and glanced at her before letting his lips brush her skin. He looked conflicted, angry almost, but he lingered over her. A little shiver shot through her as he released her hand. Whether it was a shiver of pleasure or of dislike, she wasn't entirely sure.

He made her feel things—mostly shame and embarrassment. And he was Lady Helisende's nephew. But she couldn't help admitting to herself she was intrigued.

CHAPTER THREE

"GIVE ME A moment to look this over." Lord Daniel stroked his thick, black beard as he took his time reviewing the proposed duty roster and patrol plan for the Watch.

"Of course, my lord," Victor replied. He sat across from his new liege lord awaiting orders, idly looking around the man's office, which was orderly, fitted out with clever cabinetry like the interior of a ship. It had been a week since Victor's arrival in Winchelsea, and he was still learning the lay of the land.

So far, Lord Daniel had been easy to please, unlike Victor himself. He was not pleased when his aunt, Helisende, Countess of Hastings, had wheedled him into moving to the nearby town of Winchelsea and entering the service of the earl. He wasn't sad to leave Hastings. If anything, he was relieved to get away. But he didn't appreciate how casually she'd let him go.

She wanted him to find himself a nice wife, she said, suggesting one of the unmarried de Vere daughters as a match, as if he was fit to be a husband. Before Spain, he might have been considered a good match for one of the de Vere daughters. But years of combat had changed him, and the Victor who returned to England had too many rough edges to make him a fit husband for some simpering noblewoman. Besides, he was damned if he was going to enter into a lifelong commitment just to serve his aunt's political ambitions.

He had thought about joining the Templars, not that celibacy suited him, but a simple martial life away from court intrigue had a definite appeal. But his aunt forbade him and sent him here instead. "Make yourself indispensable to Lord Daniel," she said, providing no further instruction. He suspected she might have some ulterior motive, but Victor had pledged his oath and intended to do the very best he could for his new liege lord.

"How are you getting along with the men?" Lord Daniel asked, looking up from the duty roster.

"Quite well, my lord. They're well-disciplined and good at their work."

"I'm glad to hear it. And they are welcoming your direction?"

"Indeed, my lord."

Lord Daniel tilted his head. "Though your arrival was rather unexpected, I appreciate having a man of your skills and experience working for me. I'm still quite new to governing, as you've probably heard."

Victor smiled. "My aunt told me your history, my lord. Quite unusual."

He liked Lord Daniel. His Lordship was a young man, not much older than Victor himself. Having spent most of his youth disguised as a common shipwright, he didn't have any of the arrogance Victor was used to seeing in the nobility. He was forthright, fair, and generous with his men. He was attentive to detail without being overbearing. He never pretended to know more than he did, and he asked good questions. His military knowledge was sadly lacking, but he commanded respect and was easy to follow.

"I'm not sure I want to know what your aunt had to say about me." Lord Daniel chuckled. "She doesn't like me very much."

"She says you have a sharp mind and are a shrewd negotiator," Victor said, carefully choosing the most complimentary thing his aunt had said about His Lordship.

Lord Daniel raised a skeptical eyebrow. "I'm sure she had a

great deal more to say than that, but I won't put you in an awkward position by asking you to repeat it."

Thank God for that!

"But enough about your aunt," Lord Daniel continued. "Let me finish looking this over so that we can move on to more pleasant topics. Like the new song I've been working on. If you have time later this evening, I'd love to play it for you and get your thoughts. I think you might find it quite entertaining."

"I would like that, my lord."

Lord Daniel nodded and turned back to the roster.

The afternoon after Victor's arrival, His Lordship sat down with him with lutes and ale and brought in his friend Gerard, a troubadour with whom he had some family connection. They'd sat swapping songs for several hours. Lord Daniel's wit was sharp, and his compositions were every bit as good as those Victor had heard at his aunt's court. Gerard was better with the lute and had a better voice, but his original verse wasn't as impressive. They were both far better than Victor could ever hope to be, not that either of them was anything but complimentary of his mediocre skills.

It felt odd to be so friendly with his liege lord, but he got the sense Lord Daniel was relieved to have a break from the formality and propriety of his position. His Lordship seemed grateful to have another companion and ally in this house full of women, especially as he was adjusting to life as a new father. It was good to make a new friend if he dared call him that. He'd lost so many friendships after he'd returned from Spain. They all said he'd changed, and maybe they were right. Since his return, he'd had no interest in anything but his work. He hadn't realized how much he'd missed the comfort of casual camaraderie with other men.

Lord Daniel looked up from the parchment, clearing his throat. "I'd like for you to add another guard to the southern gate. There have been rumors of bands of brigands along the road to Hastings, and one cannot be too safe."

"Consider it done, my lord."

His liege lord turned back to the parchment.

Adding another guard was a bit excessive. How much protection did this tiny backwater need? The brigands were all targeting traffic from Hastings. Why would they bother with this piddling town?

Winchelsea wasn't terrible. It was merely dull and provincial compared to Hastings. He supposed it was picturesque at sunset. The stone buildings almost seemed to glow in the evening light, with the proud lines of the castle crowning the view. The port was certainly thriving, even if it was dwarfed by Hastings's. But the place only had six streets, and everyone knew everyone. There was no anonymity in a town like this, and…well…he had a memorable face. Then again, he'd become too recognizable in Hastings too, which was part of why he'd needed to leave. At least in Winchelsea, he had no enemies. *Yet.*

"Very good. I'm impressed," said Lord Daniel, handing the duty roster back at last.

Victor smiled. "Thank you, my lord."

Lord Daniel shifted uncomfortably in his chair. "I have a favor to ask, Victor."

"I'm at your command, my lord," he said with a polite nod.

Lord Daniel exhaled and fidgeted, as if being called "my lord" made him feel itchy. "My wife is worried about her sister, Lady Alais. There's a troubadour named Gilbert who expressed a bit too much interest in her. My wife sent him away the day you arrived, but she's worried he might try to come back for her. She doesn't think Lady Alais's usual chaperone is sufficient defense, and she wants her guarded when she goes out, at least until we're sure Gilbert is gone for good. I think you're the man for the job."

Victor went rigid and swallowed hard. The night he arrived, Lady Alais was dressed in red, a low neckline offering a tantalizing glimpse of her sweet and tender decolletage and a clinging waistline showing off the generous curves of her hips. He'd never felt such a powerful attraction to a woman on sight. Her dark hair shone in the candlelight, and her warm brown eyes were filled with mischief and merriment, though he also thought there was a hint of distress she was trying to keep at bay. She tugged at his heart. Well, perhaps not only his heart. If he was being honest, other parts of his anatomy were involved as well.

But then she had to go and comment on his face.

He tried to ignore her, really he did, but she was sitting right next to him. How was he supposed to get food without speaking to her? And she was paying far too much attention for his comfort. While she pretended disinterest, he could tell she was listening to every word he said to the earl. Worse, yet, she had the nerve to start flirting with him right after insulting him. She sat there and asked cheeky questions about a bawdy song and batted her eyelashes as if he was the same eligible bachelor who'd left for Spain two years ago and not the grizzled warrior who had returned.

Fortunately, he'd managed to avoid being seated next to her again after that first night. Lady Alais was a danger to his sanity and was to be avoided at all costs. The last thing he wanted to do was to spend his days trailing after her.

"I…well…um…may I ask why, my lord? Isn't there someone in the baron's household better suited?" He wasn't a nursemaid for God's sake, but he didn't dare offer an outright refusal.

His Lordship leaned back in his perfectly crafted, high-backed wooden chair and tipped it onto the back legs, balancing as he spoke. "I've never seen anyone as cool and collected around Lady Alais as you seem to be. The night you arrived, she was doing everything possible to get under your skin, and you took it in stride. When she started batting her eyelashes, you gave her a look, and she backed down without you saying a word. I've never seen anything like it."

Cool and collected? It's a good thing he had no idea how far that was from the truth.

Bringing the front chair legs back to the floor with a thunk, he leaned toward Victor. "There aren't many men I can trust around her. She's too pretty for her own good, and she flirts with absolutely everyone. She's trouble. I know she doesn't mean to be, but she doesn't seem to be able to help herself."

Too pretty indeed. It hurt to look at her.

"My lord, I'll do whatever you need, but I'm not sure I'm the most appropriate chaperone for a young lady." There was no way to refuse. The man was his liege lord. But surely there had to be a better solution.

"I'm not asking you to chaperone," His Lordship said, tipping back in his chair again. "Her maid, Dora, will be with her. But Dora is an old woman with an unfortunate tendency to fall asleep when she should be paying attention, and even wide awake, she's not intimidating. All I need from you is to fend off any men that might try to approach her when she leaves the castle."

Victor raised an eyebrow. "Men, plural? There's more than this Gilbert?"

"She's beautiful, rich, and eighteen. Of course, there are more," Lord Daniel said, coming down with a thud. "I feel like I spend more time helping Lord de Vere swat them away than running Winchelsea, which brings me to the other thing I wanted to ask you about. We're planning a tournament next month. We're hoping it will improve our relations with our neighbors. The Archbishop of Canterbury has been trying to expand his territories near Winchelsea. The Church is getting greedy and wants to expand at our expense, and we need allies to resist him. Also, God willing, the tournament will help us find Alais an acceptable husband. I'd like you to take the lead on organizing the preparations."

Now *there* was a job a man could enjoy. "It would be an honor, my lord."

"Thank you for agreeing...on both fronts." He stood and clapped a large, calloused hand on Victor's shoulder. "Your duties with Alais should only require a few hours a day. She spends most of her time at the castle."

Victor gave an uneasy nod. He'd only intended to agree to

help with the tournament, but it was too late to take it back now. He wondered if Lord Daniel lumped the topics together on purpose to make him agree.

"Carenza will be pleased that you've agreed. She liked the idea when I proposed it. There aren't many people she would trust to defend her sister."

"I'm honored by your trust," he said with a forced smile.

"Thank you for stopping by. I'll see you at dinner. And don't forget to bring your lute for afterward."

Victor walked away thinking about how Lady Carenza was too clever by half. There were moments when she scared him a little, reminding him of his aunt. It was no wonder Lord Daniel was besotted. Lady Alais was a clever one too, though she went to great lengths to hide it. He liked women with a spark of intelligence—not that he liked Lady Alais. So far, she'd been petty and rude, and he had no time for her nonsense. But if she ever stopped putting on her act of being a silly, shallow flirt, she could be quite irresistible. To another man. He was immune to her charms, of course. And now that he'd given his word of honor to prevent anyone from approaching her, he'd better stay that way.

He wandered out of the castle and down Castle Street until the castle gate was no longer in view. Then he turned and made his way to Birdie Street, which he had just discovered three days ago. It was a narrow alley off Castle Street that was easy to miss. One entered through a small stone arch that led to a cobblestone path that wound around the steep hillside to the east of the castle. The rough and shambling buildings lining the path housed the town's poorer residents, as well as a variety of interesting establishments with names like The Dirty Horn, The Slippery Weasel, My Lady's Chamber, and The Wayward Widow. Like most port towns, Winchelsea offered a variety of entertainments for the sailors and travelers looking for a bit of fun.

Victor was headed for the Bird in Hand, which specialized in young ladies that resembled famous and noble women past and present. There was a Cleopatra, a Helen of Troy, and even a fiery, redheaded Queen Eleanor. There was a saucy version of his aunt, Helisende, Countess of Hastings, who he studiously avoided, even though she teased him relentlessly when she realized who he was. And, of course, there was a Lady Isabella de Vere along with her three "daughters," Carenza, Alais, and Iselda. After looking over the offerings of the house, he was embarrassed to find himself inexorably drawn to "Alais," though he insisted on calling her by her given name, Jane.

Like her supposed namesake, Jane was flirtatious and saucy, but in contrast to the real Alais, she was quite kind to Victor. She looked remarkably like the real Lady Alais with her chestnut tresses, soft brown eyes, and her generous figure. She blew him kisses with her full, red lips whenever she saw him.

Victor had to admit he had a definite type, and Lady Alais de Vere, unfortunately, was his ideal made flesh. If he was going to be forced to spend his days with Lady Alais, at least he could find some relief with Jane for the torture he would have to endure.

Jane took him by the hand and led him upstairs with a smile.

"What's your pleasure today, my lady?" he asked, kissing her hand.

"Do you know no one else ever asks me that, my lord? The other ladies don't know what they are missing," she said with a sultry smile as she ran her hands over his buttocks.

"*Hmph.* Well, I live to serve." He nibbled on her ear.

Opening a door to one of the compact rooms, she drew him inside. "You are an unusual man."

"I'll take that as a compliment." He closed the door firmly behind them, ignoring the sighs and moans coming from neighboring rooms. "But you haven't answered my question. Fingers, tongue, or cock?"

She whispered "tongue" in his ear, and he readily complied, making her melt and tremble with unfeigned pleasure before he would take any of his own. It had always been this way for him. He needed to see pleasure to take it. It had been frustrating when he was young, but he'd come to accept it and over time even appreciate the dedication and creativity it required of him. He had accumulated an extensive knowledge of female pleasure and used it to great effect when given the opportunity. He rather regretted that these days he only used his talents to pleasure prostitutes so they could pleasure him in return. *It might be nice to thoroughly please a lover, or perhaps, even a wife.*

He frowned. Where did that thought come from?

"You look sad, my lord. Were you not satisfied?"

"*Hmm?* Oh no. Quite satisfied. Just thinking too much." He pulled on his clothes, left his payment, and headed back to the castle, bracing himself for another dinner with the lovely de Veres.

CHAPTER FOUR

LADY ALAIS STORMED out of the castle toward the stables, sending piles of red and gold leaves swirling in her wake. Moments later, Victor came chasing after her.

"Lady Alais," Victor yelled, jogging to catch up. "Lady Alais, I can't let you leave without me. Lord and Lady Carenza were clear."

"I don't need a nursemaid," she snapped at him. She entered the stables. "If you would be so kind as to saddle Snow and Bella?" she asked the obviously smitten groom in her sweetest voice.

"Saddle Socorro first," Victor barked, determined not to let Lady Alais have a chance to escape on her horse before he was mounted. He glanced back at the castle to see a lady's maid who must be Dora watching the interaction with keen interest, ambling along in no hurry to catch up with either of them.

"My lady, do I *look* like a nursemaid to you?"

Lady Alais glared at him and turned her back. So far, this was going even worse than he expected, which was saying something.

There was a soft pressure on his arm, and he turned to see Dora smiling up at him. "I take it you are Sir Victor? It's nice to meet you. I'm Dora, Lady Alais's maid. I must say having you here makes my job so much easier."

"Dora," Lady Alais complained, giving her a betrayed look.

"A pleasure to meet you. You can call me Sir Fly Swatter. I'm here to smash anyone who buzzes too close." He said it loud enough for the groom to hear and was satisfied to see the man jump. "Aside from my fly-swatting duties, I plan to leave the two of you alone."

Dora patted his cheek and looked delighted.

The groom brought out a powerful bay courser first, avoiding Lady Alais's gaze as he handed the reins to Victor. At least the man had the good sense to know which of the three of them could break his neck.

Lady Alais gave Victor a resentful look but kept glancing surreptitiously at his horse. Finally, she gave up her pretense of disinterest and walked over.

"What's his name?"

"Socorro."

"*Help?*"

He nodded. "He's saved my life more than once."

She sauntered all the way around for a thorough look. "He's beautiful."

"He's a trained war horse, and he bites." He smiled coldly.

She cocked her head as if he'd just issued a dare. "Hello, Socorro," she said softly and reached out her hand slowly to let him sniff before petting his nose. Socorro nuzzled her hand shamelessly. She giggled and gave him an apple she had tucked away. "You're a sweet boy, aren't you?"

"Socorro, since when are you a sweet boy? You're supposed to bite my adversaries, remember?"

"Am I your adversary?" She gave him a sultry smile.

"You're not my friend. I know that much."

She straightened and narrowed her eyes at him. She must not be used to men resisting the effects of that smile. He wasn't exactly immune, just wary.

"Lord Daniel asked me to keep you safe when you go out, and I gave my word of honor that I would," he said quietly. "I'm not your nursemaid, and I'm not your friend. I'm only a guard.

Pretend I'm not here."

The groom came out with Snow and Bella and carefully avoided Lady Alais's eyes as he handed over the reins. Soon everyone was mounted, and they were wending their way down Castle Street, past merchants and peasants going about their daily business. Eyes followed Lady Alais wherever she went. Fortunately, she ignored the attention she drew.

Lady Alais turned toward Winchelsea's southern gate when they reached Fish Street, weaving through the dockworkers, sailors, and fishermen who openly gaped as she passed. Was he going to have to decapitate anyone before they even left the town? Fortunately, his forbidding glare seemed to be sufficient to make them keep their distance.

He breathed a sigh of relief as they passed under the stone arch of the southern gate. They ambled along the ancient Roman road with grassy hills on one side and the shore on the other. It was a clear, crisp day, perfect for a ride. The sun was shining. The birds were singing.

Victor was almost starting to enjoy himself when Lady Alais abruptly veered off the road, and broke into a gallop, darting out of sight into the nearby woods.

"Saint Agatha's tits on a platter," Victor grumbled under his breath and followed her, weaving through trees, and steadily catching up. She disappeared again, and for a moment, he thought he'd lost her trail. A branch whipped against his shoulder and caught in his shirt. Breaking it and throwing it to the ground, he turned around in circles, peering through the autumn leaves until he caught a glimpse of her blue gown.

There she was. She had stopped in a nearby clearing and dismounted. She stuck her hand inside a knot in a tree and then peered into a shrub. *What the hell?*

He dismounted and tied up Socorro before tiptoeing over to the clearing, sword drawn in case a man was hidden in the shrubbery. He edged into the clearing, keeping his back to a large tree, looking out for any suspicious movement. Lady Alais let out a little shriek upon seeing him.

"Why do you have your sword drawn?"

"So I can kill whoever it is that's meeting you here," he said, examining every tree and bush.

She sighed and slumped down on the grass. "Put it away. There's no one here."

"Then why did you run away from me?" He lowered his sword.

She looked up at the sky in silence for several moments before responding. "Carenza says I must marry because of what happened with Gilbert. I'm not in love with him, but he's a lot better than some stuffy lord I've never met. I thought he might leave a message proposing we run away together, but he didn't." A tear dripped down her cheek. If she didn't look so red-faced and angry, he would have been certain she was putting on a show. "He's gone, and he's not coming back, the coward. So I'm stuck. They plan to marry me off to a stranger by Christmas." She sniffed and wiped her tears. "Are you going to tell my sister I ran off?"

Mentally cursing his aunt for making him come to Winchelsea, he slid his sword back into its scabbard and sat on the ground across from Lady Alais. He was a military commander for God's sake. How was this his job? He almost wished that Gilbert had shown up so that he could detach his head from his shoulders and be done with this ridiculous assignment. He liked Lord Daniel, but this was too much to ask.

"I'm not here to spy on you for your sister," he said through clenched teeth. "My only job is to keep Gilbert and any other men who might try to endanger your virtue away. No one was here, so as far as I'm concerned, I have nothing to report. But I would appreciate it if you didn't try to come here again looking for secret messages. I can see my way to forgetting this happened once, but if it happened again…"

She wiped her eyes. "It won't. You have my word."

"Where's your maid, by the way? You and I probably

shouldn't be sitting here alone like this."

Lady Alais waved a dismissive hand, then wiped a few more tears. "She'll get here eventually. Why? Are you worried *I* might endanger *your* virtue?"

He laughed incredulously, trying hard not to imagine how pleasant it would be to have Lady Alais de Vere endanger his virtue.

She sniffed and looked him in the eye. "Since we're alone and there's no one to hear, now would be a good time to sing me the song about the cat."

"What?" *The song about the cat? Where did that come from?* "No."

"It really would cheer me up."

"No." If Lady Alais de Vere ever heard the song about the cat, it wouldn't be from him. For God's sake, where was Dora?

They stared in opposite directions in silence, looking any-where but at each other for several agonizing minutes.

"Do you think we should look for Dora?" he asked. "I'm starting to worry about her." He wasn't, but he *was* worried about being alone with the beautiful woman all this time, unchaperoned. He'd hate to be forced into marriage with her because of a rumor of inappropriate behavior.

"Fine," she said, dragging herself to her feet. "Let's get her and go home. I'm finished with my ride."

He knew he should agree and be done with this travesty of a morning. He had no business offering her distraction or comfort. Besides, anything he might propose was bound to exacerbate his profound discomfort in her presence. Nonetheless, he heard himself saying, "I have a better idea. Let's head down to the beach and race."

Lady Alais gave him a dubious look. "I love Snow, but she's no match for Socorro."

"I'll let you have a head start."

"Let me ride Socorro, and you have a deal."

"But, my lady, he's a war horse."

"He's a sweet boy."

He let out his breath slowly. "I can't believe I'm agreeing to this. Your family will never forgive me if you get hurt."

"I won't," she said with cheerful confidence as she dusted herself off. "My brother used to let me ride his destrier when I was younger."

"Your brother? No, wait. I think I knew you had a brother. I met him once or twice when I was young. His name is…Charles, I think?"

Lady Alais nodded and looked off into the distance, blinking back a tear he sensed was real, this time. "He died in a shipwreck a few years back."

"I'm so sorry for your loss." *Wonderful.* Now he'd gone and upset her more.

She shook herself and plastered on a smile. "Can I take Socorro now?"

"I'd rather wait until we're at the beach." *Or never. That would be fine too.* Why was he doing this?

She sighed and headed over to Snow as Victor mounted Socorro. They rode back to the road and found Dora on Bella looking distressed and pacing back and forth beside the road.

"Where did you go, my lady? I couldn't see which way you went. You know I'm too old for galloping. It isn't nice leaving an old lady alone on the open road like this. Brigands might accost me."

Lady Alais bowed her head repentantly. "I'm sorry, Dora. Truly, I am. I was being thoughtless and inconsiderate. Fortunately, Sir Victor found me and brought me back. We're going to the beach now. I promise we'll stay in sight."

Dora looked at her for a long moment with narrowed eyes. Then Dora's eyes flicked to Victor, and the corner of her mouth quirked into the ghost of a grin. "To the beach it is, my lady."

Victor wasn't sure he liked that look. Dora seemed altogether too perceptive for an old lady who could barely sit a horse.

They rode down a narrow dirt path to an empty stretch of

beach just south of Winchelsea. Lady Alais helped Dora settle down on a blanket while Victor adjusted the stirrups so that they could ride each other's horses.

"Don't worry, Dora," Alais said. "We won't go farther than that rock down there. You'll be able to see us the whole time."

Dora looked on with an unnerving twinkle in her eye as Victor cupped his hands to help Lady Alais mount Socorro. She stepped up and leaned into him as she swung herself up onto Socorro's back. The tantalizing shape of her lovely leg beneath her skirt pressed against his chest, and her exquisite posterior was level with his face. A tiny moan escaped him.

"Did I hurt you?" she asked, settling herself on Socorro's broad back.

He could have sworn Dora chuckled, but when he looked back, she was gazing at a seagull, all innocence.

"It's nothing, my lady." He hurried to mount Snow, hoping to hide his distress. "Are you ready?"

Lady Alais smiled, and without warning set off down the beach, looking like she was floating on Socorro's back. He watched their rhythmic motion as they pounded through the sand, hair and mane streaming in the wind. By God, she was glorious.

Remembering himself, he tore after her, pushing Snow to her limit and still falling far short of catching up. Lady Alais whooped in unladylike glee as she flew past the rock that marked their finish line. His heart threatened to pound out of his chest at the sight of her in her natural state, all artifice fallen by the wayside.

"I won, I won," she yelled and brought his horse to a halt.

"Not a fair race," he objected, sidling up beside her.

"He's magnificent. I think I'm in love."

He raised an eyebrow. "Don't listen to her, Socorro. She'll break your heart."

Thank heavens he had more sense than his horse, or she would surely break his as well.

"I would never do that to a sweet boy like you," she said,

stroking Socorro's neck.

"Race you back," he said, taking advantage of her momentary inattention to get a head start. Needing some distance to compose himself, he pelted back down the beach as fast as the little palfrey would carry him. Lady Alais was neck and neck by the time he passed the blanket where Dora was sitting, despite his early lead. Poor Snow was lathered in sweat and breathing heavily.

Victor dismounted. "I think I'd better give Snow a rest, but if you want to keep galloping around on my war horse like a madwoman, I won't stop you."

He sat down cautiously with Dora and watched as Alais tore back and forth along the beach, hooting like an Amazon warrior. The sight was enthralling. He couldn't pull his gaze away. It was a bad idea to gape at her like this, but rational thought had abandoned him. The sight of her, free and wild, tugged at something in his battle-hardened heart.

"I like you," Dora said, patting his hand. "She needs someone who can keep up with her, someone strong and fierce. Lord knows I'm not up to the task."

Victor laughed. "Is anyone? My horse perhaps…"

"I think you'll do fine. But be careful. I've watched more than one man dash himself to pieces trying to win her. Gilbert got farther than most, but he would have failed in the end even if he wasn't unsuitable. He couldn't match her spirit and passion."

"I assure you I have no designs beyond keeping her safe." He had a job to do, and he had no intention of dashing himself to pieces for anyone's entertainment, least of all a spoiled, spirited young woman like Lady Alais. Besides which, it was his chivalric duty to keep all men away, including himself.

She patted his hand again. "That's nice, dear."

"What are you two chattering about?" asked Alais, halting in front of their blanket. Both she and Socorro were breathing heavily. Her face was flushed from the exercise. She was radiant in the bright autumn sun.

Victor stood to help her down from Socorro. She slid against his chest until her face was level with his with her toes barely touching the ground, her lips so close and kissable.

No. None of that.

He released her and stepped away briskly. Oh, he was going to keep Jane busy tonight.

Lady Alais was remarkably quiet on the way back to the castle. When they got to the stables and dismounted, she put a hand on his arm, and he immediately drew back.

"I'm sorry," she said, withdrawing her hand and blushing. "I wanted to say thank you for letting me ride Socorro. And I should apologize for my behavior earlier. I know you're only doing your job. I shouldn't make it hard for you."

She turned and walked into the castle. Dora winked at him and then followed. Victor watched Lady Alais go, taking guilty pleasure in the view.

Satan's salty roasted balls on a stick.

He was in trouble.

CHAPTER FIVE

ALAIS SAT WITH four other young ladies near her age on a blanket laid on a grassy field next to Winchelsea's west gate, watching knights arrive for next week's tournament. The tall, crenelated city wall loomed beside them, showing patches of lighter stone where repairs had been made after last year's battle. Vines twined up the square sides of the watch tower by the gate. The mottled aquas and indigos of the bay rippled in the distance and the crisp, sea-salted air that rolled off of it made their blanket and clothing billow in the breeze.

Alais and her friends had an excellent view of the ancient Roman road to Hastings without being close enough to be overheard by passersby. Dora was sitting with them and knitting. Sir Victor sat at a discreet distance, sharpening his sword, looking like a thundercloud ready to ruin her sunny day.

"Are you sure you don't want to join us, Sir Victor?" Alais called over to him.

"Very sure," he called back.

"But I was hoping you'd let me braid your hair," she teased, making her friends erupt in uncontrollable giggles. Dora gave her a scolding look.

"Absolutely not," he answered, setting to work on his sword with renewed vigor.

Alais turned to Dora. "I know I shouldn't tease him, but it's so hard to resist. He's been so grumpy lately." She couldn't say why, but nothing pleased her more than getting under his skin. He tried so hard to be stoic and impassive. It was delicious fun to see his façade slip, even if it was only to express annoyance at her.

Dora shook her head and then went back to her knitting. Alais turned back to her friends.

"So what's your ideal man, Lady Alais?" Lady Eugenie asked, taking an apple from the picnic basket before looking back at the road below, and then tucking a golden lock behind her ear.

"My ideal man? Hmm." Alais smiled and looked up at the clouds, narrowing her eyes, as if she had to think about it. As if she hadn't listed his attributes a thousand times in her head. "He's brave and loyal and true—"

"That goes without saying," Lady Eugenie objected.

"He's clever and witty—" Alais continued.

"Boring!" interjected Lady Mathilda, brushing away a fly that had landed on her raven hair, and rolling her deep brown eyes.

"And handsome, of course!" Alais persevered. It was hardly the most important factor for her, but she knew what her audience wanted. The distant sound of sword sharpening suddenly picked up pace.

"Elaborate," demanded Lady Simone, her round, baby face sporting a wicked smile as she folded her arms beneath her ample, pillowy breasts.

"He's tall and lean and well-muscled. He's graceful of bearing. He has blond hair and piercing blue eyes that set my heart aflame. When he looks at me, his eyes become haunted and hungry. He can't eat or sleep for the love of me, but he's ready to fight all comers to win me. None can withstand his sword. He sings me love poems, woos me with sweet words, and gives me precious gifts, and I pretend to be aloof and unmoved but still he persists. I don't give in to his courtship or show him any sign of my affection until he demonstrates his love through some grand gesture, like slaying a leviathan, defeating an evil tyrant, or better yet, providing a dramatic rescue. *My rescue, preferably.*"

The ladies leaned in around Alais, nodding and murmuring approval as she pontificated. Their brightly colored skirts puddled around them, rustling in the ocean breeze. The sound of the sword sharpening stopped.

"And then, and only then," she added in a confidential murmur, "will I grant him the kiss he so fervently seeks. His kiss will be a delicious torment, filling us both with desire and longing, and he'll propose on the spot because he can't live without me. He needs to hold me naked in our bedchamber, or he will surely die." The sword sharpening started again.

"Alais! Don't say things like that," Iselda yelped in shocked tones, looking remarkably like their older sister, Carenza, at that moment.

"Oh, don't be such a prude," Alais said, jabbing a finger repeatedly into Iselda's shoulder.

Iselda swatted away Alais's hand. "I'll tell Mother!"

"Don't you dare!"

"At least your mother *admits* to what married people do. My mother still pretends babies are carried down from heaven by angels and delivered in baskets," Lady Simone said, rolling her eyes.

"I'm confused," said Lady Eugenie. "What do babies have to do with being naked in a bedchamber?"

Everyone was suddenly silent. They all looked anywhere but at each other. Alais certainly wasn't going to be the one to explain. Dora's knitting needles clacked, and her mouth moved. She appeared to be counting her stitches with great attention and was of no use, either.

"Oh look!" Lady Mathilda said, pointing. "There's another knight coming along the road. See his banner?"

Grateful for the distraction, Alais turned to pay avid attention to the new arrival.

"I don't recognize the banner," Lady Simone said, squinting to make it out.

Alais shaded her eyes and nodded before announcing, "Robert of Guestling. He's Sir Victor's cousin. Victor's father, Giles, is Castellan of Guestling. Robert is second-in-line after Sir Victor." She'd never met him before, but she knew the banners of every noble house within a three-day ride, along with their political allegiances. Was Sir Robert independent-minded like his cousin or a tool of Lady Helisende's scheming? She would have to listen closely to see if she could determine where his loyalty was bestowed.

The sword sharpening stopped again.

"*Eh.*" Lady Mathilda shrugged. "You can do better than second in line."

Robert was now close enough that they could make out his features.

"Blond hair, blue eyes, Alais," Lady Simone said teasingly. "Just like that troubadour Gilbert you fancied."

"Gilbert? I'm over Gilbert." If he wasn't such a coward, he would have invited her to run away with him. But as she watched the knights arrive, she started to think perhaps her marriage options wouldn't be so terrible after all. "Heavens, this Sir Robert is rather handsome, isn't he?" Alais said, appreciating the view.

The man who rode toward them seemed like her dream come to life. He had eyes the color of forget-me-nots and golden curls that perfectly framed a face full of laughter and mischief. As he passed the ladies on the hill, he doffed his cap with a flourish and winked at them, though he made a strange face when he noticed Sir Victor sitting nearby.

"Oh my," was all she could say as he rode on through the west gate and into Winchelsea. She and her companions collapsed against each other in a fit of furious giggles.

THAT EVENING, LORDS Rossignol and de Vere hosted a banquet in the great hall of the castle. Alais was forced to sit at the head table next to Carenza instead of gossiping with her friends, as she would have preferred. Worse, she was going to have to suffer through being introduced to the various noblemen who had come for the tournament as they came to pay respects to their hosts.

Candles cast warm light on the wood trestle tables in the hall, and braziers were scattered around the vast room to take the chill out of the brisk autumn air. It seemed as if half of Winchelsea was dining with them this evening. Nearly fifty people were amassed, if she had to guess. The sounds of laughter and the clinking of tankards completed the festive mood, as they all nibbled on bread and cheese, awaiting the feast. Lucky them. They weren't on display and could simply enjoy the party.

"Now remember, treat them all with equal favor," her mother whispered as they made their way to the head table. "You won't like all of them, but you must pretend you do. You can't afford favorites this early. We want them all to think they are in the running so that they bid each other up when speaking with your father about the terms of an alliance."

"I'm not a heifer at market, Mother," she murmured through gritted teeth, trying to ignore the many eyes that were turned her way. Normally, she didn't mind attention, but on this day, they weren't admiring so much as scrutinizing. Her stomach flip-flopped, and she swallowed hard.

Her mother took her firmly by the elbow and steered her to her seat. "Now smile, dear. They're all watching."

As if she needed to be reminded. Even Sir Victor was watching as she took her seat, and he usually avoided paying any attention to her whatsoever when he wasn't guarding her. Their eyes met, and he quickly looked away, turning to Daniel, and asking something she didn't catch. But she didn't miss the slight reddening of his cheeks. At least her dress was having its intended effect. If she could get a rise out of Sir Victor, then her suitors ought to be properly dazzled.

"Good evening, Lord Daniel, Lord Martin," said a tall, middle-aged, reedy man with a large bald spot and a fringe of mouse-brown hair who approached the table right after Alais sat down. "Lord Louis, Castellan of Hawkhurst at your service. Your cousin sends his respects, Lord Daniel." He bowed deeply, and Daniel inclined his head in acknowledgment. "Lord Martin, it has been too long! I see your little girls aren't so little anymore."

Hawkhurst. She had no desire to have anything to do with the place, not after last year's battle with Daniel's uncle, the Earl of Hawkhurst. Lord Raymond was gone, thank heavens, replaced by his incompetent son. She planned to avoid Hawkhurst at all costs. Still, she needed to be polite to her father's old friend.

Alais's father smiled. "Very true, Louis. I was sorry to hear about your wife. She was a good and kind woman and will be missed by all." Her mother nodded in sympathy. "I must say I'm surprised to see you here today after everything."

"Well, um," Lord Louis cleared his throat, "my son is bothering me to take another wife. He thinks his wife is overburdened taking care of us both, and so I agreed to examine my options." He cleared his throat again, and, to Alais's horror, looked hopefully in her direction.

No. Absolutely not.

A brief grimace crossed her father's face before he composed himself and said as graciously as possible, "Allow me to introduce my daughters. My oldest, Carenza, is now Countess of Winchelsea, as I'm sure you're aware. We're all proud, though I'm not sure how I feel about my own daughter outranking me," he joked, earning a strained smile from Carenza. "She's holding my first grandbaby, little Charles, our tiny future earl." He paused in his introductions to coo at the baby and make him giggle by puffing out his cheeks.

"Congratulations on a handsome grandson, my lord," Lord Louis offered politely.

"This is my second, Lady Alais," her father continued, trying to recover his dignity, "and my youngest, Lady Iselda. It's amazing how quickly they grow up."

"Such lovely young ladies," said Lord Louis, offering another bow. "I look forward to becoming better acquainted." Alais bowed her head in acknowledgment, trying to keep her inner turmoil out of her smile.

As Lord Louis returned to his table, she grabbed Carenza's arm and whispered in her ear, "Please don't let it be him. Tell Papa I won't do it."

"Calm down, Alais," Carenza answered, removing her arm from Alais's clutches.

"Calm down? He's as old as Papa, not to mention that he's from Hawkhurst."

"Appearances aren't everything," Carenza said, mistaking her concern and patting her hand.

"Says the woman married to the most attractive earl this side of the English Channel."

Carenza smiled and blushed, sneaking a glance at her husband as she bounced Charles on her knee. "Yes, but you may remember, I nearly had to marry his uncle." She put a reassuring hand on her sister's. "Don't worry. It's up to you who you choose, as long as you do it swiftly and with Father's approval."

The introductions continued, and Alais was relieved to find some acceptable candidates among the bunch. Lord Guy of Dymchurch was young, friendly, and jolly. He was a bit shorter than she would ideally like, not much taller than she was herself, but he had lovely green eyes and thick brown curls and made up in muscle for what he lacked in height. She liked his friendly, earnest manner. Dymchurch was already a friend to Winchelsea, so there was no political advantage to the alliance. He wasn't an exciting choice, but he would do in a pinch.

Sir Elias of Canterbury was tall and lithe with hair so light it was nearly white. He had pale, penetrating blue eyes. He was a little bit on the serious side for her taste. He didn't smile even once when they were introduced, but there was an intensity in his look that convinced her he was more interested than he was letting on. Relations with Canterbury had been fraught of late, and perhaps a marriage might ease tensions. Not that she planned to marry for strictly political reasons, but it would be nice to feel useful.

Lord Alphonse of Whatlington was clearly a bon vivant. He drank a bit too freely that night and feasted with carnivorous abandon, but his smiles and compliments pleased her. She found his auburn hair and hazel eyes rather appealing, and he had quite a kissable mouth. And Whatlington had rich farmland. With Winchelsea's tendency to flood, it was always helpful to have a reliable source of crops.

Then there was Sir Robert. He had a confidence that fell just shy of arrogance, and he seemed to know exactly what effect he had on women. His deep blue eyes smoldered as they rested on her, and he smiled wolfishly as she returned his look with equal boldness. He moved as if dancing. Each word, each gesture felt like it was directed at her, even if it was spoken to someone else. And much as she disliked Lady Helisende, she supposed mending fences with Hastings would pose an interesting challenge, though she rather hoped he wasn't close to his aunt.

"My lady, it is a rare privilege to behold such beauty and grace," he said. A lock of his golden curls fell in his eyes as he leaned over her hand to kiss it. He ran the tip of his tongue across her knuckles as he kissed her, and it was all she could do to remain standing.

Sir Victor cleared his throat loudly, and she shot him a glance before returning her attention to the gorgeous man in front of her. What was he upset about?

"You flatter me, my lord," she said, her voice suddenly breathy even to her own ears.

"It is no flattery. Your lips are rosebuds. Your eyes dazzle me like stars in the night sky. It is a privilege to be allowed to stand before you and drink you in. You are perfection itself, my lady. I am at a loss for words."

He most certainly was not, but who was she to object? Perhaps he was laying it on a bit thick, but as an often-ignored second daughter, she couldn't help but melt at his words.

Sir Victor cleared his throat again, looking daggers at his cousin. But what did it matter to him whom she chose? Wasn't he anxious to be rid of her?

Sir Robert pointedly ignored Sir Victor and gazed into her eyes with an irresistible smolder. Never mind that he was second in line behind Sir Victor for a tiny castle in a market village. She'd never cared much for wealth and position. She wanted passion and romance, and this was a promising start. None of the others had shown their interest as boldly as him.

As Sir Robert returned to his seat at a neighboring table, his gaze strayed momentarily to his cousin. The tense look they exchanged was so brief she almost thought she'd imagined it. Catching her watching, Sir Robert immediately adjusted his countenance, giving her a flirtatious wink as if nothing had happened.

She smiled, and her cheeks heated. Whatever that strange moment of hostility was about, it was hardly her affair. Sir Victor was grumpy at the best of times, and who knew what history there might be between the cousins? Knowing him, it was probably some matter of honor. He was so prickly about that. It was probably nothing to worry about. Was it?

CHAPTER SIX

WEST OF WINCHELSEA, in a large meadow just off the road, Victor guided Lord Daniel around the nearly finished tournament grounds, showing off the work of the carpenters. There were stands for the audience, a platform for the Rossignol and de Vere families, a corral for the horses, and booths for vendors. A group of men was currently hammering in a wooden palisade around the field of competition.

"I checked on the provisions this morning, my lord, and everything was delivered as expected. We have food, wine, and ale aplenty for your guests," Victor said as they passed the half-built booths where merchants would sell their wares to the crowds attending the tournament.

"Excellent," Lord Daniel said with a nod. "And the healer is prepared with everything he needs to treat the injured?"

He gestured to the ancient symbol of healing, a snake and staff, a worker was painting on the canvas of the healer's tent as they passed by.

"Yes, my lord."

They continued their tour of the grounds and came to a stop on the central platform where the Rossignol and de Vere families would sit.

"How are our guests from Hastings and Hawkhurst? Is everyone behaving?" Lord Daniel asked, surveying the field with a keen eye.

"So far, so good, my lord," Victor answered, following Lord Daniel's gaze, and feeling rather proud of his work. "I think you were wise to host this tournament. It's clear they're spoiling for a fight, but it's much better for all concerned if they vent their spleens in taunts and jousting rather than open warfare. To my mind, though, Canterbury is more of a concern than Hastings or Hawkhurst. The archbishop has already made more headway with my aunt than I would like. I'm discreetly keeping a close eye on Sir Elias. He's a Canterbury man through and through."

"Good thinking. I don't trust Canterbury. Your aunt and I have had our differences, but I'd rather form an alliance with her than submit to Canterbury's incursions. He has far too much land already."

"Agreed, my lord."

Lord Daniel nodded in satisfaction, then furrowed his brow. Was he dissatisfied in some way? He started pacing back and forth like he was avoiding something.

"What is it, my lord?" Victor asked, at last, worry getting the better of him.

"I was hoping you could help with another delicate task related to Lady Alais."

Victor stood very still. *Not again.* Whatever Lord Daniel was about to say, Victor was certain he wouldn't like whatever came next. He tried to stand tall and appear unconcerned. "Yes, my lord?"

Lord Daniel took a deep breath and let it out before he began. "Lord de Vere and I would like to enlist your help figuring out how suitable Lady Alais's suitors are. I don't mean what they offer in terms of lands, titles, alliances, however. Lord de Vere has that well in hand, and I've already shared my preferences with him on alliances. What we need to know is what kind of men they are." He paused.

"My lord?" Victor thought he saw where this was going, and he didn't like it.

"Setting political considerations aside, none of us want to see Lady Alais get hurt. We can't let her fall prey to someone who will make her miserable."

Victor stifled a groan. Far too much of his life revolved around Lady Alais de Vere these days. And, though he couldn't voice his feelings aloud, she was managing to make him miserable even though he had done everything in his power to avoid becoming her prey. It was no easy task defending her honor when she was temptation incarnate.

"She can't end up with someone cruel or neglectful," Lord Daniel continued, "or deceitful or unfaithful or…well, you get the idea. The thing is, the suitors are all on their guard around us, always careful to say what they think we want to hear. You, on the other hand, can go places we can't—gambling halls, brothels—"

"My lord—" he objected.

"Don't try to pretend you don't know your way around Winchelsea's brothels. I try to stay out of my men's private lives, but everyone knows where you spend your nights."

Victor gritted his teeth and clenched his fist. One of the downsides of his scar was that he attracted notice. People followed his doings with prurient fascination, even if most would never admit it in his presence. God, how irksome it was the way the gossip seemed to swirl around him everywhere he went.

"All I'm asking," Lord Daniel continued, "is that you see who else is there, see what they let slip, and let me know if there's anything I should be aware of for the sake of Lady Alais's safety and happiness."

Christ on the cross, his aunt had better be deeply grateful for what he was putting himself through here in Winchelsea.

"Fine," Victor grunted through clenched teeth. At least it didn't involve any more contact with Alais.

"I've offended you," Lord Daniel said, frowning.

"No, my lord," he said, recovering. "I'm not offended, only disappointed that my private affairs seem to be so widely known."

"What you choose to do when you are off duty is between you and God. I'm not here to judge." Lord Daniel shrugged. "Thank you for agreeing to help me out. Lord de Vere and Carenza will be quite relieved."

Victor exhaled. How did the man manage to be so damned nice while giving him torturous assignments?

"Tell Lord de Vere and your lady wife I'll learn what I can," Victor said in flat tones, doing his best to keep his irritation at bay.

Lord Daniel looked at him with a furrowed brow but said nothing.

"Now if you'll excuse me, my lord," Victor said after a moment of silence, "it's time for me to meet with my men."

Lord Daniel nodded. "You may go."

With a bow, Victor made his escape. Socorro was waiting for him by a tree, giving him a dirty look for interrupting his grazing.

"Not you too," Victor grumbled as he untied Socorro and mounted. "I've got enough trouble without my own horse giving me lip."

Pressing his heels into Socorro's sides, Victor rode faster than was strictly necessary back to the city gates, venting his spleen in a good gallop. As he rode through the city gates, he forced himself to slow down. It wouldn't do to run down the innocent citizens of Winchelsea just because he was in a bad mood.

Upon arriving back at the castle and handing Socorro over to a stable hand, Victor headed straight toward the stone building where the Watch congregated. When his men informed him that a prominent wool trader had just been found with his throat cut in a warehouse on Fish Street, Victor had to hide his delight.

Thank Christ! A distraction that has absolutely nothing to do with Alais.

He managed to refrain from rubbing his hands together in excitement as he asked his men to take him to where the body had been found.

They led him down to the dank stone building and showed him the corpse. The man's blood had spilled on the sacks of grain where he was left, and nowhere else, so he must have been killed on site. There weren't any noticeable bruises, so it didn't seem like there had been much of a struggle. Victor searched the man's pockets and found a curious token—a wooden coin with a black X painted on it. He showed it to his men, and they looked unnerved.

"Well, at least we know who did this now," said a stringy old coot named Bernard.

"Explain," said Victor.

"There's a money lender here, a usurer, goes by the name of Matthew," Bernard explained. "He works out of one of the brothels on Birdie Street when he's in town, though he travels around a lot. He's based in Canterbury, I'm told. To get past his armed men, you have to show this token. Usually, he keeps a low profile, but every so often someone winds up dead for nonpayment."

"Then why hasn't he been apprehended and hanged?" Victor had no patience for usurers.

Bernard shrugged. "He isn't an easy man to get to. He magically disappears every time we try."

"*Hmm*. Well today, *I'm* going to look for him." One wasn't supposed to hope for violence. If Victor had an opportunity to carry out some justice while working through his feelings about his latest Alais assignment, though, all the better. "You four, come with me. The rest of you deal with the body, then go back to your duties."

Bernard and three others showed him to the brothel on Birdie Street where Matthew was rumored to operate.

Victor breathed a sigh of relief that it wasn't the Bird in Hand. That would have been awkward. He stationed two of his men in front and sent two in the back. Then he took the dead man's token inside the brothel.

It was a rather sad establishment—none of the light and fun of the Bird in Hand. A meager fire failed to take the chill out of the air. The stale scent of spilled ale mixed with the acrid, burnt scent of something being overcooked in a cauldron. Most of the women who circulated amongst the clientele looked underfed. The rough, worn, trestle tables were filled with grim-looking men, a mix of sailors, dock workers, and ruffians. Eight of the men stiffened slightly and quietly reached for their weapons when he entered. So he was outnumbered. *Thank God.* He had a lot of spleen to work through.

He went up to the bar and showed the token to a bartender who was missing all of his teeth. "I'm looking for Matthew. Do you know where I can find him?"

The bartender gestured toward a hallway into the back. Victor walked down the hall, hearing the eight men from the front room closing in behind him. There was a door to his left and another door out to the back at the end of the hall. He opened the one to his left and saw a small man in velvet disappearing down a trap door into the cellar over the shoulders of two enormous men who were shoulder to shoulder, blocking the door and trying to hide the small man from view.

"Fucking suitors," Victor grumbled as he punched the two guards in the balls. He lunged for the trap door while they were doubled over. Prying the door open, he jumped down to the cellar floor, ignoring the ladder, and saw the small man frantically fiddling with the lock on a door at the other side of the cellar that must lead to another building's cellar. Victor tore across the room and pinned him, then pulled a small knife from his sleeve and held it to the man's throat.

"You're Matthew?"

"Yes," he said in a thin, wheezy voice. He was licking his lips, and his eyes were darting back and forth.

"I'm told that the murdered merchant I found in a warehouse just now might be a customer of yours."

"I don't know what you're talking about."

Victor searched him quickly for weapons and threw two knives and a short sword into a mess of crates in the corner. Moments later, he heard one set of feet and then another land in the cellar. Victor couldn't help smiling as he turned to face his opponents. Oh, they would regret crossing him today.

"You attack me, Matthew dies," he yelled to make sure everyone heard. Two large men barreled into sight with swords drawn and stopped dead when they saw the knife at Matthew's throat. "If you let me out of here with Matthew, I'll forget your ugly faces, at least until the next time we meet. You don't need to make this difficult for yourselves." He really hoped they didn't take him up on it, but he felt morally obligated to try.

"Who you callin' ugly, ugly?" said a man with stringy black hair who was all neck and no chin. "There's ten of us and one of you. Why should we do anything you say?" They began to close on him.

"Shit," Victor said, realization dawning. "This isn't Matthew, is it?"

Ugly's friend, Ugly II, chuckled. "He's quick."

Victor jabbed his knife into Not-Matthew's side. He was still hoping to interrogate the man when this was all over, so he made sure to incapacitate, not kill. Then for good measure, he knocked the man over the head, leaving him limp and unconscious. He had no such qualms about the Uglies. They were clearly hired muscle and wouldn't know anything useful, and since they were trying to kill him, he had every excuse to defend himself. Vigorously. While imagining them as Alais's suitors.

He drew his sword and carved his way through the two men in front of him, swiftly dispatching a third as he dropped down into the cellar. It was disappointingly easy. This particular Matthew really should hire better muscle.

Victor was about to jump up the ladder when Ugly IV leaped down on him. He ran his sword through the man's gut, and the man collapsed, dead, on top of him. But the dead man was not small, and it took some maneuvering for Victor to roll him off. As he was wriggling free, an unpleasant smell nearly choked him. Fluids he didn't want to identify leaked from the man's gaping wound and smeared all down his front. "Ugh," he groaned as he pulled his sword free, realizing he was now wearing the contents of the man's lower intestine.

He climbed back out of the trap door and was forced to take off Ugly V's left leg in the process. Uglies VI and VII came running at him with swords drawn. Ugly VI stopped short and wrinkled his nose. "Jesus, he stinks."

"Oh, shut up," Victor spat back, decapitating Ugly VII before stabbing Ugly VI through the neck, which spattered Victor's face and hair with arterial blood. The remaining Uglies went running into the arms of his men outside. God, what a mess. And Ugly VI had been right. He stank of another man's entrails.

Victor walked into the common room, covered in blood and guts. Hob and Ulf rushed in, swords raised.

"There's a wounded man in the cellar. Tie him up and take him to the castle dungeon," Victor ordered, and his men rushed to comply.

The horror and disgust on every single face in the common room made for a comical picture. If only Victor was in a laughing mood. "Ladies and gentlemen, I'm afraid this establishment is closed until further notice, though I will pay good coin to whoever can point me to a bucket of water to get this filth off me." Most of them fled the room, though one enterprising young woman with an admirable bosom held her nose and showed him to a well in the back. He dumped a bucket over his head before extracting his soggy bag of coins and paying her for her service.

Upon his return to the castle, he got some clean clothes from his room and went down to the bathing room for a lengthy bath.

As he emerged, thoroughly cleansed, and smelling a bit too strongly of lavender oil, a servant informed him that Lords Rossignol and de Vere wished to speak with him, and he followed him to Lord Daniel's study.

"Did you just kill seven men and shut down a brothel on Birdie Street?" Lord Daniel demanded with no preamble. Victor wasn't sure whether he was angry or impressed.

But then Lord Daniel sniffed and looked confused. *Definitely too much lavender oil.*

"The Watch informed me a money lender named Matthew was responsible for the murder of a silk trader. I went to investigate. We don't want trouble this close to the tournament. When I tried to apprehend the criminal, I was attacked by his lackeys."

"Matthew," Lord Martin mused. "We've been trying to get at him for years. This is the first time we've made any headway. The man you captured is Matthew's right hand. I'm amazed we didn't lose anyone. When we've tried this in the past, we've always had casualties of our own. Frankly, I'm astonished you're still alive. I'm told you fought your way through seven men?"

Victor nodded. He wasn't sure what to say. Other than it was the most fun he'd had in weeks, but that sounded like boasting so he stayed quiet.

Lord Daniel whistled. "I underestimated you."

"Most people do." Victor shrugged. It was hardly the first time.

"Why in heaven's name did Lady Helisende let you go?" Lord Daniel asked, running a hand through his dark hair. "She must have known what she was giving up."

"I needed to leave Hastings, and I told her so." And she had been none too pleased. "Too many people there remember me from before—" he gestured at his face—"and I got tired of all the pitying looks. I threatened to join the Templars, and she proposed I come here instead. I think this was her way of keeping me close."

Lord Daniel and Lord de Vere looked at each other for a long moment.

"Well, I'm glad you're here," Lord Daniel said. "I need a new commander for my troops. John, who holds the position currently, is getting too old for this work and asked to retire. I think we've found a worthy replacement at long last. Also, if you're willing, I'd like you to take over as my swordsmanship instructor. Seven men! Good Lord in Heaven, I would like to be that good."

Victor swallowed and nodded, trying not to grin. "Thank you, my lord." Saints above! Did he just get a promotion? His aunt would be ecstatic. So far, his mission to Winchelsea was a rousing success. If only life were simpler, and he could escape all the women who were complicating it.

⫸⫷

THAT EVENING AFTER dinner, he made his way down the winding street from the castle to Jane, proud of his success, and still smelling a bit too strongly of lavender oil.

"My lord, I hope this fragrance isn't for my benefit," she said pulling back in surprise after kissing him.

"It's for my own benefit as well. I had a messy day. You wouldn't have appreciated my stench from earlier."

He nuzzled her neck and grazed it with his teeth, making her gasp. It was so much fun to make her do that.

Grabbing the front of his cotte, she pulled him into another kiss.

"I heard all about your messy day," she murmured in his ear. "Several ladies came here seeking employment after you shut down their establishment." She hastily unlaced his cotte and pulled off his shirt, kissing her way down his chest, then unlaced his breeches so that she could stroke him. "I was worried about you." She knelt and took him in her mouth, and he moaned at the intensity of the sensation.

"Oh God...oh God... Wait, Jane!" He pulled away from her exquisite torture, panting. "You know I always insist on ladies first."

Pulling back, he lifted her to her feet, wrapped an arm around her waist, and pressed her back on the straw pallet, climbing on top. He pulled up her skirts and rendered her speechless, not relenting until he felt her convulse beneath him. "God, I love watching you come." Sliding into her, he lost himself in record time.

As they lay catching their breath, she asked, "Did something new happen with Lady Alais today? You were quicker than usual. I can always tell when she's done something new to set you off. I'm starting to suspect you have feelings for her ladyship."

He shook his head vehemently. Feelings? He couldn't afford any of those. For heaven's sake, he was supposed to be guarding her, not trailing after her like some lovesick swain. He had a sworn duty to defend her from all comers, himself included. Not to mention that she would never look twice at him when so many whole and handsome men vied for her hand.

"I hardly saw Lady Alais, but I did get a new, irritating, Lady-Alais-related assignment. Actually, I could use your help with it. Come to think of it, you may be uniquely positioned to assist me. I'll make it worth your while."

He explained about the research he was supposed to do into Lady Alais's suitors.

"If you hear of anything or know of anything that you think might be useful, let me know."

"Like, for example, a noble lord that comes to me several times a week without fail because he can't have the real Lady Alais?" She cocked her head, giving him a saucy look.

He groaned. "I already know about him. You're all the 'Lady Alais' he needs. Trust me." He pulled her into a kiss, which she returned with more affection and enthusiasm than he had any right to expect from a woman in her profession. "So you'll help me then?"

"Of course." She winked at him and smirked.

"Thank you, Jane." He left his payment and hurried out into the night, praying that none of the Rossignols or de Veres ever found out who exactly it was that he visited so often on Birdie Street. Or what it could possibly mean about him, something he didn't want to delve into too deeply. Better he ignore that and focus on what he should instead of what he could never allow himself to have.

CHAPTER SEVEN

T HE GREAT HALL was filled with troubadours, and for once, Alais hardly noticed. She was ensconced by the enormous hearth with her bevy of suitors, her mother keeping a watchful eye from a discreet distance as the other guests caroused and got drunk on wine from the de Vere cellars.

Sir Victor also looked on from the other side of the room, although he pretended to be otherwise occupied every time that she tried to meet his gaze. Surely, he couldn't be concerned for her safety in such a public setting. Did he think one of her suitors was going to leap upon her unexpectedly? The thought made her want to giggle…unlike the sorry joke Lord Guy just made.

She should be enjoying this. Wasn't this what every girl dreamed of, to be surrounded by attractive men vying for her hand? Instead, she was bored out of her mind. She wished they would talk about politics and court intrigue, but they all resolutely refused to say a word that wasn't either a compliment or a comment on the weather.

"Lady Alais," Lord Alphonse and Lord Guy said at the same time. They exchanged looks of annoyance thinly disguised as polite surprise.

"After you, Lord Guy," said Lord Alphonse.

"No, no. After you," said Lord Guy, smiling nicely but looking daggers at Lord Alphonse.

"Oh dear. I seem to have dropped my handkerchief," she improvised quickly. "Whichever of you retrieves it for me should speak first."

They both dove for it. Lord Guy got there first. Unfortunately, Lord Alphonse was holding wine and spilled a bit on Lord Guy's cotte.

"Look what you've done, you sorry oaf," Lord Guy grumbled under his breath but not so quietly that she couldn't hear every word. He seemed to realize his gaffe because he rose and announced, "My lady," he said aloud, "You are as beautiful as the morning sun. You outshine every other lady in this room."

It took every bit of her willpower not to roll her eyes. "Thank you, Lord Guy," she said politely, attempting not to show any sign of favor through word or deed.

"I was going to say you are celestial, my lady," said Lord Alphonse, not to be outdone by his rival. "You sparkle like the night sky, pure and serene as an angel from heaven."

Oh, Good Lord preserve me. "You are too kind, Lord Alphonse," she answered, taking her handkerchief back from Lord Guy.

Lord Alphonse had designated himself her wine bearer and sat by her left side, handing her goblet with a lingering touch of the fingers whenever she wished a drink. Unfortunately, he kept stealing quaffs himself when he thought she was distracted, and he was starting to list a bit to the side. She didn't want to marry a drunkard, so he was probably off the list for serious consideration, even if his mouth did look inviting and kissable.

The handsome Sir Robert stood behind her, a possessive hand resting on her right shoulder. He'd wrapped his velvet cloak around her shoulders the moment she mentioned a slight chill and had kept his hand in contact with her ever since, as if giving her the cloak gave him an excuse. Not that she minded. She found herself nestling into his touch and adjusting her posture to give him a better view down over her shoulder to her chest. He was still the front runner, though she had yet to determine what his views were on Lady Helisende. Despite her attraction to him, she hesitated to tell her family to accept on her behalf. She wasn't sure why she was putting him off, but there was no need to rush this more than her parents already were.

Sitting across from her was Lord Guy, strumming the same three chords over and over on a lute he'd borrowed from one of the troubadours. He kept mumbling, "No, wait. No, wait. Ah, here it is," every time his fingers fumbled a chord. Clearly, he fancied himself a musical genius. It was kind of adorable how inept he was, though also a little bit hard on the ears.

Lord Louis sat beside Lord Guy looking more like a chaperone than a suitor, and Sir Elias stood by the fire, saying nothing, but watching her intently with those unnerving blue eyes.

"Sir Elias," she said, attempting to draw him out. "I've heard that tensions have eased between the Archbishop of Canterbury and the Archbishop of York after the king's intervention in their jurisdiction dispute. Do you happen to know the details of how things were settled?"

Sir Elias's gaze sharpened, though she wasn't sure how that was possible. "My lady, I don't think—"

"You needn't worry your lovely head with such matters," Lord Alphonse interrupted, drunkenly. "Especially on such a pleasant, fall day. The air is quite crisp, don't you think?"

Not the weather again!

Her hands balled into fists as she struggled to bring her irritation in check. A glance at Sir Elias told her he was ready to murder Lord Alphonse where he stood.

"Lord Guy," she said quickly, hoping to diffuse the situation. "Do you know any troubadour love songs?"

She didn't really want to hear one at the moment, but she had to do something.

"Oh, uh…of course, my lady," he said. He looked thoroughly flummoxed. She was going to regret asking, she could already tell.

"By the fountain in the orchard, where the grass is green…" he began to sing. If one could call the off-key honk of a goose being strangled singing. Alais watched in alarm as Sir Victor—on the other side of the room, but never out of eyesight—turned his head in what appeared to be alarm. And, she was sorry to note, he wasn't the only one.

Lord Guy's voice was dreadful. She had to put an end to this, and quickly. Before she could think of a polite interruption, Victor joined the group and leaned to ask Lord Guy if he could borrow the lute to settle a bet.

"What was the bet?" Lord Guy demanded, obviously reluctant to surrender the lute.

"Three silver pieces that I don't know all the word for Guillaume IX's 'My friends, I had such dismal fare.'" Sir Victor reached for the lute, clearly unwilling to take no for an answer. Alais hadn't heard the song he mentioned and was hoping he might oblige with a performance. After all, she knew any song he knew by heart was unlikely to be suitable for her ears, which made it all the more interesting.

"Who was this bet with?" Lord Guy grumbled.

"Lord Daniel."

Alais smiled. Even Lord Guy wasn't bold enough to interfere with something involving Lord Daniel. Sir Victor took the lute. Alais and Lord Guy both looked around to see where Lord Daniel was. He was absorbed in a battle of verse with a troubadour from Dover who sang some clever verse earlier in the evening.

Sir Victor didn't bother to look around. He wasn't even pretending the bet was real. Lord Guy was no longer singing, and that was all that mattered. While she admired his quick thinking, she couldn't help but poke at him—he was so fun to poke at, after all.

"Sir Victor," she said, "I don't believe I've heard the song you mentioned before. Perhaps you might sing it for us while Lord Daniel finishes his business with that troubadour from Dover."

His brows furrowed and he gave a miniscule shake of his head, intended only for her, but she was having none of it.

"Please, Sir Victor. Humor me."

He took a deep breath and swallowed. Her various suitors shifted in irritation, trying to pretend they didn't mind.

Lord Guy looked askance. "I'm not sure that's suitable for—"

"I'm sure Sir Victor wouldn't sing anything unsuitable, especially to me," she said before he could finish. "*Would* you, Sir Victor?"

Sir Victor gave her a strained smile.

"See, gentlemen? He would never do anything that was not proper." She tilted her head and fluttered her eyelashes at him, almost certain she could hear his blood boiling in his veins. She smiled and she knew it was the brightest of smiles, because this time it wasn't for show. For the first time all day, she was enjoying herself.

"Surely, you don't want to hear Sir Victor sing when there is so much *other* talent in this room," Sir Robert said, caressing her shoulder and squeezing it. Something in Sir Victor's face hardened at the sight.

"Oh, I think I would," she said, tucking a stray strand of hair back into her golden hair net. "He's been hiding his talent. I'd like to hear what he has to offer."

Sir Robert leaned close to her ear. "Surely, my lady, any one of us would be a better—" Sir Victor strummed his first chord with confidence, and Sir Elias stepped back with wide eyes.

"I don't think this is a good idea," Lord Louis whispered loudly, but Sir Victor ignored him, strumming several more chords, and then plucking a lively melody.

"My friends, I had such dismal fare," he began in a gruff but surprisingly tuneful baritone. "I must my own vexation share." He caught Alais's eye for a moment but swiftly looked away. "Not that you need to be aware. It's truly only my affair."

Lord Alphonse perked up from his drunken stupor. "Hey, I know this one," he chimed in happily.

"But I shall sing, and you shall see," Sir Victor continued. "That these three things do not please me: a queen under guard, a pond without fish—"

"Those aren't the words," Lord Alphonse objected, swaying slightly in his chair. "It isn't 'queen,' it's c—"

"—and worthless boasts and flattery," Sir Victor sang loudly, drowning out whatever Lord Alphonse was about to say as his fingers flew over the strings. He was an unexpectedly capable musician, though she supposed she shouldn't be surprised. He was capable of most everything he undertook.

As he continued to sing, he winked at her, and Sir Robert's caresses became a death grip. She turned to give Sir Robert a look, and he murmured an apology, loosening his pinching fingers.

Sir Elias, she noticed, had turned his icy stare on Sir Victor. There was something smug in his look that Alais didn't like. But why would Sir Elias have views about Victor? How could they have met? Did it have something to do with the tensions between Sir Victor's aunt and the Archbishop?

Meanwhile, Lord Guy looked on with barely contained irritation. Apparently, he didn't appreciate being shown up.

In spite of the various lords' reactions, Sir Victor's performance was well received by those nearby who were not in competition for her attention. He began to draw a crowd. By the time he'd finished the song, half the room had gathered round. Alais had no idea why he was so shy about singing. He was an expert performer. Even Daniel and the troubadour from Dover were watching by the end.

"You really do know every word of everything Guillaume IX composed," Daniel said, giving an appreciative nod.

"Well, he did change a *few* words," the troubadour from Dover chimed in.

"Embellishing for the lady, no doubt, as any singer worth his salt should," Daniel said, inclining his head toward Alais. "Sir Victor, can I borrow that lute? I wanted to play something I've been working on for our friend Bertrand here."

Sir Victor handed it over, and Lord Guy looked on, defeated. With a friendly nod in her direction, he disappeared into the crowd, leaving Alais feeling slightly bereft. *No, that would be silly with five suitors sitting here with me, though I confess I'm barely interested in entertaining them.*

"Finally, he's gone," Sir Robert mumbled.

What did he have against Sir Victor? Weren't they cousins?

"Do you visit your aunt, Lady Helisende, often?" she asked, wondering if the hostility had something to do with their conniving aunt.

"She's not my aunt, I'm afraid. My father's brother married her sister, so while we're distantly related through marriage, there's no direct connection. And thank heavens for that, because she doesn't like me very much. She's always preferred my cousin," he said, casting a dark glance at Victor.

Well, that was interesting. It was a relief to know he wasn't close to Lady Helisende, but the mystery of his enmity toward Sir Victor only grew.

Abruptly, he moved to stand in front of her, offering her his hand, and when she took it, he helped her to stand. "My lady, I was hoping you could tell me about that tapestry over there. It has a most unusual floral pattern," he said, offering her an arm with the clear intent of leading her away from the other suitors. Alais took his arm and followed his lead. Perhaps they could find a quiet spot for kissing. She wouldn't mind that at all.

Unfortunately, her mother saw as they passed.

"Sir Robert," the baroness said. "Did I hear you say you were interested in that tapestry over there? I'm so flattered you find it interesting. Some of the needlework is my own, you know. I'd be happy to show it to you and tell you anything you want to know."

Defeated, Sir Robert was forced to excuse himself and take her mother's arm, and Alais had to return to the other suitors who, if she was being honest, were boring her to tears. *Sheep, one and all,* she thought to herself. *With the possible exceptions of Sir Robert and Sir Elias.* Though she didn't particularly fancy the idea of finding herself with Sir Elias. He was so stiff, and he hardly ever spoke. And she was certain he was about to dismiss her question about Canterbury when Lord Alphonse interrupted. Not to mention that the intense gaze thing was beginning to wear on her.

As she settled back into her seat, she cast a wistful gaze about, looking for Sir Victor. He'd rescued her once. Any chance he might do so again? Unfortunately, he was nowhere to be found.

Time dragged on as she waited for the evening to end. Her mother refused to relinquish Sir Robert, which meant she was stuck with the others and their tiresome conversation for the rest of the night.

To her surprise, Lord Louis was her savior. None of the others had anything interesting to say, but then Lord Louis began to regale her with marvelous stories about her father in his youth and all the mischief he used to get up to. He was still too old to consider as a husband, but he was a gifted storyteller, and that was entertaining.

At last, the evening came to an end. Hopefully, she could arrange with her mother to meet her suitors individually going forward. Managing them as a group was grueling. There had to be a better way.

As she drifted off that night, she found herself thinking not of her suitors but of that surprising performance by Sir Victor. What word should it have been instead of "queen"? Someday, she promised herself, she would get a proper answer. He was a vexing man! She would track him down the next day and see if he'd share what he knew.

CHAPTER EIGHT

WHEN LADY ALAIS left the hall, Victor finally came out of the corner where he'd been lurking. Yes, lurking. What else could he call it? He'd been standing in the shadows, avoiding everyone while watching Lady Alais's suitors fawn all over her, and trying to keep himself from marching over and giving them all a taste of his fists.

Except Lord Louis, who seemed respectful enough, looking at Lady Alais like a beloved daughter rather than a prize horse to be bought. Not that Lady Alais would ever agree to wed Lord Louis, thank heavens.

Time to go to work. Clearly, all of these suitors were unsuitable. Victor merely needed to find out why for Lord Daniel. When Lord Daniel had first given Victor the assignment, it was all he could do to conceal his cringe. But after watching this pack of idiots all afternoon, he was warming to the idea. It was time to go make some friends and sabotage all their hopes and dreams regarding Lady Alais.

Shoving off from the corner, he headed straight to the center of the pack of wolves. "Gentlemen, gentlemen," he cajoled, arms wide. "The night is young. Don't tell me you're retiring already. Come have a drink with me, and I'll tell you everything I know about Lady Alais. I'm her personal guard, you know," he said, leaning in and lowering his voice persuasively. "You might learn something to your advantage."

He was improvising, but it seemed to be working. All eyes were trained on him.

"Thank you for your kind offer," said Lord Louis. "But I must decline. You young men go enjoy yourselves. I'm too old for carousing." He bowed out with a kindly smile and headed for the door. A good man. An old man. One definitely too old for Lady Alais.

That left four—Lord Guy, Lord Alphonse, Sir Elias, and his cousin, Robert.

"Excellent proposal," said Lord Alphonse, who was already slurring his speech slightly from drink. He threw an arm around Victor. "As you say, the night is young. What say you, gentlemen?"

"Yes, an interesting proposal, cousin," said Robert, eyeing him suspiciously. "You do know more than any of us about Lady Alais. Why exactly are you volunteering to tell us?"

Of course, his cousin was wary. Robert had never trusted him an inch, even though they'd grown up together. It was disappointing, really. All Victor had ever wanted was to be friends, but his cousin always treated him as a rival. And Robert had been particularly unfriendly ever since Victor's injury, as if he was disappointed that Victor had the gall to survive, thereby snatching Guestling from his waiting hands. But his cousin couldn't possibly be that greedy and resentful, could he? After all, Victor had no plans to marry, so Guestling would pass to Robert in time. Still, his father always told him he should treat Robert as a brother, so that was what he would try to do.

If Victor was feeling charitable, which he wasn't, Robert was a reasonable match for Lady Alais. Not a brilliant one, but Lady Alais didn't seem to care about lands and position. And the two of them seemed to genuinely like each other. Victor knew he shouldn't let old family prejudices get in the way of Lady Alais's happiness. Nonetheless, the idea of the two of them together made Victor's skin crawl, though he didn't like to examine why too closely.

"I like a bit of sport," Victor said with a shrug, knowing Robert would bite. The man couldn't stand to see anyone else win. "I think the competition will be more interesting if you are well informed. Besides, you haven't had much of an opportunity to taste the pleasures Winchelsea has to offer, cooped up here in the castle. It's a very hospitable little town with a surprising variety of entertainment. It would be a shame for you all to miss out."

"Well, I'm in," said Lord Guy, rubbing his hands together. "It is rather dull here at the castle."

Robert eyed Victor for a moment, then said, "I suppose I'll join as well. I shudder to think what you might have in mind for entertainment, Cousin, but I wouldn't want anyone to gain an unfair advantage over me."

It worked. *Brilliant.*

"Sir Elias? Will you be joining us as well?"

Piercing blue eyes bored through Victor as Sir Elias stood silently observing him. "Fine. I will join," Sir Elias said at last. "Like Sir Robert said, I wouldn't want anyone to have an unfair advantage."

Victor smiled, but it must have gone wrong because Sir Elias recoiled. No matter.

Like St. Patrick, I have played my flute and secured my snakes. Now to lead them to their demise.

"Come, gentlemen. Follow me." Victor turned and led the way through the entry hall, out the portcullis, through the front courtyard, out the castle gates, and down Castle Street. He deliberately passed Birdie Street. Best to save that for later when they were all properly drunk. Instead, he led them to The Victory Cup, an establishment frequented by Winchelsea's wealthier inhabitants that happened to hire irresistibly pretty serving girls. It was important to keep temptations close at hand. He wanted to give the suitors every possible chance to trip up.

"My lords, welcome," said a saucy, red-headed wench, spreading her arms to display her decolletage and winking at them as they entered. "We are honored by your presence. Please make yourselves at ease." She gestured to an empty table, polished to a dull gleam, at the front of the candle-lit room. The floor was covered in fresh rushes, and a musician played a lute by a roaring fire.

Victor pulled out the bench and slid into a seat. Lord Guy slid in next to him, followed by Lord Alphonse. Sir Elias and Robert sat opposite. Dear Lord, how he loathed the lot of them.

"My name is Kate, and I'll be serving you this fine evening. What can I get for you gentlemen?"

Staring fixedly at her chest, Lord Alphonse said, "Your finest wine, and keep it coming."

"Right away, my lord."

"Best to bring us some bread and cheese too," Victor added. He wanted them drunk but not so much that they made themselves ill. He didn't want to have to wheel them back to the castle in carts, after all.

The serving girl returned swiftly with pewter cups and two sizeable jugs of wine. Once she finished pouring for them, Victor raised his cup.

"To the lovely Lady Alais."

"And her ample dowry," Lord Guy added, making Lords Alphonse and Robert chuckle.

"And her ample bosom," Lord Alphonse said, laughing too hard at his own joke.

Victor clenched a fist beneath the table and took a deep breath. *This is what you wanted, remember?* They were here so that he could report back on their unworthiness. It wouldn't do for him to punch them senseless for revealing themselves exactly as he hoped.

Sir Elias wrinkled his nose and narrowed his eyes. "Sir Victor, if you please, would you tell us what you have to say about Lady Alais so that I can leave these fools to their drink? Their company offends me."

Lord Alphonse sighed loudly and rolled his eyes. "Oh, come

off your high horse, Sir Elias. I've seen how you look at her. You want to tup her bowlegged as much as the rest of us. Admit it."

Sir Elias's hand flew to the hilt of his sword.

"Gentlemen," Victor said quickly, making a placating gesture. "Save it for the tournament." Though truth be told, his own blade would be drawn right now were it not for his scheme to discredit them all.

He had to take control of this conversation before the others killed each other. Lord Daniel wouldn't be pleased if his tournament fell apart because of a tavern brawl.

"Lady Alais," Victor said loudly, gaining their attention, "is looking for a handsome champion—"

"Well, that rules you out," Robert interrupted.

Why did Robert have to needle him like this? "I was never in the running. I am merely her bodyguard."

"But surely you must have been tempted," said Lord Alphonse, "spending all that time alone with a sweet little filly like that."

They didn't know, *couldn't* know, the things that went on inside Victor's head. He clenched his hand harder beneath the table, digging his nails into his palm.

"Is she pure?" Lord Guy asked.

This time, Victor's hand flew to the pommel of his sword despite his best intentions. "What did you say?"

"I heard a rumor about her and a troubadour," Lord Guy continued, oblivious to his danger. "Is she untouched? She seems almost too good to be true—beautiful with good childbearing hips and a dowry that—"

"She is pure as the driven snow." If Lord Guy finished his sentence, Victor knew he couldn't stop himself from running his sword through the wretch's throat. "You mustn't listen to gossip, Lord Guy," he said, attempting to tamp down his violent urges and speak calmly. "I heard a rumor that you feel so inadequate in your manhood that you stuff lamb's wool down your breeches every morning, and we all know that can't be true."

Lord Guy turned scarlet and clenched his jaw, staring down into his drink.

Good. That put the man in his place.

Victor didn't actually know how far things had gone between Lady Alais and her troubadour, but he would be damned if he was going to sit and listen to a bore like Lord Guy insult her honor.

"I am sure the lovely Lady Alais is above reproach," Lord Guy mumbled into his cup.

"Indeed, Lady Alais is all that is beautiful and virtuous," said Robert with an inscrutable smile. "Any man would be lucky to have her for a wife, and I aim to make her mine."

Sir Elias looked daggers at Robert, then turned back to Victor. "I tire of these fools and their posturing. What can you tell us that might aid us in wooing her? If you have nothing useful to say, I will return to the castle."

Victor took a long, deep drink as he considered how to respond. He had no intention of helping this pack of braying asses in their courtship, but he had to say something. Perhaps he would have a little fun and lead them astray.

"What would you like to know?"

"What is her favorite flower?" asked Lord Alphonse, pouring himself another cup. "Ladies like flowers."

"Violets." Victor once heard her declare violets boring. He looked forward to seeing her expression as they all brought her bunches of them.

"Her favorite perfume?" Robert asked.

"Anything rose-scented." In fact, she found rose scents cloying and wrinkled her nose whenever her friends wore it.

"But isn't it really her father we need to woo?" Lord Guy asked. "Tell us about Lord de Vere. How do we get into his good graces?"

"By pleasing his daughter," Victor answered a little too sharply. He still hadn't forgiven Lord Guy for his earlier comments. In a calmer tone, he continued, "Lord de Vere has given her the freedom to choose, as long as she does so quickly. He wants her married by Christmas."

Robert smiled triumphantly. "She'll choose me. I've already got her wrapped around my finger."

Victor took a deep, calming breath. He didn't care. He *couldn't* care that Robert was right. There was no reason for his hand to grip the hilt of his sword once again. If his stomach churned at the thought, then it must have been something he'd eaten. Where Lady Alais bestowed her affections was none of his affair. His duty was to defend her honor until she married. That was all.

Sir Elias shook his head and stood. "I've had enough of these popinjays. I bid you all good night." He headed for the door.

Too bad. Victor had failed to eliminate him from the running. *Ah well.* There was still time before the tournament.

"What a shame. His loss. What say you to moving along to a place that offers a bit more feminine hospitality?" Now to go in for the kill.

"No, thank you," said Robert, rising. "I've no interest in your idea of hospitality. I believe I shall turn in as well."

Victor knew very well that Robert enjoyed a brothel as much as the next man, but perhaps he was on good behavior for the sake of Lady Alais. And the man was his cousin. He shouldn't always assume the worst of him. His father would want him to give Robert the benefit of the doubt. He nodded goodnight to his cousin and let him go.

"Shall we, gentlemen?"

He left coin on the table and led Lord Guy and Lord Alphonse off to Birdie Street.

Two down. Two to go.

CHAPTER NINE

THE TOURNAMENT WAS three days away, and the weather was chill and blustery. This was the first day in a week with no rain. Victor would have preferred to be at the tournament grounds, overseeing preparations, but instead, he was stuck accompanying Lady Carenza and Lady Alais on a visit to Silver Street to pick up tournament prizes.

"Sir Victor, it's good to see you. I was beginning to think you were avoiding me," Lady Alais said, giving him a wink as he bent to kiss her offered hand.

She was right. He was absolutely avoiding her. The rain had given him such a lovely reprieve from her company. Spending time with her had only sharpened his absurd and inconvenient attraction, which he was determined to ignore. Not that time away lessened his feelings. It only reduced the likelihood of his slipping up and making them known in some way. And it was his sworn duty to keep that from ever happening. For today's outing, he intended to maintain as much distance as possible, keeping conversation and contact to an absolute minimum.

"A pleasure to see you as always, Lady Alais," he said with a sideways smile. "And you, Lady Carenza," he continued, bowing.

"My husband is glad you are accompanying us today," Lady Carenza said with a dry smile. "We'll try to be quick so that we don't take up too much of your time. I'm sure that you have more important things to attend to."

"Think nothing of it, my lady. I am at your service." He gestured toward the gate, but Lady Alais didn't move.

"He still refuses to tell me what word he replaced with 'queen' the other night, and he won't tell me about the song with the cat either," Lady Alais teased. "I tried to ask Daniel, but he turned me down too. Carenza, do you know those songs?"

"As if I'd tell you if I did," Lady Carenza answered shaking her head. "Give it up."

Lady Alais shrugged. "For today," she conceded, grudgingly.

The song about a cat again. Would Lady Alais ever give up?

They set out on foot. On the narrow streets of Winchelsea, it was easier to walk than to ride most places. A fall breeze caught Lady Alais's hair, and she turned her face to it, closing her eyes and reveling in it for a brief moment. Victor caught a waft of lemon and thyme, the scent that followed her everywhere, and he breathed deeply. He would have to see if he could find a perfume with that scent for Jane.

"Will you be competing in the tournament, Sir Victor?" Lady Alais asked, taking his arm.

He stiffened and gently removed her hand. "I'm sorry, my lady. I need my sword arm free to defend you from brigands." He could still feel the warmth of her hand on his forearm like a caress. Stop noticing that, he told himself.

"Oh yes, the dastardly brigands of Winchelsea! They might steal me away and ravish me if you weren't here to defend me."

He gulped, hearing her say the word "ravish."

"But you didn't answer me," Lady Alais continued, oblivious to the effect of her words on Victor. "Will you compete in the tournament?"

"Of course, my lady." God's teeth, his voice was unusually raspy. Did she notice?

"I'm sure you'll win. I heard about your exploits on Birdie Street the other day." Victor had a moment of panic before he realized she must be talking about the Matthew raid. "From what

I've seen of your practice, you're a better swordsman than any of the other competitors, except maybe your cousin. He might give you some competition."

"You've watched me practice?" That was disconcerting news. He swallowed, hard.

"It's more interesting than embroidery." She shrugged.

"Is it? It's all just poking holes in things," he said looking down at his feet.

Lady Alais giggled. "But you men take off your shirts and thrash around, gleaming with sweat while you try to poke your holes. It's all much more stimulating than a room full of ladies with needle and thread poking holes in fabric."

Victor tried to decide if he was going to keep his shirt on during practice going forward, now that he knew she was secretly watching, but then he decided he didn't much mind the thought of her gaze on his bare chest. He looked around, ostensibly to be watchful, but more so he could mark the time of day by the position of the sun in the sky. How many more hours did he have to wait before he could see Jane?

Lady Carenza stepped in and took her sister's arm. "Alais, you might want to spend less time ogling sweaty men and more time praying for salvation. I fear for your silly soul sometimes."

They arrived at the jeweler's shop. Lady Carenza turned to him. "Ignore her. She'd flirt with a boulder if she got bored enough."

Lady Alais turned to him and responded in exactly the same voice, "Ignore her. She'd lecture God Himself on moral rectitude, given the chance."

With that, the sisters swept into the jeweler's shop, past the two burly guards protecting the shop's glittering wares.

Victor had a moment of blessed peace. He nodded at the guards, and they nodded back. They recognized him, of course, and knew better than to bother the head of the Watch. Victor leaned against one of the posts holding up the shop's awning.

Why couldn't Lady Alais let him be? It would be so much

easier if she ignored him, but she couldn't seem to stop herself from torturing him. Even though she obviously didn't mean anything by it, he couldn't brush it off. He knew he'd be dreaming tonight of holding her against his bare chest while he ran his sword through brigands hell-bent on ravishing her. He couldn't escape, even in his sleep.

A tempting, savory smell wafted on the breeze, and Victor turned to the baker next door. He could do with a lamb pie about now, come to think of it. Soon he was back at his post with a delicious hand pie. As he bit into it, he tried to focus on what still needed to be done for the tournament and mused on different ideas while he ate. He was licking the last bits of pie off his fingers as the ladies emerged from the shop.

"Here," said Lady Carenza, handing him a small, but surprisingly heavy leather pouch. "You'd best hold onto this until we're back in the castle."

He already knew what it contained: a heavy gold ring set with a ruby and a gold cloak clasp set with diamonds. These were two of the three prizes for the tournament. The third was a beautiful black destrier that was already housed up in the castle stables. Lady Carenza would give away the clasp to whoever she deemed the most valiant competitor. Lady de Vere would give away the destrier to the best jouster, and Lady Alais would give away the ring to the best swordsman. Victor didn't want the clasp or the horse, but he was determined to have the ring if he had to give his own cousin a concussion to get it. He might not be able to woo her, but he could win her favor for a day. It was the most he could dare to allow himself.

As they set off back to the castle, Lady Alais turned once again to Victor. "So tell me about your cousin, Robert. Are you two close?"

Victor took a deep breath. Robert was the last thing he wanted to talk about.

"We fought together in Spain. He's the reason I'm still alive. The swordsman that gave me my beauty mark—" he said, pointing at his scar—"was trying to cut off my head. Robert deflected him just in time."

"How heroic!" Her eyes shone with admiration, which made him clench his jaw, though he couldn't say why. "You were both fighting the Saracens in Spain, were you not?"

They turned onto Castle Street, when he heard a commotion up the hill. He tried to see what was happening, but too many people were in the way. Suddenly, people began diving to the sides of the street and into doorways. Lady Carenza noticed the danger first, and screamed, "Alais, get out of the way!"

Then he saw it. A heavy cart filled with wine barrels had come loose from its chocks and was rolling out of control down Castle Street, straight toward Lady Alais. Without thinking, he launched himself at her, knocking her over, and rolled with her to the side of the street, out of the way of the cart, which thundered by before it crashed into the side of a nearby inn.

Victor realized with alarm that he was lying on top of her, his arms wrapped around her. For a moment, madness took him, and he lingered, feeling her lush curves pressed against him as the fresh scent of lemon and thyme swirled around them. But then he felt his body start to respond, and he rolled away in a rush before she could notice. "Are you hurt?" he asked kneeling beside her.

She sat up slowly, wincing slightly. "I'm a little bruised but otherwise fine, I think." She put a hand on his arm. He looked at it and back at her. "Thank you. Truly." Her eyes shone with earnest gratitude. There was none of the usual mischief or flirtation in her look. "Can you help me up?"

He tried to ignore the spark of heat as he took her hand in his and pulled her to standing. "Looks like you scraped your elbow, my lady," he said, turning her arm gently.

"Is she hurt?" asked Lady Carenza, running over.

"Just a little scrape," he answered, letting Lady Carenza see Lady Alais's arm. Then he took the deep blue scarf he was wearing around his neck and wrapped it carefully around the injury.

"Thanks to Victor, I'm fine," Lady Alais said, grasping his arm when he finished tying off the scarf.

Victor swallowed hard and began reciting the schedule for the tournament in his head, as fire radiated through his body from the place where she clung to his arm. He said a silent prayer for deliverance, uncertain how long he could stand physical contact with her before he betrayed himself in some way.

At that moment, Robert came riding up in shining armor, just cleaned for the tournament, his golden curls stirring in the chilly November breeze. He held his white plumed helm in his left arm and looked every inch the fairytale hero.

"Oh dear, my lady Alais, you're hurt!" he said, jumping down from his horse. "Please allow me to accompany you back to the castle. You can ride my horse."

Victor's heart sank to his toes. This wasn't the deliverance he'd hoped for. Robert might appear to be a perfectly reasonable match for Lady Alais, but he'd always been viciously competitive and more than a little petty in his behavior toward Victor, even if he had saved his life. It was a small wonder that at that moment, Victor wanted to run him through with a lance.

Yet, for some inscrutable reason, Lady Alais turned to Victor, asking permission with her eyes to accept Robert's offer, as if it was his to give. He stared down at her and blinked, but could offer no answer. He had no words.

Lady Carenza answered on her behalf. "Thank you for your offer, Sir Robert. I'm sure my sister would be much obliged if you saw her safely back up to the castle. I'll follow with Sir Victor."

He watched with gritted teeth as Robert helped her onto the horse and they began to wend their way back up to the castle.

Lady Carenza gave him a sympathetic look as he watched his cousin lead Alais away. "Don't let her tie you in knots. She'll be safely married and out of your way soon enough."

That's what I'm afraid of, he refrained from saying.

"Shall we return to the castle, my lady?"

They made their way back up the hill.

AT DINNER THAT evening, Victor found himself sitting next to Robert, forced to listen to him enthusing about the loveliness and graciousness of Lady Alais.

"Thank the Lord that I was there to save her! If I hadn't happened by just then she would have been forced to walk back to the castle, despite her injuries," Robert told a nonplussed Sir Elias. "I don't know what you were thinking, Victor, letting the ladies walk."

Victor focused on his roast duck in red wine sauce and tried to ignore his cousin.

Lord Guy elbowed him in the side. "I say, that wasn't very chivalrous of you. But maybe you're trying to give your cousin an unfair advantage with Lady Alais. Considering her generous dowry, maybe you're trying to enrich the coffers of Guestling."

Victor gave Lord Guy a look that made him blanche. *Weaselly fortune hunter...*

"The money's nice, but it's not the only appeal," said Lord Alphonse, oblivious, taking a drink of wine directly from the pitcher. "Spirited little filly, isn't she? Hot-blooded, I'll warrant. Such lovely lines, and those hindquarters..." He whistled. "Wouldn't mind saddling her up and taking her for a nice long ride."

A dagger pinned Lord Alphonse's sleeve to the table. "You will speak respectfully about Lady Alais in my presence unless you want to become better acquainted with my blade," Victor said in a voice cold enough to freeze Rye Harbor, even to his own ears.

"No offense intended, my lord," mumbled Lord Alphonse, hastily pulling his limbs out of Victor's reach as soon as Victor removed his blade and sheathed it.

Thank heavens he'd already eliminated Lord Guy and Lord Alphonse from the running. When he'd shared their exploits from their little night out with Lords Rossignol and de Vere, they'd readily agreed. But he still hadn't found a good reason to discredit Sir Elias and Robert. And Lord Louis, he supposed, though he hardly counted. He might be a nice man, but Lady Alais would never agree to marry him.

Meanwhile, Sir Elias and Sir Robert kept whispering to each other. What were they up to? He'd have to find out.

His reverie was interrupted by the start of the evening's entertainment. A troubadour began singing a lover's lament about a gallant knight whose lady love refused to grant him a kiss. He ignored it. He didn't have much use for love songs.

Another troubadour sang a satirical piece skewering his aunt and her court for decadence and dissolution. That was slightly more interesting, better than listening to drivel from Lady Alais's suitors at any rate.

Last, Lord Daniel got up and sang a duet with Lady Carenza about whether a lover should be subservient to his lady love or treated as her equal. Lady Carenza was positively cheeky in her performance. Victor thought that after a performance like that, "Carenza" at the Bird in Hand was likely to get extra business. Indeed, Lord Daniel appeared to fully appreciate his wife's talent from the way he looked at her.

Lord Guy murmured to Robert, "Are married people allowed to look at each other that way?"

"Lord Daniel is a lucky man," Robert replied.

"She was supposed to be a nun, you know," Lord Alphonse said, inserting himself into the conversation. "Never saw a nun look like that though. Pretty naughty nun… I bet she's—"

Victor lifted Lord Alphonse up from the table by his collar. "I think it's time for you to retire for the evening, Lord Alphonse. Allow me to accompany you to your room."

After depositing Lord Alphonse in his guest quarters with some pointed warnings about the consequences of ever saying another word about any of the ladies of the castle, Victor headed down to Birdie Street at long last and bought Jane's services for the whole night.

"My lord?" Jane inquired seeing the fire in his eye as he closed the door behind them.

"Pleasure yourself, Jane." His voice was strained and desperate. "I need relief now. It's the fastest way."

Nothing moved him like the sight of a woman taking her own pleasure. It was a revelation the first time he'd seen it. Despite the Church's condemnation, he was certain it had to be a holy thing. How could God have given such beauty and such capacity for pleasure to womankind and not intend for them to glory in it? He watched Jane close her eyes and stroke herself, his breathing growing ragged. He worshipped the miracle before him with his gaze and then stripped off his clothes, climbing on top of her. But suddenly, it was all wrong. The memory of another body pressed against him made him stop short. Jane was a lovely woman in her own right, but she wasn't the right woman. These weren't the curves he ached to caress. It was all a poor simulacrum of what he truly wanted. He let out a heavy sigh and rolled to his side.

"What did she do to you today, my lord?" Jane asked, all too knowing.

"Lord Daniel sent me on an errand with her. She kept touching my arm. It was torture. And then I had to rescue her from a runaway cart on Castle Street," he said, unable to stop himself from confessing all.

"I heard about that! What a mess."

"For a brief moment, I held her in my arms, her whole body beneath mine. I didn't mean to, I swear. It happened by accident. And then my cousin showed up with his fancy armor and his stupid pretty face and swept her off to the castle without me."

"Ouch," she said, smiling kindly.

"And then I had to spend the whole evening listening to her suitors drooling over her."

"My lord, if I'm not being too bold, I have to ask..." She paused, her face wary.

"Spit it out, Jane."

"Well…why aren't you courting her? Surely, you're as good a match as any of the others. Why not try to win her?"

Victor exhaled. Jane was too insightful by half.

"I'm supposed to be protecting her, not seducing her. I gave my word of honor. Besides, why would a lovely, young damsel want to be married to this ugly mug? She wants some paragon who is going to sweep her off her feet, a man who will compose love poems and woo her with sweet words. She had five suitors who were all willing to play her game and dance attendance on her every whim. I'm not for her. Besides, it's my sworn duty to keep her safe until she marries someone else."

"I think you underestimate yourself. And her too." She caressed his face and tweaked his nose. "Much as I enjoy your company and appreciate all the coin you shower on me, I'm not the woman you want. I think you should get dressed, go back to the castle, and win your lady love."

"Don't be ridiculous." He laughed incredulously, but everything in him yearned to do exactly as she said.

"It's not ridiculous. She flirts with you, teases you, and does her best to get under your skin. I think she rather fancies you."

"She does that to everyone." It had nothing to do with him. *Did it?* No, he couldn't afford to entertain such thoughts.

"Go home, my lord. You obviously aren't interested in me." She looked him up and down pausing on his deflated cock to make her point.

Defeated, he pushed up from the pallet, gathered his clothes, and dressed. "You and she have more in common than looks, you know. You both have a special talent for getting under my skin."

She smiled. "I'll take that as a compliment. Now go up to the castle and don't come back. I expect to hear wedding bells within weeks."

Shaking his head, he gave her all the coin in his purse. He didn't want his own lack of enthusiasm to hurt her in any way.

He bid her goodbye and made his way back up to the castle,

replaying the moment when Lady Alais was in his embrace over and over in his mind. Duty be damned. His self-control hung by a thread. But what kind of knight would he be if he broke his word and pursued her? And how would she respond? He would have to keep his feelings carefully locked away. No one could ever know.

CHAPTER TEN

HER DOOR WAS closed, and it had been at least half an hour since she'd heard the last footsteps in the hall. Alais gave in at last to the urge she'd been resisting all week. She knew it was a sin. It would be a catastrophe if anyone ever found out, but she couldn't help it. There was only so long she could fend it off. It was like trying to ignore an itch or trying not to drink when thirsty. Carenza was right. The sooner she got married, the better. It was better to marry than to burn, or so the saying went, and she burned. Oh, how she burned. Her personal hell would surely be a castle full of tasty men she couldn't touch.

She pulled up her shift beneath the covers and grazed her nails along her inner thigh. Sir Robert came riding up Castle Street in gleaming armor. Her fingers tickled the hair of her mound, lightly teasing. He pulled her onto his horse in front of him and then reached beneath her skirt to touch her most sensitive places. Rocking gently in the saddle, she felt the smooth leather between her legs and the cool steel of his armor against her back. She let her finger enter her warm folds and begin circling and stroking as she imagined Sir Robert's lips on her neck. Her other hand fondled a nipple as she imagined Sir Robert's hand on her breast.

He touched and teased, and the sensation between her legs quickened. She let the rhythm take her as her pleasure built, and he continued to caress her most intimate parts. It was bliss to be touched, to be wanted, to take relief from the touch of another instead of being all alone in bed imagining.... *Oh.* Sir Robert dissipated, and she was alone in her bed imagining. The pleasure that had been building fell flat.

Her itch was as strong as ever, though, so she concentrated and started again. Sir Robert lay beside her in bed. It was their wedding night. He kissed her lips, and she felt tiny explosions all through her body. His hands explored her naked flesh, caressing, pressing, teasing. The moment had come. The moment when he would enter her and make her his. Something pressed between her legs, something new, something she'd never seen or felt before, and—

Her mother stood before her, delivering a gruesome lecture about blood and sticky liquid and the importance of ensuring the succession. Alais pounded her fists into her mattress in frustration. Why was it so difficult tonight? How could she need it so much and find it so impossible?

She thought back on her day, reviewing the events and trying to find the point at which the itch had sharpened into something she could no longer ignore. Maybe if she could figure out what had set her off, she could find a path to relief.

Then she had it. The weight and muscle of Sir Victor stretched the entire length of her. His arms had held her for a brief moment. And then he was gone. She'd felt the absence of his embrace the entire rest of the day. And then there was the way he looked at her when she left with Sir Robert. For some reason, she felt an intimacy with Victor that was different. Sir Robert felt like a distant ideal. Sir Victor was all too human, all too real.

She imagined Sir Victor lying beside her, his fingers touching her instead of her own. Tremors shot through her. Her fingers quickened their pace. His twilight blue eye watched as she shook in wave after wave of guilty pleasure, her body finding its release at long last. She moaned into her pillow with the final spasm, unable to keep silent.

When it was done, she went over to her washbasin to scrub her fingers clean. She couldn't leave any traces of her activities. No one could ever know. She splashed water on her face as well to revive herself from the trance of fantasy and sensation, then climbed back into bed.

Sir Victor. That was unexpected. She could swear he felt something for her—something about the way he looked at her and appeared embarrassed every time she touched him. But he'd never said or done anything to indicate a more active interest. She would have to try to draw him out, encourage him to speak.

He avoided her as much as possible. Perhaps he didn't like her after all. She was still embarrassed about how he'd overheard her asking about his face when they first met. He was probably insulted, even if he laughed it off at the time. He'd had every right to be insulted. She was so rude. There had to be a way to make it up to him. Setting aside the unexpected attraction she felt, she cared what he thought of her. She hated the idea of him holding a poor opinion of her.

It was a little silly, though, for her to get fixated on a man who wasn't interested when she had five suitors who were. She'd probably end up with Sir Robert in the end, though the idea had lost some of its appeal. He was pretty, and the way he looked at her certainly made her blood race at first. But it was nothing like a moment ago, thinking about Victor. Maybe she needed to reconsider her priorities. Could she possibly entice Victor to propose? As she drifted off to sleep, it was her guard, not her suitor, that filled her thoughts.

ON HIS NARROW pallet in his spare quarters, Victor lay awake, staring at the ceiling. Why *didn't* he court Lady Alais? Other than the fact that he was her protector, there was nothing stopping him. He could speak with Lord Daniel about being relieved of his assignment and try to win her hand. Guestling wasn't an impressive holding, but it was more than some of the others had to offer, certainly more than Robert had, at least. Lady Alais even seemed to like him these days. It wasn't only that she kept flirting with him. She flirted with everyone, so that was meaningless. But something had shifted in how she acted around him.

If he were to court her, how would he do it? She wasn't as vain and shallow as he'd originally thought. She was a flirt without a doubt, but she wasn't as preoccupied with her own appearance as most young women he'd met. She knew she was beautiful and didn't fuss about it. She liked to laugh and joke. Her humor tended to test the boundaries of propriety, something the two of them had in common.

He suspected that flattery would be useless with her. Words would only take a man so far if not accompanied by action. The whole episode with Gilbert proved that. It was clear that she had no patience for cowards. Money and position wouldn't impress her either. She might like the idea of being showered in gifts, but she wasn't ambitious or avaricious.

What she wanted, as far as he could tell, was a grand romance. She wanted someone who would sacrifice everything for her sake, someone who would offer unquestioning loyalty. He wasn't sure any of her suitors would offer that. They were all thinking in terms of what she could offer *them*, rather than the other way around. But he could offer it. If he was being honest with himself, he already had. He didn't think he could deny her anything if she asked, not that he would ever admit that out loud.

She also wanted affection, attraction, a spark. Those were not the sorts of feelings he generally inspired in women these days. Robert seemed to be the one with the best chance of kindling her flame. In fact, he seemed to have succeeded already to some extent. Victor had seen the look in her eye whenever Robert kissed her hand or found excuses to touch her—helping her onto a horse, retrieving a handkerchief, pulling a leaf from her hair, clutching her shoulder after offering his cloak. There had been warm moments with the other suitors as well, but not as frequently. Each time he was forced to watch one of these moments, his gut churned and twisted, and at the first opportunity, he fled to Jane.

He shouldn't begrudge his cousin. Robert saved his life. If they made each other happy, why shouldn't they be together? But he worried about Robert's temper and his tendency toward vindictiveness. In his darker moments, Victor sometimes wondered why Robert had bothered to deflect that blade the day he was injured. While Robert made a great show of loyalty and sympathy, it was clear that he resented being second in line after Victor for Guestling.

Robert never missed an opportunity to take a backhanded dig at him. Part of why he needed to leave Hastings had been his exasperation with the way Robert and his friends all called him "poor Victor" and talked endlessly about their pity for him after his heroic sacrifice. Robert made disparaging comments in the company of ladies, questioning *poor Victor's* ability to do his duty and produce an heir, as if his wound extended well beyond his face. He'd even tried to drive a wedge between Victor and his father, accusing Victor of neglecting his family to drown his sorrow in wine and whoring. Fortunately, his father had seen through it and told Robert to stop talking nonsense, though for some reason he still expected Victor to treat Robert like a brother.

He'd had to leave Hastings to be free of it all. His aunt had wanted him to marry. She'd even specifically mentioned Lady Alais before he'd left. It would solve a political problem for both his aunt and Lord Daniel if they wed, but he was damned if he was going to marry a woman for politics, even a beautiful woman whom he couldn't get out of his head. Dear God, he wanted her! But she didn't want him, so it could never be. And he still had a duty to defend her. He'd given his word to Lord Daniel.

He would have to content himself with winning her favor at the tournament. That one kiss, which he was determined to earn, would have to last him a lifetime.

CHAPTER ELEVEN

"Have you decided whose token you're going to wear yet?" Iselda sat on the bed, looking even younger than usual. Alais was less than one year older, but they appeared much farther apart. Iselda dressed too modestly, in Alais's opinion. That high-necked green velvet gown obscured the few curves on her slim form, and all her luxuriant chestnut hair was hidden beneath a wimple and veil.

"None of them." Alais smiled and winked at her sister.

"None?" Iselda's eyes grew wide.

"Why should I let them think they've won my favor before the competition? Besides, if I singled one out, it would offend the others. And if I wore them all, it would offend them even more." Alais looked at herself in the mirror. She wore a deep-blue velvet dress with a gold brocade silk panel in the front. The square neckline and tight lacing on the sides accentuated her curves. Her mother had lent her a sapphire necklace for the occasion, which added to her overall effect, and its dangling jewel nestled between her breasts, inviting illicit glances. She let her long hair hang brazenly loose, adorning it only with a simple deep-blue scarf to hold it back.

"Where did that scarf come from?" Iselda asked, pointing to her head. "I don't think I've seen you wear it before."

"No idea."

She knew exactly where it came from and who had given it to her, but she didn't want to give herself away to Iselda. Hopefully, Sir Victor would notice. It might be too subtle, but she didn't want to do anything that might catch the attention of her other suitors. It was important to keep her options open for as long as possible. She would be delighted if Sir Victor took the hint and put himself forward, but she knew she would need to marry whether he did, or he didn't. "How do I look?"

Iselda giggled. "Scandalous, but I'm sure that's what you were hoping for."

"Scandalous is good, as long as I haven't crossed the line to shameless." Alais turned to examine herself from all angles.

"I think you're fine. Mother will approve."

"But Carenza won't?"

"No, she won't."

Alais smiled. "Good, then I've got it right. Shall we head out?"

They joined their mother and Carenza, who handed little Charles over to his wet nurse.

"You look lovely, darling," her mother said. "Your suitors won't be able to keep their eyes off you."

Carenza frowned. "Won't you be cold with that much skin exposed?"

Iselda giggled beside Alais, and Alais stifled a laugh and squeezed Iselda's hand.

"I'll be fine, Carenza." Alais led the way out to the front courtyard where a carriage waited for them. They rode down through the city, out the western gate, and over to the tournament grounds where a growing crowd was gathered.

The Rossignol and de Vere banners waved and snapped in the breeze on either side of a central platform where their families would be seated under a canopy, half of which was red striped and the other half blue striped to match the tabards of the two teams of competitors in the melee.

Townsfolk and visitors milled around the tournament grounds in a festive mood as they alighted from the carriage. The elevated stands of tiered bench seating that extended out on either side were starting to fill with revelers, and on the opposite side of the field, there was more tiered seating dotted with guests.

A double palisade of wooden stakes lined the tourney field in front of the seats to prevent horses from bolting into the crowd. Moveable barriers enclosed either end. On one side they were festooned in blue and on the other in red to match the pavilion. The field itself was covered in sand to reduce the chance of injury to falling cavaliers. Soon, proud knights would take the field to display their might and prowess, and she would have a front-row seat to the whole display.

Alais wandered away from her family to see the rest of the grounds and hopefully find her friends. She walked behind the seating on each side where vendors set up stands to sell foods, beverages, ribbons, and flowers. Attendees adorned themselves in the colors of those they supported. She was already dressed for the day, of course, and needed no further adornment, but she pulled a coin from her purse and bought a pastry.

Wine and ale flowed freely, and the scents of roasting meats and sweet treats filled the air. She wandered over to watch a puppet show for the children for a few minutes and then caught sight of Simone in the distance.

Alais made her way past a juggler who was entertaining the crowd, drawing *oohs* and *ahs* with their feats. She nearly bumped into one of the braziers placed at regular intervals so that people could warm themselves. Despite the chilly weather, the crowd was festive and raucous. Hundreds of spectators meandered through the grounds filled with excitement and good cheer.

Simone was with Lady Eugenie. What luck! Alais hurried to join them.

"I love your dress, Alais!" Lady Simone said, taking the edge of a long sleeve in her hand and fingering the velvet.

"You look lovely yourself, Lady Simone! Green suits you."

"It brings out my eyes, doesn't it?"

Lady Eugenie gasped and grabbed Alais's arm. "Don't look

now, but Sir Victor is staring at you."

He was? Alais and Lady Simone immediately swung their heads around to see.

"I said 'don't look'!"

Sir Victor stood beside Lord Daniel and was indeed staring at Alais with an intensity that made her blush and turn away.

"I think he was staring at something else just past me," Alais said, suddenly warm despite the brisk weather.

"No, he fancies you. I'm certain of it," said Lady Simone. "It's too bad about his face. I'm told he used to be quite handsome."

"I think his injuries show his valor," Alais objected, realizing it was true. Somehow, in her eyes, his scars made him all the more attractive.

"Whose valor are you commending, Lady Alais?" asked a deep voice behind her. She turned to see Sir Robert in all his armored glory, crowned with golden ringlets. "Oh dear, I see you've forgotten the pin I gave you. Here, let me give you this to wear instead."

Before she could object, he pulled off the silver clasp of his cloak and pinned it to her dress. She couldn't think of a graceful way to say no. His fingers brushed the bare skin along her neckline as he took his time fastening it in place. For some reason, she didn't feel the usual rush of warmth at his touch. She sighed as he stepped away.

"There. Now everyone will know how much I adore you. I already have your handkerchief tied to my lance." She'd lost quite a few handkerchiefs over the last week at her mother's urging. He took her hand and kissed it using his tongue once again, though this time, she didn't like it nearly as much as she had before. Her friends collapsed against her with sighs and giggles as soon as he turned his back.

"I want one of those," said Lady Eugenie, practically drooling as she watched him walk away.

"I want three of those," declared Lady Simone, not to be outdone.

Alais's glance strayed to Sir Victor, and she stopped giggling. She only caught his eye for a second but the heat and fury she saw before he looked away was enough to dispel her frivolous mood.

To her surprise, he walked over to her and offered a curt bow. "Excuse me, ladies. Lady Alais, you should rejoin your family. We'll be starting soon." He gestured for her to follow him toward her seat, careful as always not to touch her. When they were far enough from her friends not to be heard, he murmured, "You're wearing my scarf."

Good. He noticed. She gave him an inviting smile. "It matched my dress."

"Someone might think you mean something by it."

She paused and looked him in the eye, smiling flirtatiously. "Would they now?"

"Someone might think you mean something by that pin too."

Oh dear. What must he think? "I couldn't very well refuse in front of everyone."

"Why are you wearing my scarf?" His eye bored into her with smoldering intensity, and she could hardly breathe.

At that moment, her mother came up and saved her from having to invent a response. "Where have you been? They'll be starting soon. We need to head to our seats. Thank you for finding her, Sir Victor." Her mother started to drag her to the platform with their seats.

"Wait, Sir Victor!" she called after him. "Will you be on the red team or the blue team in the melee?" She already knew, but she wanted him to know she knew.

"Blue." He said gruffly.

"Good. Then I wore the right color." She grinned and turned without waiting to see his reaction, then headed to her place on the platform. Trumpets announced the start of the tournament, and the crowd settled into their places in the stands.

Alais took her place in front. While technically a spectator, her mother had made clear that she was also part of the spectacle. This was as much an opportunity for her to show off her beauty and her courtliness to the assembled knights as it was for them to show off their prowess to her. Daniel's voice rang out, asking the day's competitors to join him on the field. Servants handed pewter goblets to each of them.

"Good knights, Winchelsea welcomes you and is honored by your presence today!" Daniel bellowed. "Each of you comes seeking glory and renown, and I am certain that your valor on the field today will do each and every one of you credit. But this is a competition. Only three of you will walk away with prizes. Lady Isabella de Vere will award this destrier to the winner of the joust."

Her mother stood and curtsied to Daniel and gestured to a restive and sleek black war horse being led across the field by a stable hand. The crowd burst into applause and chatter about such a fine and costly gift.

"Lady Alais will offer a ring to the best swordsman."

Alais stood and offered a curtsy then held up the ring. While the ring wasn't as valuable as the destrier, she was well aware that *she* was part of the prize. The crowd whistled and hooted as she smiled at her admirers.

"And my lovely wife, Lady Carenza, will offer a jeweled clasp to whomever she deems the most valiant competitor outside of the other two winners."

Carenza stood, taking Daniel's arm, and holding up the clasp for all to see. The applause for Carenza was enthusiastic but respectful.

"As is traditional, the winners will receive a kiss in addition to the prize."

There were hoots and cheers from the crowd and several of the competitors at that. Four of Alais's suitors looked at her with lascivious intent. Lord Louis, much to her amusement, was looking at her mother, blushing furiously. Victor's gaze was fixed on the ground.

"Watch yourselves, my lords. Lord de Vere and I will be close at hand to see that you don't get carried away."

There were chuckles from the crowd at that.

"As a reminder, this is a friendly competition," Daniel continued. "Lances are to be directed at the body only. Heads, limbs, and horses are strictly off-limits. For the melee, you are aiming to knock down, disarm, or touch your sword to the chest or neck. You are not to wound or kill. When you are knocked down, disarmed, or touched, you will be asked to leave the field. Lord de Vere and I will be judging. If we tell you to leave the field for any reason, you must do so. If you cause serious injury to any of your opponents or disobey any of the rules, you will be removed and disqualified. Is everyone clear?"

The competitors shouted their agreement.

"Then I propose a toast to your honor and valor!" Daniel raised his goblet and took a drink.

The competitors raised theirs as well and took a quaff.

"Let the tournament begin!"

The competitors exited the field, half to the blue side and half to the red. Soon trumpets announced the first joust. Alais watched as Lord Guy and an older knight from Eastborne she'd never seen before lowered their lances and charged at each other. Lord Guy knocked the other knight off his horse, and he landed with a clatter in the sand. Daniel declared Lord Guy the victor of the first challenge.

Alais did her best to look interested, but she'd always found jousting a bit boring and repetitive if everyone was following the rules. If not, it could get bloody and gruesome quickly, which was always more interesting even as it was horrifying. She shivered, remembering the tournament she'd attended when she was twelve where a stray lance pierced a weak spot in a knight's armor and impaled his shoulder. It was supposed to be a friendly competition, but she knew the weapons were sharp and the deadly danger all too real. She said a silent prayer that no one died today.

The initial eight rounds were uneventful except for Victor and an unfamiliar knight from Hawkhurst. The knight from

Hawkhurst aimed slightly too high, and Victor was forced to throw himself from his horse at the last second to avoid being impaled through the neck. Daniel had the knight from Hawkhurst removed from the competition, but since Sir Victor didn't follow through with the joust, he couldn't continue to the next round. As Sir Victor was leaving the field, Sir Robert watched him intently. She couldn't hear what Sir Robert said, but she could see the sneer on his face. Sir Victor gave him an intent look and walked away without a word.

"I wonder what that was about," she murmured to Iselda.

"Very odd," Iselda answered, having also watched the exchange. "Didn't Sir Robert save Sir Victor's life in Spain? I thought they were friends."

"Very odd indeed."

As the competition continued, Alais found herself wondering about Sir Robert's character. She didn't like the idea of being married to someone who could behave so unkindly. The more she thought back over her interactions with him, the less impressed she was. She began to see a pattern of self-importance and pushiness. Even his insistence on pinning his clasp onto her this morning—he didn't even ask before he did it. He just reached out and did what he wanted. She would have to avoid encouraging him quite so warmly.

The field had been narrowed to two final competitors, Lord Louis and Sir Robert. They took their places, lowered their lances, and charged. Alais couldn't help a momentary smile as Robert was knocked onto his posterior with a great crash and an undignified grunt. She managed to school herself into a look of concern by the time Sir Robert looked up to see her reaction. He seemed nonplussed to have her watching his humiliation and stomped off the field with his horse. He was a sore loser too, apparently—not the most attractive of attributes.

Daniel declared Lord Louis the winner of the joust and invited him up to the front to claim his reward. A groom brought out the horse, and her mother ceremonially handed Lord Louis the reins before the stable hand took the horse back for safekeeping during the rest of the competition.

Then Lord Louis leaned in and whispered something to her mother that made her titter and blush. She bent her head to kiss him on the cheek and at the last moment, he turned so that her lips landed on his mouth.

She jumped back in surprise and said, "You naughty man!" But she was grinning like a cat with cream.

Lord de Vere shook his head at Lord Louis in disapproval. Lord Louis shrugged. "What can I say? You have a lovely wife, and you *did* give me permission to kiss her, just this once."

"Never again," grumbled Lord de Vere, as he wrapped a possessive arm around her and gave her a lingering kiss on the lips.

"Martin, everyone is watching," she objected when he released her.

"I don't care," he said, giving her a look that made her blush.

The audience loved it. They were hooting, whistling, banging on their seats, and doing anything they could think of to make a racket.

It took Daniel several minutes to get their attention again. "And now, we will begin the melee. Is everyone wearing their colors?" He looked at the competitors arrayed at either end of the field and confirmed that they were all wearing red or blue tabards over their armor, according to their team. "Remember the rules, my lords. Lord de Vere and I will be watching carefully. Are you ready?"

The men yelled in response.

"At the sound of the trumpet, you may begin."

The trumpet sounded, and the knights ran at each other. There were seven on each side. After the removal of the knight that jousted against Sir Victor, Lord Louis had graciously offered to forgo further participation so that the numbers would be even. Swords clashed, and the battle began in earnest.

Alais watched the chaos and quickly picked out Sir Victor

from the others. There was a smoothness and grace to his movements that made all the others look ungainly and awkward. Unfortunately for him, the rest of the blue team wasn't nearly so strong. He was the best swordsman on the field, but the blue team was soon outnumbered, as her father and Daniel escorted the fallen off the field.

Sir Victor danced and twisted and turned, knocking down Lord Guy and disarming another knight before he found himself fighting Sir Robert, Sir Elias, and someone she didn't recognize. Her heart raced as she watched, and she clutched the arms of her chair, craning her neck to see each movement.

He fended them off, spinning like a dervish. She was having difficulty seeing what was happening, the movement was so quick. Sir Elias jabbed at the gap in Sir Victor's armor beneath the left arm and left a vivid red gash.

"No," Alais gasped, half-rising from her chair.

Iselda reached out, gently pulling on her arm until she sat back down.

"He'll be fine," Iselda whispered once Alais was seated.

Alais nodded and took a deep breath, but her heart was pounding.

Fortunately, Daniel removed Sir Elias from the competition for an illegal strike. Alais certainly wouldn't be marrying him after such a vicious display.

Her gaze returned to Sir Victor, who continued to fight his cousin and one other remaining knight. He continued to deflect blow after blow, despite being outnumbered. The crowd was silent, and the only sound was the clash of steel against steel.

The unknown knight took a swing at Sir Victor's head and would have taken it off but for Sir Victor's last-moment deflection.

She jumped to her feet, her hands over her mouth. *No!*

Lord de Vere intervened, dragging the knight from the fight for breaking the rules by taking deadly aim. She cheered the call and then sat back down, clenching her hands in her lap.

It was down to Sir Victor and Sir Robert, and they were nearly evenly matched. Sir Victor had a slight upper hand, in her opinion, but it could go either way. Sir Robert looked at Sir Victor with the ugly sneer again, and Sir Victor narrowed his eyes and clenched his jaw. Whatever happened between them, it must have started long before the tournament and even before Sir Robert had arrived in Winchelsea. There was something going on she did not understand.

Sir Robert lunged at Sir Victor's neck with his sword, and she gasped. How dare he take such deadly aim in a tournament!

Sir Victor used Sir Robert's momentum to trip him, and he fell on his face.

A flood of relief and joy washed over her, and she cheered loudly, not caring who saw. If Sir Robert was disappointed in her, so be it. He deserved to lose after attempting such an underhanded, unchivalrous thing with his own cousin.

Sir Victor touched his sword to Sir Robert's neck, and it was over. He sheathed his sword, and Sir Robert slunk off, still sneering, yet again demonstrating his inability to lose with grace. The audience roared.

Sir Victor turned to look at her. The noise of the crowd and Daniel's announcement of the winner suddenly seemed to come from a great distance. She stepped down from the platform and made her way down to the field, holding Sir Victor's gaze the whole time. He walked toward her, slowly, steadily, still panting and bathed in sweat from the exertion of battle. As he approached, she could see blood from where he had been nicked during the fight. He was so brave, so graceful, so handsome. What she had said to Lady Simone was true. She no longer thought of his scar as a blemish, but as a sign of his valor, making him all the more attractive.

She held out a trembling hand. He took it in his and knelt before her. He kissed it, still holding her gaze, fire in his eye.

Her body went up in flame at the touch of his lips and the heat in his look. She stepped closer and whispered, "Rise, Sir

Victor."

He stood.

She took out the ring and with shaking hands slid it onto his finger. Taking his hands in her own, she rose up on her toes to kiss his cheek. She could feel his heat, smell his skin, taste the salt of his sweat on her lips as she pressed them to his prickly stubble. She desperately wanted to kiss his lips and lose herself in his embrace, but too many eyes were on them both at that moment. Hundreds of people were watching, including the five men who wanted to marry her. Sir Victor hadn't asked, she reminded herself as she released him.

She backed away, her chest heaving and her heart pounding as if she'd run a great distance. When she moved to relinquish his hands, he laced his fingers with hers to pull her back toward him. "Thank you for wearing my scarf." His voice was rough and harsh, strained by some emotion she couldn't identify.

It was too much, being this close. Fire coursed through her veins, radiating from the spot where his hand touched hers.

With a shuddering breath, she forced herself to squeeze his hand and smile, then pulled away to turn and head back to the platform with the rest of her family. Halfway there, she glanced back over her shoulder, and he was still standing in the same spot, watching her with the same intensity. She swallowed hard as she turned quickly and headed to her seat.

"Are you well?" Iselda asked, putting a kind hand on hers. "You look shaken. Did he say something to you?"

"I'm fine."

"You look pale, scared almost. It's not like you."

"I'm fine, only a little nervous in front of a crowd. That's all." *And completely addled by a man I can't have because he doesn't want me.*

"You did fine." Iselda patted her hand.

Alais smiled weakly, forcing herself to attend to what was happening around her and dragging her gaze away from where Victor had disappeared.

Carenza stood up to announce the winner of the clasp. She whispered something in Daniel's ear. Daniel laughed and whispered something back.

"Fine," Carenza said audibly. "Since you say I can't give it to you, I choose Lord Guy." Daniel nodded. "But I'd much rather kiss you."

Daniel gave her a mischievous smile and raised an eyebrow at her. "Oh, you will. Just not right now."

To the crowd, he announced, "For our final prize today, Lady Carenza, my wife, will bestow a jeweled clasp to the knight that she deems has demonstrated the most valor. The prize goes to Lord Guy!" The crowd's response was tepid. He was a dull choice, which was why Carenza chose him, Alais suspected.

Lord Guy made his way up to the platform and bowed to Carenza. She handed him the clasp, and told him in crisp, quiet tones, "I will kiss your cheek, and you will stand still for it. No sudden movement. Do you understand?"

Lord Guy gulped.

Carenza gave him a chaste peck on the cheek and sent him on his way.

"Ladies and gentlemen, that is the end of our tournament. Now go eat, drink, and be merry," Daniel announced to the crowd who started heading toward the food stalls.

Alais headed over to her mother. "May I head back to the castle and rest a bit before the feast? I'm feeling a bit lightheaded."

"You're feeling unwell, Lady Alais?" It was Sir Robert. *Of course.* Exactly who she didn't want to see.

CHAPTER TWELVE

"I WAS HOPING I might entice you to take a walk with me, my lady, but if you're feeling unwell, perhaps we might rest under those trees?" Sir Robert was all charm, seemingly recovered from the strange rage that overtook him during the tournament when he was fighting with Victor.

"I would need a chaperone."

"I'll do it," offered Carenza. For once Alais didn't mind having her do the honors. If anyone could scare off Sir Robert, it was Carenza.

Sir Robert took her hand and placed it on his arm, leading her over to a bench under a nearby tree with a brazier underneath. Carenza seated herself at a discreet distance on the opposite bench and turned her attention to the passing crowd.

"Are you cold, my lady?" He put a solicitous and unwelcome arm around her.

She shuddered and shook him off.

"No, my lord. I'm quite comfortable." She gave him a prim smile. "The tournament was very exciting. I'm relieved no one was seriously injured." Alais could tell he was about to launch into an amorous speech, which she wanted to avoid, so she cut in with, "Can I ask you a personal question?"

He smiled and looked her up and down lasciviously. She was sure he had a misguided notion of what she was about to ask.

"I couldn't help but notice that you and your cousin seemed angry at each other during the tournament. What happened between you?"

He cleared his throat and furrowed his brow. "That *is* a rather personal question, my lady."

"I'm sorry. I don't mean to pry. But I couldn't help but wonder, watching the way you two fought."

She inched away from him on the bench. He inched forward.

Taking a deep breath and letting it out, he answered, "You are perceptive, my lady. My cousin and I don't see eye-to-eye on many things. I saved his life in Spain—"

"Yes, he told me." She was in no mood for his bragging.

"Did he?" He cocked his head and pursed his lips. "Well, you'd think he'd be a bit more…friendly to me under the circumstances. I don't like to speak ill of others, especially to a lovely lady, but he hasn't been the same since his injury. He seems to feel…. How do I put this? He seems to feel inferior, jealous. The poor man resents me."

This solidified Alais's low view of Sir Robert in a way that nothing else could. It was plain to her that whatever resentment might exist was entirely on Sir Robert's side. Perhaps he was jealous of Sir Victor's status as the heir, or his superior skill as a swordsman. Sir Victor had never spoken a word against his cousin despite the obvious hostility between them, and here Sir Robert was implying Sir Victor was jealous, inferior, and resentful. But Alais was practical. She didn't expect a perfect husband, yet she refused to marry a jealous liar.

"But I didn't ask to speak to you so that I could talk about my cousin. I want to speak about us." He grasped both of her hands in his, and she forced herself not to recoil. The feel of her hands in his was so very different from Victor's touch. She just wanted to pull away. Alais tried to keep from grimacing and made herself listen to him seriously. She would hear him out and say no, and that would be the end of it.

"My lady, my affection for you can hardly have escaped your

notice." He raked her with a lecherous gaze that rested a bit too long on her chest. "And I daresay you have some feelings for me too unless I am much mistaken. Lady Alais," he tightened his grasp on her hand and gave her his most smoldering and ardent look, "Will you do me the honor of marrying me?"

He didn't wait for an answer before launching himself at her and pulling her into a sloppy kiss that made her feel cold all over.

"Wait," she yelped as soon as she could pry herself free. "You haven't heard my answer yet. That was excessively forward, my lord."

His brow furrowed, and she could see storm clouds forming behind his eyes.

"I am flattered by your proposal. I hold you in high regard, but I'm afraid I must refuse. I've given it careful consideration, but I don't think we're well suited. I'm sorry, my lord."

Carenza gasped, and Alais glanced at her. This was the right thing to do, wasn't it? Carenza gave her a little, encouraging smile as Alais turned back to her suitor.

"But your father and Lord Daniel approve," he said, scooting closer and grasping her hands again.

"They don't object, but the final choice is mine. I've decided this is not the right match for me. I'm sorry to disappoint you," she said, scooting away and pulling her hands from his clasp once more.

There, she'd done it. If he had any chivalry at all, he would accept her rejection and leave her alone.

His eyes narrowed, and that ugly sneer she saw during the tournament was back. "What did Victor tell you about me?"

"What?"

He grabbed her shoulders a little too harshly as he glared at her. "He told you some lie. That's why you're refusing me."

"He told me you saved his life, and he told my father and Daniel that you were a good match for me, that he knew of no reason why they should oppose a marriage between us." She plucked his hands from her shoulders and pushed them away, as she gave him a warning look.

He regarded her with a scowl, and his face bore no resemblance to the handsome man she'd first admired. "So after all of your flirtation, after leading me on shamelessly, you're rejecting me out of hand?"

The words hit her with the force of a slap. She gasped. "I beg your pardon?"

"After the way you behaved, riding with me back to the castle that day you were injured, accepting my gifts…You're wearing my clasp right now. I gave it to you in front of everyone right before the tournament. I don't believe this!"

How had she ever thought this man could be a match for her?

"I'm sorry if you feel I led you on. You can have your clasp back," she said, unfastening it from her dress and handing it to him. "I think I should return to my family."

"I'll make you regret this. I promise you that." His eyes narrowed to slits, and there was no hint of his usual flirtatious warmth. He was a snake ready to strike.

Alais shivered and recoiled.

"Sir Robert." Carenza moved from her bench to intervene before Alais realized she'd even gotten up. For once, Alais felt a swell of gratitude for Carenza's interference. "Don't threaten my sister," the duchess said with an imperious tone, and she gave him a glare that made him flinch. With that, she reached for and took Alais's hand. "I think it's time we go."

Alais was more than happy to let Carenza pull her away. She was trembling all over, barely aware of her surroundings as they weaved their way through the crowd.

As soon as they were out of sight and earshot, Carenza stopped and pulled her into a hug. "I'm so proud of you, Alais! You did the right thing. I was absolutely certain you were going to marry him, but I'm so glad you saw through him in the end. He's a waste of time. You deserve better."

Alais was stunned. Carenza had *never* told her she was doing the right thing.

Now her older sister dragged her over to Daniel and their father who were absorbed in a logistical conversation with Sir Victor.

"You'll never believe what Alais just did." Carenza interrupted, positively bubbly. "She turned down Sir Robert! I'm so happy she saw through him. Oh, it is such a relief!"

Her father and Daniel looked confused. Sir Victor looked at Alais, fire in his eyes. Her heart skipped a beat.

"My love, I thought you wanted Alais to get married," Daniel said hesitantly.

"Of course, I do," Carenza said. "But not to some stuffed shirt who spends more time on his hair than I do. And he threatened her when she turned him down. Can you believe it? He said, 'I'll make you regret this. I promise you that.' As if he was already plotting revenge. Good riddance is what I say."

"Lady Alais," Sir Victor said. "Would you like me to accompany you back to the castle? I don't like that he's threatened you."

Yes, she would have liked nothing better, but did she dare offend her suitors by disappearing like that?

"I appreciate the thought, but I've been looking forward to this tournament for so long," she said, straightening and squaring her shoulders as best she could.

Her father shook his head. "Sir Victor's right. I wouldn't want anything to happen to you, however unlikely it is that he would take action." Turning to Sir Victor, he said, "Can you go get her maid? You should head back quickly."

Thank heavens for her father.

"As you wish, my lord. I'll return as soon as I've seen her safely home."

Sir Victor bowed his head and disappeared. Several minutes later, he returned with Dora and a few other servants who were headed back to the castle.

Alais set off in a carriage with Dora, still shaken by her encounter with Sir Robert. She'd been looking forward to this day all month, but it was turning out so differently than she'd expected.

Sir Victor followed the group by horse. She swore she could feel him watching her through the carriage walls, but she didn't dare turn to look out the window.

"What happened, my lady? You look distressed," Dora said, taking her hand and giving it a squeeze.

"Sir Robert proposed, and I turned him down. He didn't react well."

Dora's eyebrows shot up. "You turned him down? But I thought you and he…"

"I know. I did too, but today made me realize he's not a nice person, however handsome he might be." Alais stared fixedly at her lap.

Dora looked at her long and hard then nodded. "Then you made the right choice, my lady."

"If that's so, why do I feel so awful about it?" She'd certainly learned her lesson about trusting a pretty face. Sir Robert might show a fair face to the world, but his temperament was distinctly unattractive. She felt like a fool for being taken in.

Dora patted her hand and gave it another squeeze. "You just rest and refresh yourself. I know you'll be going to the feast this evening, so you'll need your strength."

Alais rested her head on Dora's shoulder and closed her eyes. She didn't want to go to the feast, but she knew she had no choice. Hopefully, Sir Robert would opt not to attend. She would be quite relieved if she never had to see him again. Her other suitors didn't fill her with enthusiasm, but she needed to make a decision quickly now that the tournament was over. She could only hope that Sir Victor would take her encouragement and declare himself. Otherwise, she was stuck with choosing between Sir Elias and Lord Louis since her father advised her against Lord Alphonse and Lord Guy for reasons he refused to share.

The coach halted, and Sir Victor opened the door to help her down. As she put her hand in his, she searched his face for some sign that he might be moved to action. He looked at her intently, as if trying to hold something back, but what that was she couldn't guess. If only she could speak on her own behalf! But that was not how things worked. A lady could not ask a man. The question had to come from him.

"My lady, is something wrong?"

She had stood and stared too long, she realized.

"I—" She stopped, uncertain of how to proceed. "You fought bravely today. It was thrilling to watch. I admired your skill and grace." Squeezing his hand, she tilted her head slightly closer to his. His head inclined almost imperceptibly toward hers. His lips parted. It was the unconscious prelude to a kiss, she was certain. They drew closer and closer. Her breathing grew ragged.

Dora cleared her throat, and sanity returned. Of course, they couldn't follow through with their inclination, especially standing in the middle of the courtyard surrounded by servants, but she let the spell hold them for several seconds before she dropped her gaze demurely to the ground with a private smile.

"I shouldn't delay you," she said, relinquishing his hand. "I'm sure you need to get back to the tournament grounds."

He retrieved her hand and placed it on his arm. She thrilled to the feel of the muscled tendons beneath her hand, and the heat of him moving over her from his side. "At least let me accompany you inside."

She gasped. He never touched her if he could avoid it. He was always so careful to keep his distance. Now, she took full advantage, putting her other hand on his arm as well and leaning into him. His muscles tensed at her touch. Such delicious muscles.

"Have you ever considered marrying, Sir Victor?" A lady couldn't ask a man, but she could hint.

His muscles became even more rigid beneath her touch.

"I would like to marry, but I doubt I'll ever find a woman willing to have me."

"You shouldn't doubt yourself. I'm sure any woman would be proud to have such a husband." *I would, if only you'd ask.*

His face reddened, and he blinked as if surprised. "You are too kind, my lady. If only others were so kind, perhaps I might marry after all." He covered her hand with his and looked at her with such intensity, she thought she might melt on the spot.

"Women have been unkind to you?"

He gave a mirthless laugh, and suddenly she remembered her own first meeting with him.

"Oh." She turned bright red. "*I* was unkind to you."

He shrugged. "You were honest."

She took a deep breath. "I was hideous. And wrong. Will you forgive me?"

"There's nothing to forgive." He raised her hand to his lips slowly and deliberately and kissed it. She could hardly breathe. "My lady Alais, I—" He paused, running his thumb over the back of her hand ever so gently.

"Yes?" What was he going to say? Was he going to declare himself at last?

Alais held her breath, watching the complex play of emotions across his face, wondering what his next words might be. But then he blinked, leaned back, and let her hand go.

"I should go back to the tournament grounds. May I take my leave, my lady?"

Oh. He didn't want her after all. Perhaps she'd been imagining things. What a fool she was!

"Of course."

She stood frozen, watching his retreating form, unaware of the swirl of activity around her in the main entrance hall. He glanced back once, and the look he gave her would have melted stone. Maybe all was not lost after all. As he turned away, hope sparked in her heart once again. What was she to make of this man?

Dora tapped her on her shoulder, startling her. Collecting herself, she let her maid lead her back to her room where she changed out of her fancy dress and lay down for a rest before dinner.

"Do you think he'll propose?" She stared up at the canopy over her mattress before turning her head to look at Dora.

Dora gave her a long, considering look. "We're talking about Sir Victor?"

"Yes."

"I confess, my lady, I'm glad you finally took notice of him. I think you're well-suited. Until today, though, I didn't think you held him in any regard. He may not have thought so either, but I think he'd have to be blind not to see it now." Alais sat up on her bed as Dora carefully hung her extravagant dress in her wardrobe.

"Do you think he returns that regard?"

"Very much so, though he might lack the confidence to make it known."

"If I'd come to my senses sooner, I might have given him more encouragement." She stood up and started pacing. "I'd much rather marry him than any of the others, but I'm worried he doesn't think I'd consider him. I don't know how to show him, and I may not have time before I have to make a decision. Why do men have to be the ones to propose?"

"Shh," Dora said, taking her elbow and leading her back to bed. "Rest, my lady. It will all turn out for the best, I'm sure. I'll come back in an hour to help you get ready for the feast."

Alais curled into a ball beneath the blankets and stared at the wall, unable to think of anything except the hard fact that her entire future would be decided in the next few hours.

CHAPTER THIRTEEN

A S THE LAST of the crowd left the tournament grounds and the vendors packed up their stands, Victor busied himself with a thousand different tasks. Anything to avoid thinking about Lady Alais. For a moment, he'd thought... *No.* He didn't dare let his mind go down that path. Better by far to focus on the tournament.

And what an eventful tournament it had been. If he didn't know better, he would think someone was out to kill him. Was it an accident of aim in the joust? And what about Sir Elias and the stranger? One succeeded in drawing blood and the other nearly decapitated him. Robert himself seemed to be out for blood. Four men taking deadly aim in one day was not a coincidence. Someone was hoping he wouldn't survive the day.

But who would want him dead and more importantly, why? Robert didn't have a motive that he knew of. Well, aside from the obvious.... But was Robert willing to kill him over Guestling? If so, why didn't he let him die in Spain? He and Robert had never been the best of friends, but it seemed so unlikely Robert would orchestrate an attempt on his life.

As for anyone else being after him, he didn't have any debts and hadn't deflowered anyone's daughter. Certainly, he'd angered his fair share of merchants in Hastings, keeping them in line on behalf of his aunt, but not enough for any of them to want him dead. Maybe this had something to do with the run-in with Matthew's men? But how did Sir Elias come into it? Canterbury had always welcomed Victor in the past. Did something change? Canterbury might not like the link between Hastings and Winchelsea that he represented, but would he go to such lengths to disrupt it?

In the distance, he saw the knight he jousted against walking over to his horse to depart. Victor moved up from behind and grabbed his arm.

"What the—" The man spun to confront Victor, but he was too slow, and Victor pinned him against a tree with his arm twisted behind his back.

"What happened in our joust wasn't an accident. I want to know who's after me and why." Victor gave the man's arm an extra twist, making him yelp.

"I don't know who's behind it. I swear. I have gambling debts, and my money lender offered to cut me a break if you had an accident at the tournament. I don't know why."

"What's the name of this money lender, and where can I find him?"

"His name is Matthew, and he travels around. He's from Canterbury, but he comes to an inn in Hawkhurst called the Sword and Shield on the Kalends of every month. That's all I know. I promise."

Victor shoved him away and drew his sword, pointing it at the knight. "Get out of Winchelsea, and never come back."

The man rushed off to his horse and escaped as quickly as he could manage.

Lord Guy came walking toward the paddock and stopped short when he saw Victor with his sword drawn. "Good heavens, man! The tournament is over. You don't have to go brandishing that thing at innocent people."

"Not so innocent. He tried to kill me," Victor said, sheathing his sword.

"What, here? In front of all these people?"

"During the tournament. He admitted moments ago it was no accident his lance was aimed high."

"Heavens! Well, I'm glad I'm getting out of here then." Lord Guy made for his horse.

"You're not staying for the feast? I thought you were still hoping to try your luck with Lady Alais."

Lord Guy instructed a stable boy to saddle his horse, then turned back to Victor, beckoning him closer. "Just heard a nasty rumor that she's compromised," he said in a loud whisper. "Apparently Sir Robert had his way with her, and then she rejected his proposal of marriage. Can you imagine? Murderous knights and compromised ladies… I'm getting out of this place as soon as I can."

Victor was shaking with rage by the time he finished. "Where's Robert?" he asked in a quiet voice filled with violent intent. It was a slanderous lie. Victor had guarded her well. He was certain his cousin never had the opportunity.

"Left hours ago," Lord Guy said, mounting his horse. "Didn't want to stick around after she rejected him. Can't say I blame him. How humiliating. I'm afraid I must be off. I bid you adieu."

Victor watched Lord Guy depart, unable to move, fury rooting him to the ground. Robert was behind this. There was no doubt in his mind. It was exactly the sort of vindictive thing his cousin would do to get back at her for rejecting him. In fact, Victor strongly suspected he'd done it before. In Hastings, there was a lovely young wife of an aging nobleman who'd caught Robert's eye. When she'd rejected his advances, a rumor had begun circulating that they were lovers.

Victor had never been certain that the rumor originated with Robert. His attentions to her had been sufficient to cause a stir even without her requiting. Even so, he'd always thought Robert was behind it somehow. And now, the similarities in the two situations were too great for it to be a coincidence.

Poor Alais. Poor, sweet, innocent Lady Alais, who was wearing his scarf, who had kissed his cheek, and given him a ring. He knew she was only being kind to him. There had been a moment in the castle when he almost let himself hope, but he'd realized he was imagining things. He felt too much for her, and it was clouding his perception.

But she didn't deserve this. *No one* deserved this. He thought about his visits to Jane. However annoyed he was by the interest of the town in his personal business, it hadn't escaped his notice that they excused him. He was allowed to seek solace. He wasn't proud of it, but he wasn't punished for it either. A woman who was even rumored to seek pleasure, though, was doomed. Robert's lie would ruin Lady Alais's life.

Thinking of Jane gave him a pang. A woman of her profession was the lowest of the low. He went to her because he was hopelessly in love with Lady Alais, but he wasn't blind to the kindly affection Jane had for him. In a different world, he might have married her and lived quite happily for the rest of his life with her as a beautiful and adoring wife. In this world, however, it wasn't possible for one of his station to marry one of hers. Besides that, his heart was bestowed elsewhere, hopeless as that might be.

Victor stood by the paddock, hoping Lord Guy was wrong and that he might catch sight of his cousin. He watched as each of Lady Alais's suitors came for their horses, except for Sir Elias, who seemed to have left early. Each one mumbled about being misled or her being "damaged goods". Lord Alphonse had the temerity to grumble about her questionable virtue, as if he himself hadn't spent the entire last week making inappropriate remarks about her. Victor fought the urge to challenge them to combat to defend her honor, realizing that it was probably for the best if they all left. None of them were good enough for her. None of them deserved her if they were scared off so easily, especially if they believed she was a woman of easy virtue and low morals.

Especially when he was sure that they—like him—would easily lie with any comely woman who was willing to let them.

Lord Louis was the last to ride off. He apologized to Victor repeatedly, saying he didn't believe the rumors, but couldn't continue to pay court to someone with a damaged reputation. Victor knew Louis was trying to be conciliatory, but he wanted to smack the man over the head for being so cowardly. What was the point of chivalry if you abandoned your lady love in her hour of need?

Victor rode back to the castle slowly, weighed down by dread. He didn't know what he would find there, but he knew he had to come to Lady Alais's defense. He'd given his word of honor to safeguard her. Robert couldn't be allowed to sully her like this. Her family had to be made to understand that this was an invention. This was not of her doing. There had to be a way to fight it. There had to be a way to undo the damage. He couldn't think of one, but he was determined to try. Even though he knew it was all a lie, he couldn't help feeling he'd failed to defend her as he should.

But this was no time to dwell on his failing. Lady Alais needed a champion, and he was ready to be that for her, whether she recognized his efforts or not. He'd long since given up hope of her returning his affection. He would fight for her while everyone else ran away. He would stand by her when everyone else fled. He was hers, come what may. She wore his scarf. She gave him a ring and a kiss. He would happily spend the rest of his life serving her for the favor she'd shown him that day.

Chapter Fourteen

WHEN ALAIS WALKED into the grand hall for the feast, it was clear that something was wrong. At her entrance, all conversation stopped. All eyes were on her. She could see fury radiating from her mother's eyes and cold disapproval from Carenza. Iselda stared at her, wide-eyed. Daniel and her father were whispering together with furrowed brows. Ladies Mathilda, Simone, and Eugenie all looked at her like she was covered in plague sores. What was going on?

Her mother swept over to her with a false smile plastered on her face and grabbed her elbow, guiding her from the room. But she dropped the smile as soon as they were out of sight and dug her nails into her elbow, dragging her down the hall to her receiving room. She shoved Alais onto one of the low cushioned benches that lined the walls. Alais stared at the colorful medallion patterns on the carpet, knowing from experience that looking her mother in the eye would only enrage her further.

"What did you do, Alais?" her mother demanded, looming over her, her fists clenched.

"I...I don't know, Mother." She began crumpling her skirt in her hands, trying to imagine what could have happened to produce such a reaction. "Honestly, I have no idea what this is about."

"Sir Robert left town in a fury after you turned down his

proposal, and on his way out, he apparently told anyone that would listen that he compromised your virtue."

"What?" Alais yelled, standing to face her mother with balled fists. "That lying, no good, rotten, conniving…"

"Did he?" her mother interrupted.

Alais looked at her mother in horror.

"Of course, he didn't," she screamed. "How could you believe him? You're my mother!"

Her mother began to pace, wringing her hands. "He said he was alone with you the day you were injured because of that runaway cart. He helped you onto his horse and brought you back to the castle without a chaperone."

"I was hurt, and Carenza told me to! It was only a short distance. I was with him for a trice. Nothing happened, I swear."

Her mother stopped pacing. "I have been forthright with you about the specifics of what a man and a woman do together. I need to be absolutely sure. Did he touch you between the legs?"

"No." She shivered in revulsion.

"Did he press any part of himself between your legs?"

"No."

"Was there any sticky white liquid?"

"No. I told you, nothing happened." *My own mother doubts me?*

"He didn't spill the blood of your maidenhead?"

"How could he if he didn't touch me?"

Her mother stood still and glared at her. Alais glared back with all of the outraged fury she could muster.

"None of this would have happened if you'd only said 'yes' to his proposal."

"I'm sorry. What?" Her mother might as well have sprouted another head; it was incomprehensible.

"He was a perfectly respectable match. I can't understand why you turned him down."

Alais was speechless. "I can't talk about this." She rushed to run from her mother's study and flee down the hall. Her mother grabbed her arm before she could leave the room.

"Go wait for us in the solar. I'll send Dora. The rest of us have to go through with this farce of a dinner. We'll speak in an hour or so. Stay out of sight."

Alais made her way to the solar, her eyes blurred with tears. She sat in a dark corner, wishing she could disappear into the wall. Dora came in to see to her but wouldn't make eye contact. When Alais begged her for a hot mint infusion to calm her nerves, Dora finally offered a brief, sympathetic look.

"Nothing happened, Dora. You know nothing happened. You do all of my laundry. I couldn't have hidden it from you."

Dora blinked. "You're right, my lady. I'm so sorry for doubting. I'll get you that infusion." She gave Alais a quick hug and scurried out. At least one person believed her, not that the word of her maid was likely to be sufficient to clear her name with anyone else, but it was something.

Her marriage prospects were doomed. No one would want to tie themselves to her now. She felt hot bile in her throat as she thought about Sir Victor hearing Sir Robert's lie. Shame coursed through her veins. She didn't want to see the look on his face, didn't want to see the shadow of disapproval in his eye. For some reason, his disapproval would be the most damning of all.

WHEN VICTOR ARRIVED at the castle, the whole family was gathered in the solar. Lady Alais sat weeping silently in the corner. She looked up briefly when he came in, deep shame in her eyes, but she immediately dropped her gaze back to her lap. He ached for her, certain she thought he was one more person, come to condemn her.

"Sir Victor, I'm glad you're here," said Lord Daniel. "I'm sure you've heard." He glanced at Alais. Her eyes were squeezed shut.

"I have, but I don't believe it. I think this is Robert's revenge for Lady Alais's rejection." He risked another glance at Lady Alais, who was now staring at him with wide, hopeful eyes. He tried to convey faith and courage to her as he returned her gaze.

"Whether it's true or not hardly matters if everyone believes she's compromised," Lady de Vere said, glowering at Lady Alais. "If you'd only accepted his offer…"

"Isabella, enough," said Lord de Vere. To Victor's surprise, Lady de Vere relented and took her husband's hand. "It's clear what needs to happen. She needs to marry immediately, or, if no one can be found, she needs to go to the abbey."

"No, Papa, please, not the abbey!" Lady Alais's eyes filled with tears again.

Forcing her to live a religious life would crush her spirit, and the mere thought filled him with dread on her behalf. If only Victor could sweep her up in his arms and carry her far away from their accusing stares!

"Sir Victor, are any of her suitors still here, or have they all left?" Lord Daniel asked, looking like he'd rather be anywhere but where he was.

"I'm sorry to say they've all left, my lord." Victor exhaled. "Cowards," he added through gritted teeth.

"Then, Alais, I'm afraid you'll have to go to the abbey," said Lord de Vere as gently as he could manage.

Lady Alais looked like a caged animal. "Wait! No! There has to be some other way. Carenza, you know I'm not cut out for life at the abbey. I hate it there."

"You have to go somewhere until this blows over," said Lady Carenza. "In a few years, maybe—"

"A few *years*?" Lady Alais wailed.

Victor had to clench his fists by his sides to resist the urge to reach out for her.

"I'm sorry, Alais, but you brought this on yourself." Lady Carenza shook her head.

Lady Alais stared at her sister in horror. "You don't believe me?"

"I want to believe you, but you haven't exactly been a model of restraint." Lady Carenza mouthed something that looked like "Gilbert."

Lady Alais looked like she was about to gouge her sister's eyes out, and Victor couldn't blame her. He wondered if he should step between them. Fortunately, Lord Daniel got there first.

"Alais, I'm sorry," Lord Daniel said, "but I don't see an alternative right now. You can't stay here, unmarried. None of us want to see you go through that kind of humiliation. At least at the abbey, you'd be safe from gossip."

Victor watched Lady Alais sag as Lord Daniel's words sank in. As the earl, he was her last recourse. She was defeated. Hope disappeared from her eyes and her lip began to quiver. Iselda started toward her to offer sympathy, but her mother held her back. No one else came to Alais's defense or comforted her. She folded in half in her chair and her head dropped into her lap. He had to do something but had no idea what.

And then she sat up abruptly and looked at him. The plea in her gaze sharpened. There was one way he could save her reputation, but did he dare offer?

He was about to speak when she beat him to it. "Sir Victor, marry me. Please."

Her words left him thunderstruck. For a moment, all he could do was stare, his mouth hanging open.

"What?" asked Lord Daniel. "Alais, he hasn't asked for your hand. What makes you think—?"

"I'll marry her." Victor heard the words coming out of his mouth but had no recollection of forming them. Though he spoke to Lord Daniel, his gaze was fixed on the woman he loved.

Lady Alais closed her eyes for a moment and whispered, "Thank you."

Lady Rossignol and her mother gasped.

"If you and Lord de Vere will grant me your approval," he added, glancing at Lord Daniel when his brain caught up to his mouth.

"You have my blessing and my thanks," said Lord de Vere.

"Sir Victor, I'd like to speak with you privately for a moment," said Lord Daniel. Victor followed him to a small room across the hall.

His heart and mind raced. Was he really going to marry Lady Alais de Vere? It seemed so obvious to him that it was impossible, that she would never consider him. But moments ago, she'd asked for him. Yes, she was desperate. Yes, he was a solution to a problem for her. But she was willing, had even proposed it.

Lord Daniel invited Victor to sit and took the seat opposite. He always made the furniture he sat in look uncomfortably small. "Are you sure you want to do this? She put you on the spot. You don't have to agree just because there's no other way."

Victor appreciated that he didn't prevaricate. "I'm sure."

"You already know the details of her dowry. Under the circumstances, do you require more?"

He shook his head in vigorous refusal. Lord Daniel observed him in silence for a long moment.

"Did you make the foolish mistake of falling in love with her despite our warnings?"

Victor looked at the ceiling. He'd tried so hard to keep it all hidden. He closed his eyes and nodded.

Lord Daniel chuckled and shook his head. "We're all fools for love, I suppose. Welcome to the family." He clapped a meaty hand on Victor's arm. "One last thing." He looked Victor in the eye. "No more trips to Birdie Street."

Victor exhaled. "One more trip, and not for pleasure. I need to do right by someone who has been kind to me." Jane would be well taken care of. He would see to that.

"One trip."

"Thank you, my lord."

"Call me Daniel."

They returned to the others. Lady Alais's eyes were wide with apprehension, following his every movement. He wanted to go to her and speak with her, but he wasn't sure if he was allowed. Would they have a chance to speak before they wed? There was so much he ought to know but had never even considered. Most of all, he wanted to reassure her that he understood his role and would not press for anything she didn't want to give. She must be terrified. It had all happened so fast.

"We've reached an agreement," Daniel announced. "I'll speak to the priest to see how quickly we can schedule the ceremony. I'm hoping we can do this tomorrow unless there are any objections."

Lady de Vere clapped her hands and said, "I do love a wedding!" as if nothing was amiss in the world. Lady Carenza and Lady Iselda rolled their eyes. Lady Alais stared at her mother in obvious disbelief.

As the family started to go their separate ways, Victor asked Daniel if he might have a word with Lady Alais. Daniel gave a nod and asked his wife to stay and chaperone. She was not the chaperone Victor would have chosen, given the naked hostility in Lady Alais's eyes when she looked at her sister, but he would take what he could get. He moved to stand beside her.

Lady Alais still sat in her corner, crumpling the fabric of her dress in her clenched hands.

"Lady Alais, I was hoping we could talk for a moment."

She looked up and then, before he even realized her intentions, she threw herself at him, wrapping her arms around him and resting her head against his chest. "Thank you," she murmured.

He folded his arms around her gingerly, uncertain how to respond, especially with Lady Carenza watching. She fit well against him, and the delicious scent of lemons and thyme rose up to his nostrils. He inhaled deeply as his heart began to pound.

"I'll be a good wife, I promise! You know the rumor is a lie. I can't tell you how much it means to me that you believe me. But I'm untouched. I swear. And I'll always be faithful. And I'll give you as many babies as you want. And—"

"Lady Alais, slow down. I wanted to check that you truly

want to go through with this. I'm yours if you want me, but if you change your mind, I promise I won't be offended."

"Change my mind? I don't understand." She pulled back to look up at him. Her cheeks were pink and her eyes luminous.

"You were cornered. I was your only escape, but I'm under no illusions that you would choose me were circumstances different. I know I'm scarred and that you don't think I'm—"

She raised a hand to his face and caressed it. He froze. She traced a finger along his scar, down his cheek, across the bridge of his nose, and down to the corner of his mouth. Then she trailed it along his lower lip. He closed his eyes as she traced his scar, fearing what he might see in her eyes. The thought that she might pity him twisted like a knife in his gut while her gentle touch pulled him in closer. It was agony, and he couldn't pull away.

Their lips met. He knew he should step away. She must have been doing this out of gratitude rather than true affection, but there was no escape. His body wouldn't respond to his mind's frantic pleas. Her lips brushed against his, sending lightning to his extremities. He didn't respond. It was all he could do to keep breathing.

"Is something wrong?" she whispered, pulling away slightly. "Why won't you kiss me?"

Everything was wrong. He was wrong for her. She was doing this out of desperation. She could never feel for him what he felt for her. But his body wouldn't listen. Ferocious need flooded his veins, and he could no longer hold back.

His hands cupped the back of her head. He pulled her to him, and he kissed her as he'd dreamed of kissing her, night after night. He lost himself in her. He was no longer a man but merely a collection of impulses and sensations. And in some distant corner of his mind, he became aware that she was kissing him back with equal fervor. There was no hesitation, no resistance. She was hungry for him.

It wasn't possible. He must be mistaken. And yet there was

no denying the heat that had sprung up between them. Her hands clutched at him. Her body pressed against his own. Her mouth was soft, sweet, and demanding as they tasted each other for the first time. It was unbearable, and he needed more. He pulled her closer, his hand caressing her curves with hungry reverence, but at that moment, Lady Carenza cleared her throat.

They pulled away from each other, trembling. Victor tried to think of something, anything, that would calm his body's desperation before he had to face Lady Carenza. He closed his eyes and imagined jumping into a frozen pond.

"Are you done with your talk?" Lady Carenza asked with dry amusement.

"Carenza, I'm going to kill you," Alais said through gritted teeth.

"Don't worry, Alais. You don't have long to wait. You can survive for one more day. And as for you," she said, turning to Victor, "you had me worried for a moment there, but you'll do fine."

He had no idea what she meant by that and continued to focus his attention on icy things as he exited the room, avoiding eye contact with Lady Alais.

He made his way to his tiny room in a daze. He collapsed on his bed and lay staring up at the ceiling without bothering to undress. Lady Alais de Vere had kissed him. She. Kissed. Him. Passionately, too. And tomorrow, she would become his wife. But it made no sense. None of it made any sense.

Before the sun set on another day, he would be the husband of the woman he loved. Did he dare hope that someday she might grow to love him too? But he couldn't get ahead of himself. She was wedding him out of necessity and was probably terrified. It was his chivalric duty to give her the time and space she needed to accustom herself to marriage.

He groaned as he realized what that meant. He was going to have to sleep in the same room as her without touching her, all the while knowing he couldn't visit Jane to keep his urges at bay.

It could go on that way indefinitely. In fact, it had to because he couldn't face the consequences of giving in. The only thing worse than Lady Alais's pity would be her regret. This was going to be absolute hell, and there was no going back.

CHAPTER FIFTEEN

THE WEDDING CEREMONY was quick and quiet, carried out in the family chapel in the castle instead of at the church. Late afternoon sun poured through the stained glass and dappled the small group of attendees. There was no time for a new dress, so Alais wore her favorite red one, the same dress she wore the day she met Sir Victor. She carried a bouquet of white autumn crocuses from the castle garden that she'd picked herself. Sir Victor wore a black velvet cotte with gold embroidered trim over plain black breeches. She couldn't help thinking how lucky she was to be marrying such a noble and honorable man, and she admired his striking figure and warrior's face.

Her heart raced as he promised to be hers to have and to hold until death parted them. The holding part sounded especially delicious. She'd hardly been able to think of anything else since their kiss the night before. Throughout the ceremony, he kept giving her inquiring looks, as though expecting her to interrupt or stop the proceedings. He himself went through every step and spoke every word of his vows without hesitation, his face full of devotion, which was surprisingly tender, considering he was only marrying her to help her save face and her reputation, and especially keep her out of the nunnery. She was marrying a good man, she thought to herself as he took her hand and led her from the chapel. And he certainly wasn't a sheep.

There was no wedding banquet, only a family dinner. She kept glancing at her new husband, looking for some sign of affection or the passion she had tasted so briefly when they'd kissed the day before. She even reached out during dessert and put her hand on his thigh beneath the tablecloth. He stiffened and reddened at her touch, gently removing her hand without looking at her. She risked another glance. He looked pained. Perhaps he was worried her family might see. She could be patient, within reason.

At long last, they were alone together. A large canopy bed dominated the modest room where they were to spend their first night together, just down the hall from her own. Alais turned to look at the man who was now her husband, giddy with anticipation of what was to come. But his jaw was clenched. He averted his eyes, refusing to meet her gaze.

"Don't worry, Lady Alais," he said to the floor. "I won't trouble you tonight."

"Call me Alais. We're married. What do you mean you won't trouble me?"

"You married me to salvage your reputation. It's safe now. I've served my purpose. I don't expect you to take things any further."

"But—"

"I'll sleep on the floor. If you don't mind, I'd like to go to sleep. It's been a long day, and I'm tired. I'm sure you are too."

He pulled some blankets and pillows to the floor, stripped down to his breeches, lay down, and closed his eyes, all without looking at her. She stood still, watching him, unable to wrap her head around what was happening, or rather what *wasn't* happening. Her mother had been quite clear on what was expected. So had Carenza. And most of all, she wanted him so much. How could he simply refuse?

She took off her dress in plain sight, hoping he might watch, but he didn't. She climbed into bed wearing nothing but her shift, and he lay on the floor with his eyes firmly shut. She blew out the candle and stared into the dark, wondering what she could possibly do now. Sleep would not come. She was too aware of his presence, of every minute human sound, of the possibility that he could come to her, and the undeniable fact that he had not.

An hour passed, and Alais could hear Victor's deep, regular breathing. At least *he* was sleeping soundly. She was still staring at the ceiling in the dark. It was intolerable. This could not continue. So she got up, pulled off her shift, and silently laid herself down, naked, by his side. She leaned over him and brushed his lips with her own. He gave a start.

"Lady Alais, what are you doing?" he mumbled.

"Just Alais. We have to consummate the marriage," she said quietly. "If we don't, it's not legal."

She twined herself around him, the rough fabric of his breeches grazing against her inner thigh and the heat of his chest against her bare breasts. She nuzzled his neck.

"Oh my God, you're naked," he gasped, his whole body tensing.

"Isn't that usually how this works?" She touched her lips to his and ran her fingers through his hair, and she felt a rush of relief as he kissed her back. His lips touched hers with a tenderness and reverence that stirred her to her core. She let herself dissolve into his kiss, surrendering to the moment. Yes, this was what she'd dreamed of. At last, she was free to unleash her passion.

"Oh, sweet Jesus," he rasped, trying to pull away after a moment, but she leaned in for another kiss, this one hungrier, more desperate. His hands explored her shape and pulled her to him, caressing each curve. She felt heavenly as he awakened her body with his touch. She moved to close the tiny gaps that remained between them, her fingers digging into his back in hunger.

"Wait. Lady Alais, wait," he said pulling away, panting. "You married me out of necessity. It wouldn't be honorable for me to force myself on you under the circumstances. You don't have to do this."

Alais stared at him in the dark. He must be joking. Was she not making it clear that she wanted to do this? She pulled him into another kiss, determined to put an end to doubt, but he pulled back again.

"My good name is yours. I don't expect anything in return. I won't take advantage of you when you've already been through so much."

"But I married you." She made vows. So did he. Was he having second thoughts? "You don't want me?"

"Of course, I want you. Dear God, I want you so much."

"Then take me." She placed one of his hands on her breast, and he groaned as she leaned into him, welcoming his touch. His hand felt so good against her bare skin, she reached out to pull the other one toward her.

"No, I can't," he pleaded quietly, removing his hand, leaving her panting in desperation.

"Why?"

"Lady Alais, please don't." He extracted himself from her embrace and sat up, his back to her.

How could he do this to her? He wanted her as much as she wanted him, she was sure of it. She had felt him spring to life beneath his breeches, and his body, hot and hard pressed against her thigh before he pulled away. She knew what it meant. While she'd never seen a naked man, she understood the mechanics. If he wanted her, what was the problem?

How dare he pretend this was about what she wanted when she was throwing herself at him. It was insulting, humiliating.

In a fury, she got up, lit a candle, and started pacing. He turned his face away, as if he couldn't stand to see her nakedness. "How do you think this ends, *Sir Victor*? Imagine we decide not to consummate this marriage. How is that any better for me than living in an abbey? I don't want to spend my life alone, un-touched. Believe me when I tell you I am not cut out to live like a nun." She shuddered. "Why won't you consummate this marriage? What is it you are so afraid of?" She dropped to her knees so that she could look him in the face. He looked hard, determined, as if bracing himself for extreme pain. And then a realization hit her.

"Oh, no. Oh, no, no, no. You believe Sir Robert, don't you? You think I'm compromised, and you're ashamed to be married to me." It all made sense now. And here she'd been so certain he was the one person who believed her without proof. She'd clung to it. The fact that he knew she'd kept her virtue had made all the rest bearable. Except that now he doubted her. He was *ashamed* of her. Tears stung her eyes, and she dashed them away with her fist.

"Of course not." His eyes met hers at long last. "I knew it was a lie. And even if it wasn't, I wouldn't care."

"Then *what?*"

There was a long silence. He gritted his teeth and clenched his fists in some inner struggle. She tried to be patient. She tried to understand, but with each passing second, she was more convinced that somehow, she had failed him. He was ashamed of her, or disappointed. She'd let him down, and she didn't know how.

"I'm not the man you wanted, and I don't want a pity fuck, Alais. I can't do it. Not with you."

Oh. She took a deep breath and another. She didn't begin to know how to argue with him. If marrying him didn't convince him, she didn't know what she could possibly say that would help him see the truth.

"I don't pity you, and I don't regret marrying you. I *wanted* to marry you. I've never met anyone so brave and honorable. Didn't you see me wearing your token at the tournament? Why do you think I did that? Everyone else treats me as a pretty, brainless fool. But you see the real me. You respect me. You see me as more than a pleasing face. And I *want* to give myself to you."

"It was my duty to guard and protect you then, and it remains my duty now. Believe me, I know you're so much more than a pleasing face. But I also know I'm not the husband you dreamed of. If not for my cousin's lies, you could have had your pick of eligible men. You could have had someone whole and undamaged."

She couldn't let that stand. "You are whole and undamaged in every way that matters. You see more in me than my appearance. Why is it so unthinkable that I would see more in you? I know I was unspeakably cruel to you the first time we met, but I've learned the error of my ways. You've been my champion without asking anything in return. Let me show you how much that means to me."

Still, he shook his head. "It would be dishonorable for me to take advantage when you were forced by circumstance into this marriage."

She'd never seen him look so miserable.

There had to be something she could do, some way to move past his overblown sense of duty and chivalry. She'd bared her heart, and he still didn't believe her. The situation would be funny if she wasn't so desperate. She stood up and started pacing again. "You're worried about honor? Then why won't you take me? If there's no blood on these sheets in the morning, they'll all think Sir Robert's stories were true. Victor, I'm begging you. Please."

She climbed on the bed and waited. He still didn't join her.

"Even begging isn't enough?" She thought in desperation of one last thing she could try. It was a risk, but she was prepared to do anything to bring him to her. "Let me prove to you that I'm not cut out for a life of celibacy."

She couldn't believe what she was about to do, but it was the only thing she could think of to lure him to her. She'd been so careful never to let anyone catch her. She knew it was wicked, knew that what she was about to do would prove that she was exactly the wanton that everyone thought she was, even if a man had never touched her. But she also knew he was a man who visited Birdie Street, a man who might respond to a provocative act. It just might work to overcome his resistance. She reached her hand between her legs and began to stroke herself.

"I may be a virgin, but I have a very bad habit, Victor." She gasped in anguished pleasure. The knowledge that he was there, that he was watching her do this forbidden thing made the pleasure and shame so much sharper. "*Now* do you believe I'm not cut out for life at the abbey?" She moaned as the sensation intensified.

"Holy Mother of God," he whispered. "This can't be happening."

"I want you to touch me. I want you to take me. I'm yours to have and to hold. Be with me, Victor," she purred as waves of sensation shook her.

At last, he undressed and stepped toward her, lowering himself to the mattress beside her. She could smell his musk of leather and wood smoke.

"Please, I'm begging you."

He pulled back, taking her hand away, and looked at her, serious and wary.

"You want me?" His voice was rough, hoarse with emotion.

"Yes, I want you."

"Because I won't take you if you have any doubts."

She raised her hand and cupped his cheek. "Do you know whose face I was picturing as I touched myself?"

"Alais, please don't—"

"Yours. I want *you*."

He took a shuddering breath as he hovered above her. "Before we do this, I want to be absolutely clear. Do you want me as your husband, or did you marry me to solve a problem? Because I thought this was a marriage of convenience. Or maybe desperation. You needed my name, and I've given it to you. But are you saying you want to be with me, that you truly want to be my wife?"

She stared in disbelief. "I *am* your wife."

"Alais—" he began but then closed his mouth at the look she gave him.

"Do I strike you as unwilling, hesitant? I'm lying naked beneath you, begging you to take me. Why are you humiliating me like this?" She was shaking with fury and overwhelming desire.

"Alais, I'm sorry. I truly didn't expect this." He caressed her cheek. "If you want me, I'm yours."

"I want you."

Something shifted in his face, like a dam breaking. Suddenly, he clutched her with furious strength, grinding his hips against her. "And if I'm yours, then you're mine." He pulled her into a desperate kiss, squeezing her too hard and nearly suffocating her with his ardor. "Mine, Alais. No going back. No annulment. No lovers. Only I touch your body. Only I kiss your lips. Anyone else tries, and they die. Do you understand, Alais?"

Oh, for God's sake. "Yes, I understood the vows I made to you before God and my family in the chapel today. Did you? Because it seems like you have a lot of questions."

"I can't take this anymore. I need you. Now."

He reached down to replace her hand with his own. She cried out as the intensity sharpened at his touch.

"Kiss me," she begged as her body arched beneath his touch. Suddenly, his lips were on hers, his tongue tasting her, twisting, and teasing. He stroked like a master musician, playing a subtle melody and then strumming deeper chords that touched her very soul.

"You are exquisite," he murmured, nibbling on her ear. "Every last inch of you."

His mouth traced a trail of fire down her neck, her shoulder. He kissed his way down her chest, between her breasts, then traced the crease beneath one breast with his tongue, swirling up to the peak until it brushed over the bud of her nipple.

And then he pulled back. She gasped at the sudden absence, feeling a cool sensation where his tongue had traced, the tips of her breasts hardening as if straining toward the absent warmth of his mouth. His fingers continued their tantalizing dance, making her moan and wail, awash in sensation.

"More," she pleaded, barely able to form words. Moments later, his lips brushed against her breast again, followed by his tongue, flicking and circling, teasing her nipple until she was writhing with need. She'd never known her breasts were so sensitive, that she could feel such joy and desperation in every part of her body from such a delicate sensation. Then he grazed it gently with his teeth, and she lost her mind. Her back arched off the bed. Her whole body trembled. The pooling heat between her legs pulsed and throbbed. He put a finger inside of her, and she moaned, "Oh, Victor…"

She looked into his face. As he drove her to the brink, she saw a swirl of emotions in his eyes—hunger, tenderness, desperation, and even, love. As she thought the word "love," something within her squeezed, and she convulsed from head to toe. He made a quiet noise that sounded almost pained, as he slid another finger inside of her.

"This can't be real," he murmured as he moved his mouth to her other breast. "I've dreamed of you so many times, but all of my dreams fall short. So far short. Oh my God." He gave a desperate moan as he suckled her and her back arched again. Her body trembled. She was so close, and she wanted all of him.

"Victor, I need you. Take me now, please," she begged, desperate for him to fill her and bring her to fruition.

"Not yet. First, I want to watch you melt. I want to see you fall to pieces. Let me take you soaring through the heavens."

Something shifted in the way he was touching her, and she couldn't take it anymore. It was too much, the intensity too great. She writhed to escape, but his fingers were relentless, pushing her to the brink and then over it. And then…. And then everything dropped away. She soared, floating through sparkling stars, her body a vessel of pure sensation.

"My God, that was gorgeous," he said in an awed whisper as she came back down to earth, tingling and catching her breath.

Her body was warm and languid, but she knew they were far from done. He had to enter her. They needed to consummate, and however lovely she felt, it wasn't enough. Not yet. She reached out and ran her fingers lightly down his chest and his belly and grasped his naked flesh, running her hand up and down the hard and velvety skin that felt so different from any flesh she had ever touched. He made an odd squeak and took deep, rasping breaths.

"Now take me," she demanded, as his flesh twitched in her hand. She pulled him toward her center, and he shifted to hover over her, placing his legs between hers. Wrapping her legs around him, she pulled his hips against hers, opening herself, offering herself.

He slid into her, pressing forward slowly until she felt him reach some unseen barrier.

"Oh God, I can feel it. After this, there's no going back."

By way of answer, she put her hands on his buttocks and pulled him into her with as much force as she could muster. She wanted this done, once and for all, and she gasped at the welcome pain as he broke through her maidenhead. It was such a precious vindication, the final proof that Robert's lie was just that.

He cried out, embedded to the hilt within her.

"Did I hurt you?" she asked, not sure whether the sound he made was pleasure or pain. Her own moment of pain quickly disappeared in a flood of profound relief that the deed was finally done.

Panting and gasping, he whispered, "I'm supposed to ask you that."

"I'm fine. Just don't stop."

And so she watched his face as they started to rock together. "I'm yours, Victor, all of me," she murmured to the rhythm of their coupling. "I'm your wife. I want you just like you want me. No one will touch me but you. No one will kiss me but you. You are the only man I want. Take me. Make me yours. Love me."

And he did.

She could feel the ripples of each thrust on top of her head, in her fingertips and toes. Like the body of a lute, she vibrated at his strokes. The pace of the music quickened, and she thrummed beneath him, chords feeding into each other, driven by his steady rhythm. Their music grew wilder and more raucous until her whole body stretched taut, like a string being plucked, just before its release. And then everything dissolved in an explosion of sensation far beyond anything she had felt before.

As if from a great distance, she heard Victor cry out her name as his flesh within her spasmed and pulsed and then slowed. He lingered inside her as his release subsided, each tiny pulsation from him creating an answering frisson in her. He rolled to the side at last, and they both lay panting.

"I can't believe that just happened," he whispered.

She curled against him, resting her head in the crook of his arm, and tried to sort out her tangled thoughts and emotions. One tear and another dripped down onto his chest. She tried to hold them back, but it was no use.

"Alais?"

She didn't respond. She couldn't.

"What is it? Do you regret—?"

"No."

"Then what?"

What could she say? She wasn't sure she knew the answer herself. It wasn't regret. There was no one else she would rather have given herself to. But when she'd imagined her wedding night, she never dreamed she would have to plead with him at every step. There was blood on the sheet now. She was vindicated, but somehow, she still felt like a disgrace.

"What is it? Please tell me. I need to know." There was an edge in his voice, an undertone of panic.

"Why did you make me beg?"

"What?"

"Everyone thinks I'm ruined, but I didn't feel that way until you made me beg. Why did you do it?"

He looked stricken.

"My God, Alais, I'm so sorry. This was your first time. I

should never have done that to you. I truly didn't realize…. I still can't quite believe…. But that's no excuse. This should have been a very different night for you. I should have treated you with tenderness and affection, not made to beg and plead. You're not ruined, Alais. You take joy in your body, and that's a beautiful thing. I don't ever want you to feel ashamed of your pleasure with me."

For some reason, this made her cry even harder.

"What do you need? I'll do anything. Please tell me what you need from me."

"Just hold me, please. That's all I want."

He blew out the candle and held her in the darkness. As the tears petered out and she drifted off to sleep, she snuggled into his warmth, praying tomorrow would be better.

CHAPTER SIXTEEN

Alais woke up right after dawn to a gentle kiss. Victor was up and dressed and smiling. His twilight blue eye had a hopeful twinkle.

"Good morning, my lovely, luscious wife." He took her hand and kissed it, then sucked on her pinky, grazing it with his teeth and making her sigh and giggle. She felt a wave of desire at his touch.

"Victor, what are you up to?"

"I did everything wrong yesterday, so today I want to try again and hopefully this time get it right." He pulled a bouquet of hellebores from behind his back. He plucked one flower out and tucked it behind her ear then handed her the rest.

"These are lovely! Thank you, my husband." She sat up and buried her nose in the blossoms, then set them aside on the bedside table before folding her hands and resting them on her lap, at the same time making sure her hair didn't cover her breasts at all. She smiled at him, sure that the picture she presented to him would stir his manhood in no time. "I'm intrigued. What did you have in mind?"

Victor swallowed hard and made an inarticulate noise, his gaze lingering on her exposed chest. It was delicious how easily she could stun him into speechlessness.

There was a quiet knock on the door.

"That would be breakfast," he said, waking from his reverie to retrieve the tray from the servant at the door. "I thought we should get an early start."

Alais got out of bed, stretched, and ran her fingers through her hair, angling herself to provide him with an unobscured view of her naked form. There was a satisfying clatter as the tray slipped from Victor's hands onto the table. "Dear God, I am never going to get used to this."

Alais sauntered over to Victor and threw her arms around his neck. "You blaspheme a lot." She nibbled on his ear.

"That's the least interesting of my many sins," he mumbled into her hair as he finally gave in and took her back to bed.

Touching her exactly where she needed him, he pressed her back into the bed, making her come and come again as he pulled off his clothes and joined her beneath the blankets. When she was frantic for more, he sank into her and made sweet, gentle love to her, treating her with a delicacy that drove her mad. As she tipped over the edge a third time, his control began to slip, and she trembled in release as he thrust deep and hard, again and again, until he groaned and collapsed on top of her.

They nibbled on breakfast as they dressed and kissed and then kissed some more.

It was mid-morning when they emerged from their room and rushed down to the stables to avoid her family. Nonetheless, Carenza saw them in the halls and gave her a wink that made her cheeks burn.

Soon they rode through the west gate of Winchelsea and out into the surrounding farmland. Alais was on Snow. Victor was on Socorro. He broke into a gallop as soon as they were on the open road. "Beat you to the next farm," he yelled over his shoulder.

"Never," she yelled back, urging Snow faster and faster along the well-trodden Roman road as the wind whipped through her hair. Snow had no chance against Socorro, of course, but it didn't matter. It felt like heaven to race through the cool autumn morning, galloping with abandon after Victor as he whooped like a barbarian. He and Socorro moved together like a single creature with one mind, a graceful blur of lean muscle and movement.

"I win," he crowed, turning sharply, and circling back to ride alongside her.

"Not a fair contest! Let me ride Socorro, and we'll see who wins," she objected with a laugh, slowing Snow to a walk.

"Would you like to? I'm happy to trade. Anything to please my lady…"

"That depends. Where are we headed?"

"I thought we'd start with a visit to Hastings."

"What?" She came to a halt.

"We won't go anywhere near my aunt, I promise." She started walking again, giving him a wary look. "I thought I might spoil you some, given that you didn't have a chance for the usual pre-wedding shopping spree. I know the best merchants in the city. Their wares will put what you can find in Winchelsea to shame. My lady deserves only the finest."

"Heavens!" Alais didn't know what to say. She thought back to the occasions when he'd been forced to accompany her and her sisters out into Winchelsea on shopping expeditions. He'd always looked so miserable, but then, in retrospect, maybe that had nothing to do with the shopping.

"Then I'd like to take you to meet a talented friend of mine whom I think you might find entertaining. And this afternoon, if you're willing, I'd like to take you to Guestling to meet my father. He'll adore you. But beware, he will feed you within an inch of your life. His cook is an artist of rare skill, but you will feel like a stuffed capon by the time my father is satisfied that you've eaten enough."

"I would love to meet your father, and I'm sure I'll have quite an appetite after everything you described. What's your father like?"

Victor narrowed his eye and then raised an eyebrow. "A fat goat."

Alais burst out laughing.

"It's true! You'll see for yourself soon enough. He is a hairy man with voracious appetites and no shame. You think I blaspheme? Brace yourself. He's far worse. But he's a good man. He might have left me to the servants after my mother died, but instead, he gave me a happy childhood until I was old enough to foster." He looked off in the distance.

"And what were you like as a child?"

He laughed. "Trouble." *Of course, he was.* "You?"

"Also trouble."

He smiled. She flushed as she returned his smile. She was tempted to sneak behind a tree with him and do wicked things. But no. Plenty of time for that later.

"So what's the worst thing you got caught for?" he asked, a smolder in his look as if he knew what she was thinking.

"When I was seven, I got mad at Carenza for tattling on me about stealing a honey cake from the kitchen, so I cut off all her hair." Victor sputtered and snorted loudly. "It took months for it to grow back. She had to wear a wimple the whole time. Mother made me wear one too for punishment. To this day, I still hate covering my hair, though I suppose I'll have to, now that I'm a respectable married woman." She made a disgusted face.

She could see the boy in him when he laughed. She could just imagine him as a tiny troublemaker with twilight eyes, an angelic face, and a sandy mop. He could probably have gotten away with anything.

"Your turn." She grinned. "What's the worst thing you didn't get caught for?"

"Good question. I rarely got caught. I was sneaky." The mischievous look he gave her made her bite her lip.

"I believe that."

"All right. If I tell you, you have to swear you will never reveal my secret to another living soul." He looked so serious, she couldn't help but burst out laughing.

"I swear on Carenza's hair."

"Oh, you'll have to do better than that."

"Fine. I swear on my deepest, darkest, and best-kept secret."

"Which is?"

"You already know it."

"No I… Oh."

She watched him replay the events of last night in his memory. The laughter disappeared from his face. There was a fire in its place. And guilt. She shouldn't have mentioned it. It was like a piece of broken glass between them, injuring them both with its jagged edge.

"So? What did you do?" She forced a smile and raised an eyebrow.

"I…" He stopped and exhaled, gritting his teeth. "Alais, you have to know your secret is safe with me. You're my wife. What happens between us is no one's business but our own."

She halted her horse, and he did the same. She looked him in the eye. "I trust you. You stood by me when no one else would. I know I'm safe with you."

She started forward again. He didn't move. His gaze was burning a hole in her back. She turned to look over her shoulder and beckoned for him to join her. At last, he did.

"You trust me?"

"Is there some reason I shouldn't?"

"I can think of at least a dozen reasons. Why do you?"

She sensed that her answer mattered a great deal and took the time to compose her thoughts before responding. "Every single time I have been in danger of any kind in your presence, you have come to my rescue. You've protected me from harm. You've defended my honor. Even the first day we met, you saved me from my own rude curiosity by turning it into a joke and laughing it off. I don't know what I've done to deserve your loyalty and protection, but you have always offered it without question and without expectation of anything in return."

She searched his face for some indication of his response. He stared back, his expression unreadable. "Even last night," she continued, "I know you were trying to protect me. I know you thought you had my best interests at heart. How could I not trust a man who was willing to marry me when no one else would, and who obviously desired me, but had no expectation of consummation? It's true we hardly know each other, but I know who you are to me." He still stared, inscrutable. "Victor, say something."

Finally, his serious expression softened. "I'm yours, utterly and completely, for as long as I live."

"And I am yours."

He took a deep breath. "Good God, I want to drag you off and do sinful things to you right now." Alais wished he would. "But I promised you a day out, and a day out you shall have. We're nearly there."

Alais had been to Hastings before on several previous occasions but only to Lady Helisende's castle. She'd never spent time in the city proper. As they rode through the city gates, surrounded by a steady stream of colorful riders and wagons, she couldn't help thinking Victor was right. This was so much bigger than Winchelsea.

He guided them away from the central road up to the palace and into winding side streets that seemed to have no rhyme or reason. She soon lost all sense of direction. The streets were so narrow that she couldn't imagine how a wagon could fit through.

They stopped in front of a stone building that looked exactly like all the others crammed together in these narrow streets. He was certain of his destination, though, and helped her down. They entered a tiny shop filled floor to ceiling with bolts of cloth in every imaginable color and texture.

"Sir Victor! What an unexpected pleasure," squeaked a short, squat merchant dressed all in green velvet and who had only the slightest fringe of white hair. Alais didn't think he looked pleased at all to see Victor, unexpectedly or otherwise. "Is your aunt looking for something special? I just made a large delivery to Lenore up at the castle. Is anything amiss?"

"You'd better hope it's not. As you well know, my aunt

doesn't appreciate mistakes, but today I'm here on personal business. Allow me to present my wife, Lady Alais."

The merchant bowed and licked his lips. "An honor to make your acquaintance, my lady. May I offer you a seat?" He gestured toward a tall, padded stool beside a large, wood table marked with measurements. "Let me show you a sampling of my wares."

He began pulling down a bewildering array of fabrics in a rainbow of rich colors. There were silks, brocades, satins, velvets—every luxurious fabric she could imagine.

"You can do better than that," said Victor, shaking his head. "Show me what you show Lenore."

The merchant blanched, but there was also a gleam of greed in his eye as he put back all the dazzling fabrics he'd pulled out and shuffled into the back of his shop. He returned with a much smaller pile, but each one was fit for a queen. Victor rejected half of them for minor flaws in weave or dye that Alais couldn't even see, leaving only the finest for her to choose from. She chose fabric for two winter dresses, two summer dresses, and a cape, and gave Victor a worried look, not sure if she'd over-indulged. He just smiled.

"Are there any of these fabrics you don't like?" Victor asked her.

She pointed to three, leaving six.

"We'll take these six as well," Victor told the merchant. She watched Victor loom over the merchant's shoulder as he measured and cut, making sure he didn't skimp. They haggled over the price, but Victor still paid a sum that made her heart skip a beat. The merchant heaved a sigh of relief as they left with a large, wrapped bundle.

"I caught him cheating on his import taxes last year," Victor explained after they left. "He's dishonest to the bone, but he has the finest selection in Hastings. My aunt is his biggest customer. She used to send me along with Lenore to make sure he didn't cheat her."

"Who's this Lenore? Should I be jealous?" Alais teased.

Victor laughed. "Lenore is a fifty-year-old grandmother who's missing her two front teeth. She's my aunt's chief seamstress." He pulled her into his arms and kissed her forehead. "It's sweet, though, that you think there's anyone you need to be jealous of."

He put the cloth in a saddle bag and led her through the winding streets to a cobbler, then a furrier, then a milliner. Each one had run afoul of him at some point, avoiding taxes or cheating customers, and they all fell over themselves to provide Alais with their finest wares and keep him happy.

Last, he led her to a shop with an elaborate display of bottles of all shapes, sizes, and colors. "Ah, here we are. Esteban's perfume shop is the best you'll find outside of the Mediterranean. And he has other useful skills too."

A tall, thin man with dark skin and a long, white beard stepped out of the shop. He was wearing a spotless white robe and had a scarf wrapped loosely around his head. His eyes lit up when he saw Victor, and they embraced like old friends, exchanging a few incomprehensible words in what she assumed must be Spanish. She watched Victor gesture toward her, and Esteban's eyes went wide.

"Congratulations, my friend! My lady," Esteban said in English, turning to her with a bow, "felicitations on your marriage. I wish you joy." He turned back to Victor. "Come inside. Come inside. Let me take a look at that scar."

Alais's eyebrows raised at that. Few people dared refer to Victor's scar, let alone ask to look at it. And here she'd thought she was here to buy perfume.

Esteban sat Victor on a low leather stool and lit a bright lantern. Then he removed Victor's eye patch. Alais's jaw dropped. She'd never seen Victor without his eye patch. She stood back in the shadows and watched with fascination as Esteban examined the dark pit and discolored flesh where Victor's left eye used to be, as well as the scar on his face, in minute detail. Esteban nodded and smiled as he sat back and let Victor put the patch back on.

"Some of my finest work," Esteban said, clapping Victor on the shoulder.

Victor turned to Alais. "Esteban is the finest physician I've ever met. He stitched me up when I was wounded in Spain. You can thank him for my handsome face. Without him, it would have been far worse. I still say it's a pity you went into trade, Esteban."

Esteban shrugged. "The money's better, and I like sleeping through the night." He handed Victor two bottles.

"Onion extract and lavender oil?"

Esteban nodded. "Onion in the morning, lavender at night, as before." Esteban turned to Alais while Victor put his patch back on, and he inhaled deeply. "Lemon and thyme with just a hint of citron. Am I right?"

Alais smiled and nodded.

"You favor fresh scents, yes? Bright and sweet?"

"I do, though I'm open to other options as well. Nothing too heavy or cloying, though."

"Nothing with roses," Victor added, which surprised her. She hadn't realized he knew her disdain for heavy floral scents.

He brought her bottle after bottle with different mixes until she started to sneeze. In the end, she chose two scents. The first reminded her of a spring morning with light floral and citrus notes and a hint of rosemary. The second was a heavier, more sensual scent with sandalwood and subtle herbal notes. It made Victor smile, which was all she needed to make her decision. Victor paid for their purchases, said goodbye to his friend, and they headed out.

She would never forget this day, she thought as they made their way through more narrow streets. It wasn't the gifts he'd purchased but the way that he'd revealed a little bit more about himself with each stop. Who would have expected Victor to be such an expert in silks and millinery or to be such a sharp negotiator? Then there was the visit to Esteban. She had no doubt that he had deliberately chosen to let her see him vulnerable, to see the injury he had always kept hidden in her presence. It spoke to the trust he placed in her, trust she wasn't entirely sure she had earned.

Their next stop was an elegant inn called the Lute and Tambour, filled with intricately carved tables and chairs, and lit with silver sconces. Everything was polished to a shine, and the uniforms of the serving staff were all spotless and neatly pressed. Victor requested a private dining room and asked the innkeeper to bring wine and refreshments and to find someone named Richard.

As soon as the door closed behind them, Victor pressed her against it and kissed her with a passion and ferocity that made her wish they'd asked for an actual room instead of just a dining room. But before she was ready, Victor stepped away, leaving her panting. "Richard and the food will be here soon. I can't let myself get too carried away. Have you been enjoying your day so far?"

"It is fun to watch you torment merchants. You've bought me more finery than I could wear in a year. But Victor, you do know you don't have to buy my affection, don't you?" It was all a bit much. She liked a pretty dress as much as the next woman, but he'd showered her in silks like he had something to prove.

He pulled her close again. "I would never mistake you for a woman who could be bought, Alais." He tucked a strand of hair behind her ear and caressed her cheek.

"Am I interrupting?" asked a man with a wry smile who was wearing blue and yellow motley and carrying a lute. He had dark curly hair and an outrageous mustache. "Paul told me you had a woman with you. I was hoping you might have thought to bring one for me too, but it looks like I'm out of luck."

Victor's grip on her tightened as he answered through clenched teeth, "She's my wife, Richard."

The man gave Victor a disbelieving stare. "Wife? *You?*"

"Alais, please forgive my friend for his ignorance and insults. He's one of the finest performers at my aunt's court, but sometimes he's a complete lout."

She cleared her throat and gave Richard a haughty glare.

Richard looked dubious, but he bowed in apology. "I did not mean to offend, my lady. I made a mistake. I hope you will not hold it against me." He looked at Victor. "Perhaps you would care to explain why you invited me here. I like drinking with you, and you always bring me good songs. But I can't imagine why you'd bring your wife along to spoil our fun."

"I have a fabulously filthy song for you, courtesy of my new brother-in-law, but first I am hoping you will satisfy my wife's curiosity about a certain song about a cat. She's been after me for over a month, and I can't do it justice."

Alais gasped and clapped her hands together. The song about the cat at last! It was the best present of the day so far.

"You must be joking. For your *wife?*"

Victor nodded with a mischievous smile.

Richard stared for another moment then shook his head and sighed. He checked the tuning of his lute, then began singing a long tale of two sisters who found a pilgrim in Auvergne who pretended to be mute. They thought him the ideal candidate to satisfy their lusts without any risk of being found out. To make sure he was mute, they went and got their cat.

"When we had drunk up all the wine,
They shed their clothes, and I shed mine.
They brought the cat up from behind,
Its claws dug in. It was unkind.
The ladies pulled it down my side,
It hurt so much, I nearly cried.

It scratched again. I almost screamed.
It hurt more than I ever dreamed.
They gave my flesh a hundred sores.
I crumpled down onto their floors.
But I would not cry out. Oh no!

Despite the way they hurt me so.

'Oh, Sister dear,' one of them said,
'He's mute, all right, and safe to bed.
So, Sister, let us bathe right now.'
The evil cat just said, 'Meow.'
Eight days and more I stayed with them
And laid with them and played with them.

I fucked them both repeatedly:
One hundred eighty times, you see.
I nearly broke my saddle strap
And harness as they rode my lap.
They fucked me raw. It hurt so much!
But I could not ignore their touch.

They fucked me raw. It hurt so much!
But I could not ignore their touch."

Alais sat with wide eyes and a hand over her mouth, unable to believe what she was hearing. Victor was doubled over with laughter. It was an admirable performance, right down to the ridiculous falsetto Richard used for the sisters. She wasn't sure what she'd expected, but this was certainly far beyond anything she'd ever imagined.

"And that, my dear wife, is the song about the cat. Are you satisfied at long last?" Victor was still heaving with laughter.

"What diabolical mind would compose such a thing?" she demanded. Surely this went beyond the usual troubadour excess.

"The queen's grandfather, Guillaume IX, Duke of Aquitaine, if you can believe it," Richard announced in a bored voice. "But, Victor, you said you had something new and filthy for me?"

"Oh yes," said Victor, borrowing Richard's lute. "It goes like this…"

CHAPTER SEVENTEEN

I T WAS MID-AFTERNOON when Victor led Alais through the village of Guestling to the round, crenelated stone tower that dominated it. For the first time in a long time, he was looking forward to coming home.

"I still can't believe Daniel composed that," Alais said for the third time since they left Richard and the inn. "Does Carenza know?"

"I couldn't begin to guess." The truth was he strongly suspected she did, but he wasn't about to admit he'd given the matter any thought. "Oh, and that song I sang in front of your suitors? The word was supposed to be 'cunt', not 'queen'."

"'That these things three things do not please me: a cunt under guard, a pond without fish...' I see now why they didn't want you singing it. It was quite clever of you to change the word. It all sounded quite innocent to me."

Victor smiled. "Yes, and I am destroying your innocence quite thoroughly now, aren't I? Although I've always thought it hypocritical that men aren't expected to remain innocent, but women are. And really the word 'innocence' is disingenuous. What they really mean is ignorance. Now that you're my wife and not my charge, I'm going to take great delight in ruining you with forbidden knowledge."

She laughed. "You sound like my brother, may he rest in

peace. He always encouraged us to read and explore and do things we weren't supposed to. Like ride his destrier, Valor, when I was only ten. Valor was even bigger than Socorro."

"He wasn't worried you'd get hurt?"

She shook her head. "He trusted me to know my own capabilities. I was good with horses, always had been. And still am. He reminded me of the risks, said he thought I could handle it, and let me make my own decision. It turned out Valor loved me."

Victor laughed. "Everyone loves you, man and beast."

She chuckled and shook her head. "Tell that to Carenza."

"Carenza is neither man nor beast. Oh, and speaking of Carenza, please don't tell her or Daniel that I sang that song about a peach in front of you."

Victor was feeling pleased with how the day had gone so far. It was risky, introducing her to Richard, but oh, had it paid off! The look on her face after the cat song was priceless. And she even complimented his own lackluster singing and mediocre lute skills when he sang the song by Daniel, though Victor was a bit worried he'd made a mistake there. Daniel almost certainly didn't want that song getting back to his sister-in-law.

"I'll never look at a peach the same way again," Alais said with the same expression of scandalized fascination she'd worn since the cat song. "Oh my goodness, *Carenza's* peach…"

"Best not to think about it too hard."

"You are surely going to hell. Daniel too."

"Oh, without a doubt."

At that moment, a familiar form emerged from the castle gate and began ambling their way. "Brace yourself. Here comes my father."

A tall, hairy man with an ample belly and skinny legs started bellowing his name. He had described his father to Alais as a fat goat, but now that he was staring at the man, Victor thought he was more like a once-proud lion gone to seed. His blond hair and beard were unkempt and streaked with white. His face had the permanent flush of someone always in their cups. His father had never had the healthiest of habits.

"Good God, Victor, can it possibly be you? I'd given up on ever seeing you again. It's been months since you visited. And who is this beauty you bring with you—a de Vere by the looks of her unless I'm very much mistaken."

Victor dismounted, and let his father embrace him and thump his back hard enough to make him wheeze momentarily. "Father, let me introduce my wife, Lady Alais, daughter of Lord and Lady de Vere."

He enjoyed watching his father's expression at the word "wife." It was all he'd hoped. His father stood speechless for several moments, blustering and spluttering, turning redder by the second.

"Wife?" he roared as the words sank in. "Are you telling me my only child went off and got married and didn't invite me?! *Who raised you?*"

"I'm sorry, Father. It all happened rather suddenly, just yesterday in fact. I came as soon as I could manage." Truth be told, he was relieved that it had happened too fast for his father to attend. He loved his father, but he was hardly fit for polite company these days. He'd gone feral, living alone in the castle with only the servants for company.

His father gave Victor and Alais a sharp look. "Sudden, eh?" Then he burst out laughing. "By God, your mother and I got married suddenly too. Sometimes you can't help yourself. She is a pretty little thing, isn't she? I can't say I blame you." He swept into as gallant a bow as his portly shape would allow. "I am Lord Giles. It is an honor to welcome you to Guestling, my lady. I see you have your father's eyes and your mother's loveliness."

"It's a pleasure to meet you too, my lord. You know my parents?" Alais asked, curtsying.

"Of course, I know your parents! We live too close not to know each other. In fact, I've met you several times, though you may not remember. You couldn't have been older than six the last time I saw you. I seem to recall Victor here rescuing you from a large mastiff that barked at you and gave you a scare."

Servants led away their horses, and they made their way into the castle.

"I remember that!" Alais said, taking Victor's arm and squeezing it. "I had no idea that was you." She kissed his cheek. He must be getting used to her company because he only froze for a few seconds before he recovered.

His father elbowed him in the side. "Your mother used to look at me like that."

Inside the castle, everything was clean and tidy but shabby. The upholstery was faded and worn through in places. Paint was chipped and stained. Rugs had bare patches. Victor knew Guestling brought in a modest but comfortable income, and he'd added significantly to their collective assets from his time in Spain and his work for his aunt. His father could afford to have things repaired and replaced. He just didn't bother.

As expected, they retired to the great hall, and his father called for his cook, Marie, and consulted with the shy, plump widow in whispers for several minutes before sending her off with a playful spank and then pouring generous flagons of wine for all three of them. Soon the food began to arrive, starting with a fresh, golden baguette, still warm from the oven, served with fresh goat cheese, duck confit, and gherkins. Victor always had had a weakness for Marie's duck confit, and he dug in with relish.

"So tell me how this all came about, my boy. When Robert went off to that tournament, I thought he might be bringing a young lady home, but it seems you beat him to it!"

Alais stiffened beside him at the mention of Robert's name. He gave her hand a reassuring squeeze beneath the table, and she squeezed back. Before he could respond, Alais spoke up.

"Robert asked for my hand, but I turned him down. Victor had already won my heart with his bravery and his kindness toward me." It was sweet of her to spin this tale for his father. The truth would come out eventually, but he was grateful to her for the lie.

And then she turned to him. "He was shy about courting me, but it was his scarf and his colors I wore at the tournament. I can't tell you how my heart was pounding as I placed the ring on his finger for his triumph at swordsmanship. I was his before he dared to speak a word."

He knew she was embellishing for his father's sake, but the look in her eyes took his breath away. If he didn't know better, even he would have been convinced by her performance.

A tray of fresh oysters arrived with an assortment of sauces. "Always knew you had it in you, my boy," his father chuckled before loudly slurping down an oyster. "Christ, you took your time about it, though! Didn't think you were ever going to get the deed done." He slurped another oyster. "A man reaches a certain age, and he wants grandchildren, for God's sake!"

Victor nearly spit out his wine. He glanced at Alais to see if she was about to run away in horror, but he found her grinning and raising her glass to him. He opened his mouth to say something and closed it, opting for more wine and duck confit instead.

Bowls of rich and beautifully spiced pottage were placed in front of them. Victor inhaled deeply. Marie's pottage had always been the smell of home. When he was in Spain recovering from his wounds, he thought he smelled it on the breeze once, and it reduced him to tears. He knew if he ate the whole bowl, he would have no room for the courses yet to come, but there was no hope of holding back.

He was pleased to see Alais savoring each bite. It brought him joy to share this meal with her, to see her pleasure in the food that fed his soul. He laughed about his father stuffing visitors like capons, but he understood it. There was something so intimate about breaking bread together. It created a connection that went beyond hospitality. And beautiful food like Marie's was a sensual experience, a teasing of the tongue every bit as beguiling as a kiss. He used to wonder if his father was sleeping with Marie, but he'd long since realized that their relationship was far more intimate than that. He made love to her food, and she made love to his appetite. Whether they touched each other was entirely beside the point.

"How have you been, Father? I'm glad to see you in good health."

"Same as ever. Nothing new to tell. I'm getting older and slower." His father took a bite of pottage. "And fatter, thanks to Marie. She takes good care of me." He helped himself to another oyster. "If you want my advice, which you probably don't, you'll be on the lookout for a good cook now that you have a wife. With a good cook and a good wife, a man can be truly happy. Can't have Marie, though. She's mine."

"I wouldn't dream of taking Marie away from you."

"Who's taking who away from whom?" Victor's head whipped to the door where Robert leaned against the doorframe, arms crossed, taking in the scene. Alais's hand clutched his arm like a vice. "Lady Alais, what an unexpected surprise."

"Robert, I thought you were coming by tomorrow," his father said. "Victor stopped by unexpectedly to introduce me to his new wife. I gather you and she are acquainted already."

Alais's grip tightened even further on his arm. Her nails dug in painfully. Every muscle in his body tensed.

"Congratulations, my lady. I see now why you turned me down. I didn't think you had it in you to be so calculating and cold-blooded. He might be the heir, and I'm only second in line, but I never thought a woman would be able to get past his face. You proved me wrong."

Victor sprang to his feet, pulling free of Alais's grasp.

His father rose at the same moment. "Victor, don't touch your blade. Robert, I think you'd better leave." His voice was ice.

"And you, Victor," Robert continued, ignoring the warning. "I'm surprised you're willing to sully this house with damaged goods. I had my way with this little whore before she turned me down, or didn't you hear?"

"Oh, I heard, and I know for a fact that it's a lie. If we weren't beneath my father's roof, I would kill you for it right now. Out of respect for him, I'm giving you a chance to leave, but if I ever see you again, you are a dead man."

"So ungrateful," he said, crossing his arms and leaning against the door. "I saved your life in Spain."

Victor's hand flew to his sword, and it was halfway out of its sheath when he felt his father grab him by the collar with an iron fist.

"Leave now, Robert," his father growled.

Robert gave a sullen shrug and left.

Blood pounded in Victor's head, screaming for him to chase after Robert and end him. He shook with rage and the urge to shed blood. Only his father's hand on his collar kept him still. He was tempted to break away but knew his father would never forgive him.

"Peace, Victor. Let him go. He's bitter and disappointed. It's no excuse for what he said, but I can't let you do something you'll regret." His father released him at last. "You should see to your wife. She looks unwell."

Oh God. Alais.

All the color had drained from her face. She sat hunched in her chair, squeezing the fabric of her skirt into balls.

He gently pulled her hands away from the fabric and into his own. "Alais?"

A tear dripped down her cheek, and then another.

"Come here," he said, pulling her into his arms and thumbing away her tears.

He led her away to his old room. His father had never changed it, even though it had been years since he had lived in it. There were the old swords he collected in his youth over the mantle. Three bows of varying sizes were propped up in the corner. A dusty lute sat on a threadbare chair. The bed was small, but the bedding was freshly laundered. He helped her lay down, taking off her shoes and loosening the laces of her dress so that she could breathe more freely. He took off his boots and joined her on the narrow bed, pulling her to him and wrapping his arms around her.

"I'm never going to escape this, am I?" she asked, burying her face in his chest. "It's going to follow me forever. Now your father's going to wonder, just like my father did. It's never going to end."

She rested her head beneath his chin, and he caressed her hair. He didn't trust himself to say anything. He wanted to tear Robert limb from limb.

"I was having such a lovely day too." She propped herself up to look at him. "Thank you for today. It was wonderful." She kissed him with aching tenderness. Her sweetness only intensified his fury at Robert. How could he hurt her? How could *anyone* ever want to hurt her?

"I'm going to kill him." He probably shouldn't have said that out loud.

"No, please don't! I don't want anyone to die over this. I already feel awful enough. That would only make everything worse."

Victor gritted his teeth. He couldn't take revenge against her wishes, but everything in him urged violence. He was done with Robert.

"Victor?" She hovered above him and stroked his hair. He was undone by the plea in her eyes.

"Yes?"

"You won't, will you?"

He took a deep breath. "Not if you don't want me to."

She closed her eyes and then settled back down against his chest. "Maybe we could leave him with those sisters with the cat from the song, though. That seems like a fitting revenge."

He chuckled. "Or cut off all his hair and make him wear a wimple."

She giggled. She was so beautiful when she giggled. He kissed her. It felt strange to be able to just do that. He did it again to prove to himself that he could. Her whole body curved toward his when he touched her lips.

"*Mm.* Did you have anything else planned for today?"

"I did, but I don't imagine you'd be interested under the circumstances."

"Oh? What was it?"

"I wanted to make amends for my hurtful behavior last night by worshipping every inch of your divine form as you deserve."

Her eyes flashed with desire at his words. It still felt like a miracle that he could make her feel such things, and he prayed it always would. He traced a finger along her jaw, and her lips parted. Her chin inclined toward his. As he leaned in to kiss her, he stopped short, holding the tension, feeling the sweet pull as she leaned closer, hungry for him, eager for contact. Giving in at last, he touched his lips to hers, welcoming the soft pressure and the gentle tug followed by a delicate taste.

"I'm interested," she murmured between kisses.

"Are you sure?"

"Very sure."

CHAPTER EIGHTEEN

LAST NIGHT, SHE said he made her body sing. Today, he wanted to make her feel like an entire heavenly choir. He would set aside his own body's needs for as long as he could stand and devote himself to giving her the introduction to lovemaking she deserved. It's what he should have done last night. His behavior was unforgivable, and yet, by some miracle, she was still here today, wanting him. He wouldn't take his good fortune for granted.

Getting up, he stoked the fire. He wanted to make sure the room was warm enough for her comfort. The room had been unoccupied for a long time, and the November chill had permeated the stone walls. It would take time to heat up sufficiently, but he wouldn't rush this, not today.

He poured some water into a basin and set it by the fire to warm. Alais gave him a puzzled look. "Trust me. I have a plan."

He took off his cotte and hung it over a chair, leaving him in his linen shirt and breeches. The air was noticeably warmer already. He went over to the water and tested the temperature. In another few minutes, it would be perfect. Remembering something, he searched in the pocket of his cotte, pulling out the two small glass bottles of scented oil Alais had chosen. Opening the lid of each to find the one he was looking for, he dripped several drops in the warming water, and the room was filled with the scent of sandalwood. He tested the water again. It was just right.

He brought the basin of warm water over by the bed and went to grab a piece of plain linen and a small lump of soap. He invited her to sit up, offering her a hand. "I want to wash your feet."

"What?"

"Trust me."

There were any number of ways to help her relax and give him the chance to slow the pace of their passion and explore. He didn't want this to be only about immediate satisfaction. He wanted to learn her and give her a chance to learn him. It was important to him to show her how much more the joining of their bodies could be than a mere satisfaction of urges, how many pleasures there were besides the strictly carnal.

After a day of travel and activity, he thought she would be footsore and would appreciate the indulgence. Besides, he knew he was really good at massages. He considered it something of a specialty. He gently placed her feet in the basin of warm, scented water. Then he ran his hands up her calves to her knees, pushing up her skirt. A shiver ran through her at his touch.

"Are you cold?"

"No," she said, giving him a languid look.

He dipped the cloth in the water and tenderly bathed one calf and ankle, then lifted her foot from the water to bathe it. Her foot was slender and flexible, ending in shapely, delicate toes. She was slightly ticklish, he noted, something he would need to be careful of as he worked. He caressed her foot with the warm, wet cloth, then soaped his hands and began to massage, his touch slippery with lather.

Starting with her toes and working his way down to her heel, he made circles with his thumbs to loosen any tension. He explored each contour, listening carefully to changes in her breathing to learn where she was most sensitive and what gave her the most pleasure. When he'd explored every inch, loosened every muscle, and made her moan twice, he rested her calf on his shoulder and repeated his treatment on her other foot.

Every so often, he kissed her calf or nibbled on her inner thigh. The sounds she made when he did that made him want to abandon his careful plan and take her right then, but he held back, focusing on the details of her body's reactions. She was so responsive to his touch. He'd never been with a woman so sensitive to his every caress. With Alais, he felt almost as much a novice as she. There was so much he had to learn about her, so many ways in which she was unlike anyone he'd ever known.

When he finished her second foot and placed it over his other shoulder, he leaned in, enjoying the deeply arousing view of Alais with her legs spread around him and skirts pushed up nearly to her hips, open to him in every way. She was completely his, improbable though that still felt to his doubting mind. He let out a low, appreciative *"Mm"* at the sight of her. He intended to continue his massage, but instead, he found himself nuzzling and kissing his way up the soft flesh of her inner thigh. Her breathing grew more ragged by the moment.

"Victor, what are you doing?"

"I'm going to taste your peach," he said with a mischievous smile that she couldn't see.

"What?" she squealed.

Instead of answering, he took a taste. She jerked beneath him, grasping his hair, and letting out a yelp. He had fantasized about this so many times. It was hard to believe this was truly happening. He buried himself in her tender folds and feasted with abandon, struggling to regain control and focus. By God, she was delicious.

He needed to keep his head to do this right, but her response was so gloriously wild. She was straining and writhing, as if not sure whether she wanted to escape his torture or invite more. He slowed his tender onslaught and took a deep breath, focusing all his attention on her and away from the increasing urgency of his own body. It didn't matter that he was painfully aroused. Nothing mattered but her.

Bringing himself back under control, at least for the moment, he experimented with all the care and attention of an alchemist, seeking the right combination of sensations to produce the reaction he sought. He tested and teased, making mental notes of how each variation changed her breathing, the sounds she made, the way her body writhed around him. With each experiment, he refined his technique until he found the optimal combination and rhythm to drive her to the brink of insanity and over it, as he held on to her bucking hips, preventing her escape.

She went rigid beneath him, moaning his name, and gave a violent shudder. He nearly came himself watching her, but somehow he held back, determined to go slowly and do this right.

"How do you feel?" he asked, caressing her thighs, and tickling her calves.

All she could manage in response was, "*Unh.*"

"Oh good," he said with a smug grin. "We started at your toes, and we made it up to here." He wriggled a teasing finger to tickle her between the legs, causing her whole body to lurch. "Shall I continue working my way up?"

"*Mmhmm,*" she murmured, still apparently unable to form words.

"As you wish. Of course, that means we'll have to get this pesky dress out of the way."

Her skirts were already pooled around her waist, and the ties of her bodice were already loose. It was a simple matter to pull her to sitting and whisk her dress away over her head. She was fully revealed in the waning sunlight, so lovely it made his heart ache.

"You too," she mumbled, stretching out seductively on the bed.

"What was that?"

"I want to see you too," she said more clearly. "I haven't had a chance to take a proper look at you. We've always been…"

"Too busy?"

She nodded.

"Would you like to undress me?" he asked.

Whatever insecurities he had about his face, he had no such worries about his body. He knew he was lean and fit. His long limbs were muscular, shapely, and well-defined. He wasn't excessively hairy, with a sparse sprinkling of blond curls on his chest. He had reason to believe he was more than adequately endowed. She would not find him wanting, he was sure.

"I'm guessing you've never seen a naked man before me?"

"Of course not."

He smiled at that. "I must be quite a mystery."

She bit her lower lip as she stood and stepped toward him. Tracing a finger along his jaw, drawing his mouth toward her, she took her pleasure, tasting him at length and without shame. His chest heaved with desire, but he remained passive, letting her lead the way.

Pulling his shirt over his head, she raked her nails gently down his front. He gasped as she touched his nipples. She noticed immediately and ran her thumbs over them again, watching his reaction closely. He moaned at the intensity, another part of him stiffening further in response to her teasing. She reached for him beneath his breeches, and all of him snapped to attention.

Unlacing and pushing down his breeches, she took him in her hand, not moving, but simply holding him. He thought about frozen locales to keep himself from bursting at her touch. She took a long look at what she saw before her, running a finger up the side of his stiff, hot flesh. "It's longer and thicker than I imagined. I didn't get a proper look at it before. That really fits inside me?"

"Oh, dear God," he murmured, trying to imagine the icy land of the Vikings to keep from bursting.

She took him firmly in hand and whispered in his ear, "You seem to know all about what to do to make me writhe. What does that to you?"

His permanent half-smile spread into a full smile. He murmured in a strained voice, "Why should I tell you when you can figure it out for yourself?"

"Hmm," she mused, stroking her finger along his shaft. "You tasted my peach. I wonder what happens if I return the favor." She knelt in front of him and boldly kissed his soft, satin tip, licking away the salty drop of liquid that had formed there.

"God's bones, woman," he gasped. In the back of his mind, he vaguely remembered having a plan, but everything was obliterated by the feeling of her mouth on his cock. Alais de Vere was…*oh dear God*. It was too much. "Stop," he yelped, pulling her up. "I need to be inside you."

He sat on the bed and pulled her down to straddle him. She knelt above him on the edge of the bed and lowered herself onto his hungry flesh. As she slid down onto him, they both cried out; the sensation was too much. They were both too far gone. They moved with grasping desperation, all subtlety lost in all-encompassing need. "Oh God, I can't hold on."

"Neither can I." She heaved and throbbed around him, as pleasure overtook her and shook her.

His whole body pulsed, and all reason left him. He'd never felt anything like it, even the other times he'd been with her. Something was different this time. That something still held him after his release, carrying him along on a wave entirely unrelated to what was happening to his body. Some barrier within him had given way, and an agonizing torrent of love nearly tore him apart.

He knew he was in love with her, had known it for some time, but he'd never allowed himself to feel it fully. He had always held it back. But now it all came pouring through him, as undeniable as a river.

It wasn't time to speak. He couldn't say it aloud yet, but he felt like it must be leaking out, visible to her in some way. There was no chance she returned his feelings. He didn't want to burden her with his messy overpowering emotion. It was, frankly, terrifying to feel like this, but there was no more pushing it away.

He held her in his arms and breathed her in, trying to feel his way through the moment. She rested against him, eyes closed, breathing softly. Each tiny movement she made set off a new whirl of dizzying emotion.

He knew the instant her sadness returned. There was a slight catch in her breath, an almost imperceptible slump of her shoulders, and a tightening of her embrace. He caressed her hair. The relief and distraction he had offered her was temporary. It solved nothing. His love solved nothing. He couldn't fix this for her, and it caused him profound pain.

But there had to be some way to help. He couldn't just watch her suffer through this. She didn't want him to take revenge on Robert. He would respect her wishes, but he couldn't stand back and watch. She was worried about what his father would think. He could start there. His father would listen and be reasonable. He could fix this one thing for her and make sure she had at least one ally besides himself.

He kissed her forehead. "I need to go speak to my father. You should stay here and rest. We'll spend the night. I'll send a messenger to Winchelsea so that your family doesn't worry. Is there anything I can get you? If you're still hungry, I could have Marie send something up."

She sighed and released him. "I'm fine. I don't need anything. But don't take too long. I'll miss you." She traced a finger down his back as he sat up to get dressed.

He rose and put on his clothes and took one last look at her, curled in his bed beneath the blankets. "I won't be long. I promise."

Thank you, Jesus, for my wife.

He headed downstairs to find his father who was, unsurprisingly, still at the dinner table.

"Join me," his father said, gesturing to the chair beside him. "Marie is about to bring out some roast pork." He was still picking at the remains of a pheasant. He poured some wine for

Victor and nudged him to take remaining wing. "How is your wife?"

"As well as can be expected under the circumstances. She's been slandered, and there's nothing either of us can do."

"And you didn't marry her to save her honor after a fall from grace?"

Victor looked at the ceiling and took a deep calming breath. Even his own father wouldn't take his word for it. He looked his father in the eye. "It's true that she married me to save her honor, but she didn't fall from grace. Robert was lying. I took her maidenhead on our wedding night. If you need proof, you can ask Lord and Lady de Vere to see the bloody sheet."

"All right, all right, I believe you! No need to go talking about bloody sheets." He poured himself more wine, and the pork arrived along with more bread. "I wouldn't fuss too much about a little mishap anyway as long as she's good and faithful to you now you're married, and as long as you two get busy making grandchildren. I was starting to worry you wouldn't marry at all."

His father always had too much faith in him. Perhaps that's why he was so reluctant to visit. Every time, it felt like he was letting the man down. "I always wanted to marry. I just didn't have any prospects after I came back from Spain."

"Well, she's certainly fond of you. That's plain as day."

Victor smiled. "And I'm very fond of her."

"Ha! You're more than fond, my boy. You're so in love you can hardly see straight. I'm happy for you. She's a lovely young woman." He raised his goblet in a toast, and Victor reciprocated.

"We're going to stay the night, if that's all right with you."

"Of course! Of course!"

His father was well in his cups now. It was as good a time as any to broach a sensitive subject.

"I was also wondering," Victor said carefully, "if I might give her mother's ruby necklace. It would mean a lot to me to be able to give her something from mother."

"Give her all the bloody jewels. I don't care. It all just sits in a strongbox in the cellar moldering. Besides, it would warm my heart to see them on a pretty young thing like her. Dear God, this is delicious," he said stuffing a large bite of pork in his mouth. "Have some."

"Thank you for the jewels, father. I appreciate it." Most of the time, his father was generous to a fault, but occasionally, he was a maudlin fool, especially when it came to Mother. He was glad he caught his father at the right moment.

That concluded, he took a bite of pork. "Oh God, this is good. How does she do it?"

"She's magic."

"I'll have to take some up for Alais."

His father held up a hand as Victor started to rise. "Son, we need to talk about Robert. I know he's offended you and your wife, and he'll hear from me about it. But I don't want you going after him. He's still your kin. He's been good to me. Visits me more than you do."

Victor started to offer an apology, but his father interrupted. "I know, I know, you're busy. I'm not finding fault." He took another bite. "He's always been jealous of you, you know, even when you were boys. You both made your fair share of mischief, but you were always better at avoiding getting caught. On the rare occasions when you did get caught, you faced the consequences without flinching. He, on the other hand, got caught constantly and tried to weasel out of it every single time.

"The thing is, you were better at everything— swordsmanship, riding, flirting with pretty girls, at least until your injury—and to top it off, you were the heir. It's not his fault his father gambled away everything of value except the house in Hastings and the flour mill."

"I don't see how that excuses telling a lie to ruin an innocent woman's life."

"It doesn't. Of course, it doesn't. But she hurt him, and he told a lie to hurt her back. And now you bring her home as your wife, succeeding where he failed. That has to rankle. You've bested him again, and worse, you're now in a position to produce heirs of your own, putting Guestling even farther out of his reach. He's never had your strength of character. He isn't capable of taking this gracefully. I'm not asking you to forgive him, only have a little pity on him, and especially, not to kill him."

"Pity. God, I hate that word." Victor sighed. "I already promised Alais I wouldn't kill him."

"Smart woman, your wife," his father said, gesturing with his knife. "Killing him doesn't solve anything for her. The lie is already out. All you can do is wait for people to forget or lose interest."

Victor nodded and said nothing.

"You should take the rest of this pork up to her. Take some wine too. Newlyweds need their strength. Go make me some grandbabies."

He dutifully took a plate and a pitcher of wine along with two goblets and headed back upstairs to Alais.

CHAPTER NINETEEN

ALAIS LAY WITH her eyes closed in a happy reverie, her body still tingling with delightful sensations in the aftermath of their lovemaking. She'd put her dress back on but wondered if maybe she should have left it off. Victor's reaction to her nakedness was something she didn't think she would ever tire of.

Who cared about the rest of the world? Especially Robert and his vicious rumors. It was so mortifying that she'd ever even considered him as a suitor. There was a snake hiding beneath that pretty face. It took her longer than it should have to see him for what he was. And now, she'd spend the rest of her life living down his lies. Thank God she came to her senses before accepting his proposal. Other people might whisper behind her back, but at least she had the right man by her side to defend and comfort her.

But why was she spending time thinking about Sir Robert when she could be thinking about Victor worshipping her body in ways she'd never dreamed of?

There was a noise at the door. It began to open. Victor was back. Time to entice him to bed for a long, decadent night.

But the head that appeared was not Victor's.

Sir Robert closed the door behind him, and she stifled the urge to scream. What could he possibly want? Why was he in Victor's bedroom?

"Victor will kill you when he comes back and finds you here," she said, mustering her iciest tones.

"But he won't find me here," he answered, stepping toward her. "Because I'll be gone by the time he comes back. And you'll be with me."

"No, I certainly will not." She stood up and backed away from him.

"But I'm here to rescue you," he said, putting on his most smoldering smile. It filled her with bile.

"Rescue me?" she asked, incredulous.

"From spending the rest of your life with my hideous cousin. This was obviously a marriage of convenience to save your reputation. Come with me, and I'll get rid of him for you, and we can live happily ever after, as we always should have."

Could he truly be this self-important? Or this delusional. It was astounding.

"I would never go anywhere with you after what you did to me, and I'll have you know this is no mere marriage of convenience. I wanted to marry Victor."

His face took on an ugly sneer. "You *wanted* to marry me, but for some reason, you lost your mind and refused me. I'll forgive your momentary insanity if you come with me now like a good girl. There's no way you can choose that beast over me."

She backed closer to the fire, within arm's reach of the poker.

"I *did* choose Victor over you, and I'll never regret my choice. He's everything you aren't—noble, loyal, loving. There's nothing you could say that would ever make me betray him."

He recoiled as if struck. "I don't have time for this," he said, lunging toward her.

She grabbed the poker and brought it up between them.

He laughed. "I'm an expert swordsman, Alais. You think you can fend me off with a poker?"

As he made a grab for it, she backed away, breathing hard. "All I have to do is keep you at bay until Victor returns, and then we'll see who's laughing."

Her heart thumped loudly in her ears as terror and determination coursed through her. She brandished her poker as he stepped closer.

Sighing, he said, "Fine, we'll do this the hard way."

He grabbed the poker and yanked it from her hands, letting it clatter to the floor. She looked from him to the poker and back to him as he closed in. Dropping to the floor, she grabbed for the poker once again and managed to jab him behind the knee. His knee buckled, and he momentarily lost his balance. She scrambled up and kicked his shin, and he groaned as she circled closer to the door.

"Oh, no you don't," he said, an ugly grimace on his face as he grabbed the poker once again yanking it, and her, toward him.

The poker fell to the ground, and he wrapped his arms around her, trapping her. "So feisty. Too bad I don't have time to make proper use of you," he said, grabbing her buttocks and pressing her against his obvious arousal. "I want you, Alais, and I mean to have you. But that will have to wait until I get you away from here. Satisfying as it would be to see the look on your dear husband's face when he sees me fucking you senseless, I know he'd run me through with a sword. And I don't intend to die tonight."

She fought with all her strength, struggling against him, but he was too strong for her. His arms wrapped around her like bands of iron as he pushed her toward the door. Frantic, she tried to scream, but he clapped a hand over her mouth. She bit down as hard as she could. He roared and loosened his grip briefly. It was enough. She slid down through his arms and bolted for the door. *Almost there. Almost.*

A heavy weight tackled her from behind, pinning her to the floor. Robert's hot breath tickled her ear, as he bent her arm painfully behind her back. She couldn't move.

"Good. I have you now. I just need to tie you up."

His knee pressed her to the ground as tore a strip of cloth from the hem of her gown and bound her hands painfully tight behind her back.

Kicking and thrashing, she tried to squirm away, despite her bound hands. She landed a few good blows before he wrestled her into compliance and tied her legs and ankles. He tore off another strip from her skirt and turned it into a gag for her.

"Now I'm afraid I must leave you for a moment, my dear, to make sure the halls are clear."

He disappeared out the door and she lay on the floor, tears streaming down her face, wondering what she could do to fight him off. She looked around for anything that could help her, and she saw Victor's old swords in the far corner. If only she could scoot over there, maybe she could slice open her bonds.

She inched across the floor, ignoring the abrasion of the rough stone and her screaming ankles and wrists. Relief was across the room. She only had to reach it. As she wriggled her way forward, she said a silent prayer that Victor would come back and find her before Robert succeeded in his plan to carry her away.

To her amazement and relief, she reached the swords propped up in the corner, sat up, turned her back, and began to saw, praying they were sharp enough to cut through her bonds. Then the door opened. *Please let it be Victor. Please let it be Victor.* Robert walked through, and she couldn't stop a new burst of tears from rolling down her cheeks.

"Oh no you don't," he said, yanking her away from the swords, then lifting her and tossing her on the bed. He added another length of rope to the bonds around her wrists, making it even tighter than the last. "You know, you're turning out to be far too much trouble awake. I'll need to knock you out before I move you. But first, I have to lay my trap."

His trap? What did he have in mind?

Victor, please save me. Come through the door right now and run Robert through with your sword. I take back what I said about not killing him. I will not regret his loss one bit.

Sir Robert took a strip of parchment from his pouch and placed it on the bed. She couldn't turn to see what it said.

"That should do what I need it to," he said, with an obnoxious, self-congratulatory grin. Dear Lord, she wanted to run him through with a sword herself.

"And now to take care of you."

She shrank away from him, but it was no use.

Crash!

Everything went black.

CHAPTER TWENTY

WHEN VICTOR TURNED into the hallway with his bedroom, he sensed immediately that something was wrong. The bedroom door was wide open. It seemed unlikely Alais would have gone anywhere on her own. He turned into the room, and she was gone. There was a broken piece of crockery on the floor beside the bed and several drops of blood on the pillow. There was also a note on a thin strip of parchment resting on the pillow.

"I took her. R"

His blood ran cold. The food and wine crashed to the floor, and he grabbed his sword and a heavy cloak. He ran down the hall, down the stairs, and stopped momentarily in the great hall to tell his father. "Robert kidnapped Alais. I must find her. I'm going after them. Search the house to see if anyone saw them."

"What?" His father started to rise from his chair, but Victor didn't pause to talk to him or say anything else. There was no time to waste. Instead, he ran out of the castle to the stables and saddled Socorro before the groom even realized he was there, and he went riding out into the night.

It was too dark to gallop, but he trusted his horse to see where he couldn't and he did it anyway, knowing the road so well he could walk it blindfolded. He was headed for Hastings. It was possible Robert would have taken another route, but Hastings was his most likely destination. And anyway, there was no way he could track him in the countryside in the dark.

Victor guessed Robert would be headed home. He wouldn't want to stop at an inn with a kidnapped noblewoman in tow, and camping out with Alais wasn't a practical choice either. The mill would be Victor's second stop if he didn't find Robert at home.

The sound of his horse's hooves thundered in his ears in the otherwise silent night. A fog descended, hiding the moon and stars, and giving the air a close and stifling feel, forcing him to slow down when he was desperate to race ahead. When he'd been traveling for half an hour, a group of three unsavory-looking men blocked his way forward, and another three closed in behind. Those were the ones he could see. He suspected more were hidden in the trees on either side of the road. *Oh, for God's sake.* The last thing he needed right now was a delay fighting with brigands.

"Well met, good sir," said the largest of the bunch in a low voice oozing with threat.

"I'm in a hurry. Delay me at your peril," Victor replied with a cold certainty that made several of the men shift uneasily.

"Now, now. It isn't polite to hurry. We're only getting acquainted, and there are so many of us you haven't met yet."

One of the men tried to grab Socorro's reins. His horse tossed his head and danced away, giving Victor the opportunity to draw his sword in a flash and slice a deep cut in the man's wrist with a swift sweep. The injured man staggered off into the woods wailing and bleeding heavily. "I said I'm in a hurry. Move now or die."

"Hear that, boys? He thinks he can threaten us."

Apparently, the leader of the group hadn't noticed that Victor had nearly sliced off the hand of one of his men. "It's not a threat. It's a promise."

There was a rustling in the trees, and the outline of a rider emerged and turned to face him. "I told you idiots to take him by surprise. It's going to be so much messier this way." There was no mistaking that voice. Robert. "It was far too easy to lure you out, Victor. She's pretty, and by God, she's a good fuck, but is she really worth all this?"

Victor's vision went red, and there was a roaring sound in his ear. It was a lie. It had to be. But the words still filled him with horror. "If you've touched her, you piece of shit, I'll—"

"Now now, cousin. I'd watch my tone if I were you. You wouldn't want your wife to come to any harm."

It took all the self-control he could muster to refrain from disemboweling his cousin on the spot. It would be easier to find Alais with Robert alive. And he'd promised both Alais and his father not to kill him.

"Where is she? Is she here?" Victor growled.

"Of course not. I'm not a complete fool."

"Where did you take her?"

"Wouldn't you like to know! All you need to worry about is that I'll take good care of your tasty little morsel after I dispatch you once and for all. Then I can take her to wife because 'till death you do part'. Wouldn't want her to break her vows, after all. You know, you're an annoyingly hard man to kill."

Victor was motionless. "It was *you* at the tournament. You're in league with Matthew."

Robert startled and looked around at the men surrounding them. Then he laughed, but it was a weak, nervous laugh. "Figured that out, have you?"

There had to be more to this than pride, Victor realized. If he was in league with Matthew, there were money problems. His father had mentioned Robert's father's gambling debts... "How much do you need, Robert? Father and I can help you."

Robert laughed. "It's not about what I need, but what I want. I want Guestling. And, I want Lady Alais. Somehow you convinced her to turn me down. Even after that, I hoped I could go back after I got rid of her other suitors by telling them I'd taken her and then offer to marry her to salvage her virtue, but you beat me to it."

Victor shook his head. "I never said a word against you. You managed to lose her favor all by yourself. In fact, I have you to thank for my good fortune. I don't think she'd ever have even considered me, if not for you and your little lie." He waved his sword. "I'm giving you one last chance to tell me where she is."

"Says the man surrounded by a dozen armed men." Robert shook his head dismissively. Victor wasn't fooled. Assessing the scene surreptitiously, he'd seen it was only eight—the five on the road, the one he injured, an archer in a tree beside the road, and Robert. Only Robert was mounted. Only two besides Robert had swords. The others were armed with clubs. Robert would be a challenge, for certain, and the archer would be tricky. But the rest would be all too easy to subdue. He smiled in the dark. Now that Robert was within his reach, he didn't mind the prospect of a fight so much.

"All right, men, let's end this," said Robert, signaling.

A cold thrill went through Victor as he braced for battle. He cleared his mind and let his fury course through him as he prepared to end this sad party of brigands. They would pose him no problem. The main danger was that they would get in the way of his real target, Robert.

The man before him with a sword struck out. Victor smiled coldly as he ran the man through the neck. Robert backed away on his horse. Victor rode over the corpse and sliced. The harsh ring of steel against steel rang in his ears. *Time to take you down, Robert.*

Someone grabbed Victor's foot and tried to drag him off his horse. Victor yanked his sword away from Robert and relieved the poor bastard of his head. Again, Victor leveled a blow at his cousin. Robert blocked, but barely. His cousin was off his game this evening. He didn't know how to use the group to his advantage. Now it was time to remove that advantage.

Victor whirled round just in time to see the other man with a sword trying to hamstring Socorro. He saw red. "Don't you dare touch Socorro, you filthy pig." He punctuated the word *pig* with a thrust, which the man parried. Tingling at the back of his neck told him Robert was closing in from behind. So he wasted no time swinging at this minion, striking off his sword hand, and then piercing him through the eye, ending him.

He spun Socorro just in time to duck a swipe from Robert aimed at his head. He struck back. Their swords rang in the night with the force of the blow. *I promised not to kill you, cousin, but you are not leaving this fight whole.* Victor shoved Robert's blade away and swung at his sword hand, missing by a hair.

"Nice try, Cousin," Robert said as he struck Victor's head again. The tip of his blade nicked Victor on the jaw. First blood, damn him. But Victor was filled with an unholy rage that overtook him and guided his sword as if it were an extension of his body.

Another henchman tried to grab Victor's leg and pull him down. At the same moment, Robert thrust and pierced his shoulder in a shallow cut.

"You little shit. If you think you have me, you are sorely mistaken." Swinging his sword in a long arc, Victor slit the throat of the man at his heels. *There. No more minions with swords.* Though there was still the archer to worry about, but the remaining brigands with clubs looked at the carnage and the crazed look in Victor's eye and ran for the woods. As they scrambled, Victor turned back to Robert, slicing through his cotte, and drawing blood.

Robert struck back wildly. The fury of his onslaught put Victor on the defensive. Momentarily.

Just then, an arrow whizzed by Victor's ear. He swore but didn't pause in his fight. Returning as good as he got, Victor pressed Robert back and cut him deeply in the leg. Robert yelled in pain. Victor took the moment of distraction to pull out the throwing knife he always kept in his boot. He rode to the spot where he had the clearest shot at the archer. But the archer also had the clearest shot at him. The archer let loose a moment before Victor. The arrow ruffled his hair as he threw his knife.

The archer fell out of the tree, on top of his bow, breaking it, and moaned. Not a kill, but no more arrows would come his way.

He felt rather than heard Robert's approach. They were alone now. No more distractions. Battle fury roared in his ears. *Whatever you did to Alais, I promise to pay you back tenfold.* Their swords clashed. Victor could see the gleaming black line of blood on Robert's leg in the pale moonlight. Robert's movements were wilder now. His discipline was slipping. It was Victor's chance.

Victor executed a series of strokes calculated to get inside Robert's guard. He almost had him. At the last second, Robert pulled away and sent his horse galloping into the night at a dangerous pace. "Fuck." Victor tore after him, yelling, *"Rob-errrrrt!"*

Socorro was tiring beneath him, but Victor continued to gallop hard down the road past Hastings and continuing on toward Westfield. They came to a portion of the road that was covered in grass. It muffled Robert's hoofbeats in the night. Victor began to worry he'd lost him.

Where could he be headed? Alais wasn't with him, so where could she be? Robert hadn't had time to take her very far. Should he turn back and search around Guestling? But Robert was his best chance at getting answers and ending this quickly. He continued on.

Alais must be so scared. Had Robert hurt her? He'd called her a "good fuck." Victor's stomach twisted into a knot at the thought, but his cousin had lied about it before. Surely, he was lying again. But if it was true…

No. She didn't leave voluntarily. Everything suggested an abduction. If she didn't leave voluntarily, she didn't give Robert her body voluntarily, either. Unless…

No. He wasn't going to doubt Alais. He had to see her. He had to hear from her own mouth what happened. He wasn't going to be taken in by Robert's lies. It made no sense for her to go to Robert after everything he did to her.

He'd seen her face when his cousin had appeared at Guestling. She'd been scared. He could tell—it wasn't an act. The look on her face after Robert's insults was enough to prove she wouldn't go with him voluntarily.

But they'd only been married two days, and he'd blundered so badly on their wedding night. Maybe she was having second thoughts. Maybe she regretted her decision.

Still, he didn't think she'd go to Robert. Would she?

Reaching a fork in the road, Victor paused, squinting at the foggy darkness as he pondered which road his cousin was most likely to take.

"It's eating at you, isn't it?"

Victor's sword was out of its sheath and pointed at the voice in the blink of an eye. Robert's shape took shape out of the fog.

"You didn't notice me because you were too busy wondering if she ran away with me. Even after all my insults, maybe she prefers me to you. Maybe she regrets marrying you enough to come with me. She only married you because I left her no choice. You said so yourself. No sooner were you out of the room than she came to me, begging me to save her from a lifetime married to you. She threw herself at me, and I admit I enjoyed myself quite a bit. Such a sweet, tight little pussy she has. It's a pity we had so little time."

"She asked me not to kill you, but she didn't say anything about serious maiming." Victor moved closer to Robert.

"Serious maiming is not as satisfying as you'd think. Just look at you."

Victor inhaled sharply. "What do you mean?"

"I meant to kill you in Spain and take Guestling. I've never been very good at living within my means, and I'll admit to having enjoyed the thought of getting rid of my smug, perfect cousin. You've always been a pain in my arse. But Lord Amalric came riding by at the critical moment, and I had to make it look like I was saving you. I would have rather you died, but I thought at least with your new face, there was no chance of your producing an heir. Now, look where that's gotten me."

Victor blinked. The last year and a half rearranged itself in his mind through this new lens. So many things he'd forgiven Robert for took on a malevolent light. It wasn't only the injury. It was also the extent to which his sense of himself and his circumstances was built on a lie.

His injury wasn't an accident of luck. Robert had done this to him and then complained about his ingratitude and spread petty rumors about him, driving wedges between him and people he used to be close to. He lost so many friendships. He'd thought their distance was a reaction to his face and to other changes in him, but what role did Robert play?

And then there was Alais. He'd vouched for Robert as a match for her. But for her good sense, she would be Robert's bride. He'd done nothing to prevent it. But if he'd tried to stand in the way, would it have worked? Would Alais have listened, or would she have seen him as jealous and needy, undermining Robert in a sad attempt to gain her attention? That was exactly the seed that Robert tried to plant with her, accusing him of telling her lies to undermine his suit. *Poor Victor, so sad and desperate.*

He meant to follow Robert, not kill him. At least, not yet. He wanted Robert to lead him to Alais. But the last thread of his control snapped. He lunged with his sword, and Robert ducked, then struck back, cutting a shallow wound across Victor's chest. The pain sharpened his senses.

He struck out once again at his cousin, making contact. Robert cried out in pain and took off again at a gallop. Victor tore after him, all caution discarded, determined not to lose him in the fog. He came up even with him and slashed once again. Robert yelped but didn't slacken his pace. Instead, he made a sharp and careless turn to the right, his horse plunging into the woods.

Victor tore after him, heedless of the dangers of chasing through woods in the dark in the fog. Then Socorro let out a scream of pain and stopped short, throwing him from the saddle. Victor picked himself up off the ground with a deep growl of frustration. It was no good following a man in the dark, in the fog, in the woods on foot. Nonetheless, he followed the retreating sound of Robert as long as he could manage before he acquiesced to necessity and started up the road to Westfield for help.

Chapter Twenty-One

BLINDING LIGHT STREAMED through the window as Alais awoke, sharpening the severe headache that throbbed behind her squinting eyes. She slowly became aware of her body, bound, and tied to a bed, her hands bound above her head to one bedpost and her feet bound to the diagonal opposite bedpost. Her hands were numb and tingling as she moved her fingers to bring back circulation.

She looked around the room, searching for some clue as to where she was. It was made of stone, with stone walls and a stone floor. It was sparsely furnished and bare of any adornment or personal items that might give her some hint. A thick layer of dust lay over everything. The room clearly hadn't been used in a long time. There was no fire, and she ached with cold. She heard a seagull outside, so she knew she was near the ocean, but how far from Guestling? And how did she get here?

"Help," she yelled as loudly as she could. No one came. She yelled again. Nothing.

She was freezing. Her whole body was trembling with the cold she was aware of now that she was conscious. She tried to find a way to escape her bonds, but they only pulled tighter. She wasn't sure how long she went on like this, alternating between struggling with her bonds and yelling. Just when she was starting to lose her voice, she heard shuffling footsteps outside the door.

"Help me, please," she croaked. A timid young housemaid peered around the door, saw Alais, and ran away without a word.

She groaned in frustration. She could only hope that the girl brought back help, though she suspected she would bring the opposite. Closing her eyes, she prayed.

Several minutes later, she heard footsteps again. The maid came back along with another servant, a man this time. "Stay still, my lady. If you promise not to run, I'll untie you," the man said. She nodded her agreement, too hoarse to speak. "His lordship said to see to it you were well tended to until he can return. You're not to leave, but we'll make your stay as comfortable as we can. I'll bring up some food."

As the man untied her bonds, blood rushed into her hands and feet, and they throbbed and prickled.

"Where am I?" she whispered, shivering violently. She grabbed the dusty bed cover and pulled it around herself.

"Our master said not to tell you anything, but that you'll be safe here as long as you don't try to leave."

She had to get away, but it was no use running without a plan. First, she needed to observe her prison to decide how best to escape.

"I'll cooperate," she whispered, nodding meekly.

The man nodded. "I'll be back shortly with some refreshment. The garderobe is to the right at the end of the hall, should you need it."

She did and was grateful for the opportunity to relieve herself and to get a better look at her surroundings.

The hallway looked as unused as the bedroom where she'd been imprisoned. Everything was dusty and bare. Nothing adorned the walls. She noted that her room was the middle of three and that there were three doors on the opposite side of the hall as well.

There was nothing notable about the garderobe other than the small round window at the top, open to allow air to circulate to relieve the smell. In this private moment, she took stock of her body. There was a bump on her head and bruises all over. Her wrists and ankles had angry red welts where she'd been tightly bound, but there was no sign of anything else. At least Robert had stopped short of compromising her virtue while she was unconscious. At the thought of him, a shiver ran through her. How could two men so closely related be so different?

She returned to her room. A tray of food had been placed there—some bread and cheese, an apple, and mulled wine. While there was no sign of the servant that brought the food, it seemed too much to hope that she wasn't being watched. After taking several bites to stave off hunger, she went to the window and looked out. There was a modest walled courtyard below with a small kitchen garden on one side. Another building of similar size was directly across, but what caught her eye and gave her hope was at a somewhat greater distance.

From her vantage point, she could see the unmistakable outline of Countess Helisende's castle, which meant Sir Robert must have taken her from Guestling to Hastings. If she could get out of the house, she could flee to Countess Helisende easily enough, even if it was a case of jumping out of the pot and into the hot cauldron. The countess was hardly trustworthy, but she was unlikely to do anything too terrible now that Alais was married to her nephew. Hopefully, the countess would contact Guestling, and she could return to Lord Giles.

Another hopeful thought occurred to her. Victor must be on his way to rescue her. She suspected he would cut down an entire army to find her, but he likely had no idea where she was. *She* had no idea where she was, aside from Hastings. She was clearly in Robert's house but knowing that didn't help her much. Her familiarity with the city was limited.

It didn't appear possible to sneak out via the window. She was too high up. The lower floors were likely well-guarded. If she had an opportunity, she would assess the situation, but she thought it unlikely she would be allowed out of this vacant third-floor space.

If sneaking out wouldn't work, was there a way to get a message out? Perhaps to Lady Helisende? She could say she was expected at the castle and needed to make her excuses or else risk the possibility of search parties looking for her. Sir Robert was unlikely to want to risk Lady Helisende's wrath. As he'd told her, he didn't have the advantage of being her nephew, being a cousin on Victor's father's side rather than his mother's.

Alais decided she had best fill her stomach. Whatever was ahead, she needed her strength and her wits. Eating her fill of the simple meal, she continued to mull over her plan. Despite her thirst, she drank sparingly from the wine, knowing she needed all her mental resources to orchestrate her flight.

Half an hour later, the male servant she met before came up to take the tray.

"Pardon me, good man," she said. "Might it be possible for me to have parchment and a quill brought to me? I need to send a letter to Countess Helisende to let her know my visit is delayed. Victor and I were supposed to pay our respects after our marriage two days ago. If I don't reassure her, she'll surely send out her guard to search for me. She might even search house to house if she learns I've been abducted. For your own good, I beg you to let me write. You can read my letter yourself to make sure I don't say anything I shouldn't."

The man narrowed his eyes.

"You wouldn't want trouble with the countess, would you?" she added for good measure.

"I will discuss it." With that, he took the tray and left.

Who was the man consulting? Was Robert here in the house? If so, she could only pray he didn't see right through her ruse.

A short time later, he returned. "We don't want any trouble with the countess, but we can't risk your sending any secret messages. We'll send a messenger on your behalf and see to it that no mention is made of your current whereabouts."

"But—"

"You are here as a guest as long as you behave as a guest.

Should you attempt to escape, your circumstances would change. Do you understand?"

She bowed her head in defeat. "Yes."

The note might help, even if she didn't write it herself. Lady Helisende might suspect something. Victor and his father both knew she'd been taken and by whom. Surely it was only a matter of time before one of them came to the rescue and searched Robert's house with Lady Helisende's guard at their back.

As soon as the man was gone, she ventured out to further explore her surroundings. She tried the doors on the other side of the hall, hoping to get a view into the street. Two of the doors she couldn't open, but one gave at her push. The room was empty of any furnishings. There were cobwebs in the corners.

She hurried over to the narrow, arched window—too narrow for a person to climb through but big enough for her to see the street below. It was a quiet, narrow street with stone houses exactly like this one crowded along either side of it. A dairy cart was making deliveries below. Otherwise, the street was empty.

Weighing her options, she decided not to call out. Yet. The dairyman was unlikely to come to her rescue, and it would only bring on the ire of her captors. She needed a better plan.

Turning back to the hallway, she tried the door at the end that presumably led to the stairs. Locked. She would need to get through that door to escape. If she surprised whoever came through the door next and knocked them out, maybe she could get down and escape.

What she needed was some form of weapon, something small and heavy she could hit with. She returned to her room and examined its contents. It was sparsely furnished—only a bed, a small table, and a chair. Perhaps she could pry off a chair leg, but it would be better if she could find something smaller, like a rock. She looked at the stone walls long and hard, testing the stones to see if any were loose. At last, she found what she was looking for. A stone the size of an orange shifted loose at her touch.

She took it in her hand and waited by the door to the stairs.

Hours passed, but she didn't dare move for fear of missing her opportunity.

At long last, she heard footsteps coming upstairs. This was her chance. She said a silent prayer as the door creaked open. Then *crack,* she hit the servant over the head, and he crumpled to the floor.

As she stepped over him, she took in a shaky breath. It was the first time she'd hit anyone, and she didn't like the feeling one bit. But there was no time for regrets. She tiptoed down the stairs to the ground floor, every sense alert. Voices pierced her awareness. They were coming toward her. Desperately, she looked around for a place to hide. With moments to spare, she ran and hid behind a door.

The voices passed.

She let out the breath she hadn't realized she'd been holding.

So far, they suspected nothing. *Thank God.*

Opening the door ever so slightly, she peered out. The coast was clear.

She tiptoed out and made for the front door only to find it guarded by a disheveled but muscular man sitting on a barrel. She froze just out of his line of sight.

You can do this, Alais. He's all that stands between you and freedom.

The rock was still in her hand. If she could sneak up on the man unawares, maybe, just maybe she could escape. This was her chance. She would not get another. As silently as she could, she snuck up behind the beefy guard.

Cold sweat trickled down her back, and her heart thudded loudly in her ears.

Just as she raised the rock, his head jerked around. "Hey, what are you doing?"

Holy Mother of God, she was caught. She thought her knees would give way, but this was no time to succumb to weakness.

The man lumbered to his feet and made a grab at her. Summoning all the courage she possessed, she ducked, then swung and whacked him over the head as hard as she could.

"Ow," the man said, still conscious, but momentarily distracted by the pain. It was the best chance she was going to get. She raced through the door, ran down the street, and ducked into an alleyway. Immediately, she heard pursuers. She slunk deeper into the shadows, hiding behind some broken barrels.

It wasn't a good hiding spot. Surely, they would find her.

Her whole body trembled as she tried to calm her breathing and her racing heart.

Footsteps approached, then passed her by, missing her, just barely.

Hardly able to believe her luck, she slipped out from her hiding spot and slunk away, praying no one found her before she reached Lady Helisende.

CHAPTER TWENTY-TWO

MORNING CAME, BUT the fog remained, leaving the forest an impenetrable morass. Victor was unable to find anything useful in the gray morning light, and on foot leading his lame horse, his range and speed were limited. He decided he would have to enlist the aid of others to succeed in his quest.

He'd had dealings with the Templars of Westfield in the past on behalf of his aunt. In fact, more than once, the Templars had tried to recruit him. They'd almost succeeded before he went to Winchelsea. While he had no appetite for becoming a holy warrior, before Alais, he didn't know what else to do after his miserable year attempting to return to normal life in Hastings. He'd seen enough slaughter in the Lord's name with Lord Amalric to want no part of it ever again, but there was an undeniable appeal in walking away from all earthly possessions and earthly ties when no one wanted you around anyway.

He walked up to the castle, leading Socorro, and gave his name to the guard at the gate. Shortly thereafter, he was ushered inside. A groom took Socorro to the stable, offering assurances his injuries would be seen to.

"Sir Victor, we are honored by your visit. To what do we owe this unexpected pleasure?" The man who was speaking wore a rough white monk's robes with the red Templar cross on the front.

"Brother Stephen, thank you for receiving me. I would have let you know I was coming if I had known myself."

"Dare I hope that you've finally decided to join us?"

"I'm sorry to disappoint you, but I'm here on a personal matter. Is there somewhere we can sit and speak?"

Brother Stephen led him to a small room with bare walls, a square wooden table, and rough wooden benches. A particularly gruesome crucifix was the room's only decoration. "Have you eaten, my lord?" he asked, offering Victor a seat.

"I haven't, and I don't have time to. My mission is urgent."

Brother Stephen seated himself and folded his hands in front of him. "Of course. Then tell me what brings you here at the break of dawn."

"I was married two days ago to Alais de Vere of Winchelsea."

"Congratulations, my lord. Though I must say that makes your presence here even more of a mystery."

"My cousin, Robert, was jealous of our marriage and kidnapped her yesterday evening from Guestling. I tracked him through the night and lost him in woods just south of here several hours ago. She wasn't with him last night, but I think I know where she is. I'm hoping you'll be willing to lend me aid in finding her. You know the people and the territory for miles around."

Brother Stephen gave him a look of mixed sympathy and calculation. "I'm sorry to hear about this terrible family tragedy." He emphasized the word "family."

"My family," Victor continued, echoing Brother Stephen's emphasis, "would be very grateful for any assistance you provide locating my cousin. The Earl of Winchelsea and Lord de Vere will undoubtedly also be...grateful." He was mentally calculating how grateful he could afford to be. While the Templars individually pledged to live a life of poverty, collectively they never missed an opportunity to enrich the order. The castle where they sat, and the labor of the tenants that farmed the land, were a gift from a grateful noblewoman some thirty years before.

"I see," Brother Stephen answered, not quite hiding the mercenary gleam in his eye. "Of course, we'll help you. I'll send someone at once to notify the tenants to be on the lookout, and I can help you organize a search party to look for her. Take your ease. I'll be back shortly."

As Victor sat, the full weight of his exhaustion began to press down on him. He'd barely slept on his wedding night and hadn't slept during the night while hunting for Robert. But he couldn't afford to rest yet. Alais needed him.

Victor closed his eyes and imagined holding her in his arms, her shape, her scent, her warmth. Taking a deep breath, he opened his eyes, full of renewed determination to find her, no matter the cost. If he had to promise the Templars Guestling to get her back, he would do it, though he didn't think it would come to that.

Whatever happened, though, he needed money. When he'd left home, it didn't occur to him to bring any. He wasn't expecting this chase to extend into the next day. Now the Templars would want a guarantee of his gratitude payment. He would have to write his father. Daniel and his father-in-law should also be informed of what had happened, and, depending on how much gratitude he was expected to show, he might need to ask them for contributions as well. Perhaps Brother Stephen might be willing to lend him some coin to continue his pursuit, if needed, with a promise of repayment from the sum his father would send.

Brother Stephen returned and sat beside him. "I've sent out word to be on watch for your cousin. I have six knights ready to join you in your search for your wife this morning."

"Thank you, Brother Stephen."

"I imagine you must have received a handsome dowry for such a marriage. Certainly, one-tenth of the dowry would not be too much to part with, in gratitude for aid in finding her."

Victor offered a wry smile. It was a hefty sum but far less than he was willing to sacrifice if needed. "Thank you for your help.

You will have my gratitude within the week if you will lend me parchment and a quill to send a note to Guestling."

"Of course, my lord."

"I would also like to send a message to the Earl of Winchelsea. I'm sure he will also be grateful once he hears."

"No trouble at all, my lord." Brother Stephen came back swiftly with parchment, a quill, ink, and a blotter.

"One more thing. I left home without any coin. Would it be possible to borrow 20 silver pieces and add them to the amount my father is sending from Guestling?"

Brother Stephen narrowed his eyes. "We don't lend coin. But we know and trust you, and we know that your father or the earl will make good on your debt in the end, if you are unable for some reason. And your aunt has long been a generous donor. Given your extreme need for haste, I will agree to it this once."

"Thank you," Victor said, clapping Brother Stephen on the shoulder. Then he turned to writing his letters.

Father,

I chased Robert to the woods just south of Westfield last night. He doesn't have Alais with him, but I'm certain he knows where she is. The good knights at Westfield are helping me in my search. I wish to donate 100 gold and 20 silver pieces to their cause in gratitude for their assistance. Please send as soon as you are able. I suspect Robert left Alais in Hastings. If you find him before I do, send word to Westfield.

He paused, his quill hovering above the parchment. A drop of ink dripped from the nib, leaving a mark beside his writing. He dabbed at it with a blotter to keep it from smearing before adding to his final sentence.

...and give her my love. My heart is hers no matter what Robert may have done.

Your loving son,
Victor

Next, he had to pen his letter to Winchelsea. He took a deep breath. If he was a praying man, he would pray for inspiration. Was there a graceful way to tell your wife's family that she'd been abducted?

To the Earl of Winchelsea and Lord Martin de Vere,

It is with deep sadness and anger that I must share the news that my cousin, Robert, abducted Alais while we were visiting my father at Guestling, paying our respects the day after our wedding. I pursued Robert to woods just south of Westfield where I lost him. She was not with him, and I am certain he stowed her elsewhere before heading out to meet me on the road. My father is searching for her near Guestling. If you can send anyone to aid him, I would be most grateful. I have enlisted the help of the good knights at Westfield to search for her in Hastings. I'm trying to keep my aunt out of this, if at all possible, given the strained relations between your families. My deepest apologies for failing in my sacred duty to keep Alais safe. I will find her, and I will bring Robert to justice.

Your humble servant,
Victor

When both letters were sealed with wax and stamped with his signet ring, he handed them both to Brother Stephen to convey to messengers. "I would like to move out as quickly as possible. Can you show me to the men that are going to help me?"

Brother Stephen nodded and led him out to the stables where six knights were saddling their horses, their breath fogging the air in the morning chill. While the men varied greatly in age and appearance, something about the economy and precision of their movements along with a certain look in their eyes told Victor at a glance that they were all veterans. They were all in fighting form, lean and strong, and they moved in concert as if long accustomed to each other from training and campaigning together. He paid dearly for their assistance, but he could not imagine a group of men better suited to aid him in his task.

"Brothers, this is Sir Victor of Guestling. He'll be leading today's search. I'll let him share the details. I have urgent messages to send out." With that, Brother Stephen bowed his head and took his leave.

Victor asked a groom to saddle a horse for him, since Socorro was injured, then addressed the men. "Thank you for your assistance today. I am honored by your company. I can see that you are experienced campaigners. That will be useful as we attempt to rescue my wife from my cousin, who kidnapped her. He and I both fought together overseas on behalf of Lord Amalric of Wessex. Robert is a capable fighter and a clever foe. Wherever my wife is, I am certain she is well-defended. We're going to start our search at Robert's house in Hastings. Questions?"

A middle-aged man with a salt-and-pepper beard and receding hairline raised a hand.

"Yes, sir," Victor said, nodding at him. "Tell me your name and your question."

"Brother Eustace, sir. Can you tell us what your wife looks like?

We want to make sure we've got the right woman if we come across her."

Victor took a deep breath and pushed away the heated memories of the last time he saw her. "She's this tall," he said, raising his hand to the level of his chin, "with thick, lustrous chestnut hair, sparkling brown eyes flecked with gold, long lashes, and an impish face." He stopped himself before rhapsodizing about her luscious lips, her full breasts, or her round, delicious bottom. From the amused looks on some of the men's faces, he could see he'd already gotten somewhat carried away. "She's beautiful and spirited, and we have to rescue her before my cousin harms her any further. Any other questions?"

A man with flaming red hair and a nose the shape of a potato spoke up. "My name's Hugh, my lord. Can you tell us what your cousin looks like and what you would like us to do if we find him?"

Victor clenched his hands as he said, "If you see him, kill him. I can assure you he will not hesitate to kill you. As for what he looks like, picture me but with a pretty face and curly hair. Before I got this," he said, gesturing to his face, "people used to think we were brothers." Before he gave me this, he thought with renewed fury. "I injured his left arm in a sword fight last night, but that is unlikely to slow him down. If you find yourself fighting him, I recommend you call for help. He is deadly one on one. Any further questions?" He looked around. "No? Let's go."

They mounted and set out for Hastings. A brief exploration of the place where Robert left the road yielded nothing. Rain had obliterated his tracks. No matter. Robert could slink off to nurse his wounds for the moment. Victor would have his revenge before this was over. All that mattered now was Alais.

The group made good time in spite of the morning drizzle. By late morning, they were at the gates of Hastings. A guard stopped them as they made to enter.

"Halt! Explain your business in Hastings," the man said, eyeing the armed contingent warily.

Dismounting, Victor got a good look at the guard and smiled. "Philip, my good man, how are the wife and children?"

A grin spread across the guard's face. "Victor, it's good to see you! I thought we'd seen the last of you. It's been months."

They clasped hands and thumped each other on the back. "I can't seem to stay away."

"How are they treating you in Winchelsea?"

"Quite well, thank you. Listen, Philip, I am on a mission of some urgency with the Templars. It has to do with my cousin. You have my word no harm will come to the good citizens of Hastings. This is strictly a family matter. Can you let us pass?"

"For you, anything," Philip said, waiving the Templars through.

"Thank you, my friend. Give my best to Mathilda and the boys."

Philip was a good man. Once Victor had Alais back and had dispensed with Robert, Victor resolved to come back for a proper visit.

Mounting again, he led the Templars through the winding streets until he stopped in front of the stone edifice that belonged to his cousin.

Nodding to the men following him, he watched as they drew their swords and arrayed themselves behind him. He banged on the door.

Moments later, a man as hefty and oily as a ham hock opened the door, blinking. Victor couldn't help but notice the goose egg bruise on the right side of his head. The man made a motion to draw his sword, but Victor was too quick. His blade was at the man's throat. "Bring me my wife, and I'll let you live."

The man laughed. "Sir Robert knew you'd come."

Only the slightest noise alerted him to danger from above as boiling oil came pouring down, inches from where he stood. Slicing as he stepped forward, into the protection of the doorway, he ended the man in front of him.

The Templars stepped back as yet another cauldron of boiling oil rained down from above. So it was him alone against Robert's thugs, at least until he put a stop to those cauldrons of boiling oil. That was fine. He almost preferred it that way.

Three swordsmen came running toward him. Bloodlust roared through him as he blocked two and kicked the third one in the chest hard enough to throw him against the wall. Only three? Victor expected more. He stepped around his attackers so that he was behind them, hamstringing the first and piercing the second in the sword arm, making him drop his sword, which Victor kicked to the far corner of the room.

The man he'd kicked came lunging back, and Victor parried, then returned the attack with such a vengeance that the man lost his nerve and started flailing wildly. Victor drove him back into the arms of a suit of armor displayed in the vaulted entry hall. The idiot lost his balance and fell on the floor, with the suit of armor on top of him. Victor would have laughed if he wasn't so furious.

With all three attackers disabled for the moment, Victor ran for the stairs. Time to take out the person with the boiling oil so that the Templars could come in and finish things off.

Taking the stairs two at a time, he raced up to the third story and quickly found the room he sought. A stout serving woman stood at the window, poised to dump another cauldron. *Christ on the cross.* He couldn't stab a woman in the back.

Hearing him, she turned around and hurled the cauldron at him. He dodged and turned just in time to see her draw a throwing knife from a sheath on her calf. Before he had time to react, she threw, and the blade bit into his left shoulder. She tried to make a run for the door, but he caught her. Ignoring the pain in his shoulder, he wrapped his good arm around her throat and squeezed. She wriggled and writhed trying to escape, but Victor was far stronger. He held her firmly until she passed out, and he let her drop to the floor. He could hear the Templars downstairs and knew he had won.

Footsteps sounded on the staircase, and Victor stiffened, blade in hand. Brother Hugh's flaming red hair appeared, and Victor relaxed his stance.

"We've tied up the ones we found downstairs," said Hugh. "Is she…?" Victor could see Brother Hugh's disapproval written all over his face.

Victor shook his head. "Only passed out. I want her alive for questioning."

The clouds cleared from Brother Hugh's face. "I see you're injured. Would you like me to remove the knife?"

"Please." Victor was going to do it himself, but it would be cleaner if someone whose shoulder wasn't screaming in pain did the honors.

"Ready?"

"Ready."

With a quick pull, Brother Hugh removed the blade. Blood

poured down Victor's arm. "Tear off the arm of my shirt," Victor suggested, as Brother Hugh looked around for something to use as a bandage. "But before you do, tie her up. We don't want her waking and causing trouble."

Brother Hugh tore off a piece of fabric from the hem of her dress and used it to bind her wrists and ankles. Then he used the throwing knife to cut off Victor's sleeve and bind the wound. He must look a horror, Victor thought with a wry smile. But then, what was one more scar when he already had so many?

The woman began to stir. Victor brought his blade to her neck. He had no intention of killing her, but she didn't need to know that.

"Where is my wife?" he demanded as she opened her eyes.

"You must be Sir Victor. Sir Robert said you would come."

She looked defiant despite the sword at her throat. He pressed the blade, and she hissed. "We would have had you if not for that little bitch you married. She escaped last night. Most of the household is out looking for her."

That explained the curious lack of resistance. Victor had expected much more of a fight.

"Where is Sir Robert?"

"Ain't seen him since he left to kidnap the lady. He's probably headed up to Canterbury. Spends a lot of time there at an inn called the Black Rooster."

Victor lowered his sword.

"Brother Hugh, we need to search the house to make sure my wife isn't tucked away in some corner. Given how few are defending the house, I'm inclined to believe this woman, but we need to be certain."

If Alais was out on the streets of Hastings with most of Robert's household after her, she was in grave danger. He needed to find her as quickly as possible. Unfortunately, that likely meant enlisting his aunt's help. Alais wouldn't like that one bit.

He and Brother Hugh searched the third floor, then the second floor. On the ground floor, they found the rest of the

Templars with Robert's men tied up. "Have you searched this floor?" he asked them.

"We have. And we've searched the cellars. Nothing," said Brother Eustace. "I'm inclined to believe their story that she escaped."

Fear gripped his heart as he thought of Alais alone and unarmed in the city, pursued by armed bandits. Victor nodded, his course decided. "All of you, fan out and search the surrounding area. I must pay a visit to my aunt and enlist her aid."

CHAPTER TWENTY-THREE

I T TURNED OUT darkness was as much a hindrance as a help in an unfamiliar city whose streets Alais did not know. She could no longer see Lady Helisende's castle in the moonless night, and the twisting alleys of Hastings soon had her thoroughly turned around. Her pursuers, however, seemed to know the streets well, and they had not given up their search. Her wandering route took her from one dark alley to the next, driven more by the need to avoid detection than any sense of geography.

Alais was acutely aware of her own vulnerability as a woman alone at night, unarmed and dressed like a noble, even if she was disguised.

Shortly after she escaped, she found a clothesline in an alley. There was a cloak, and she took it. At least it would hide the fine make and fabric of her dress along with the ostentatious gold embroidery on the trim. It kept her warm too in the November chill, even if it did have an unsavory smell clinging to it.

Despite her disguise, however, she didn't dare walk openly on the streets. Her pursuers questioned everyone they saw about her whereabouts. She'd watched them. Now word of a missing noblewoman had spread far and wide, and anyone who saw her might deliver her back to her captors in hopes of a reward. Avoiding major thoroughfares, she wended her way through side streets, ducking away to hide any time she saw someone coming.

She tried to keep her course uphill. She knew the castle was the highest point in Hastings.

For the hundredth time, she wondered where Victor was at that moment, praying that he was safe and that he was coming to find her. They had so little time together before they were torn apart. What would he think of her now?

He hadn't believed Robert's lies before, but surely he would suspect the worst after her kidnapping. Better by far, though, to face Victor's suspicions and ask for forgiveness than to become Robert's for life.

Approaching footsteps sent her scurrying to find another hiding place. She ducked into a half-built building with no windows or doors, crouching down in the darkest corner, next to a pile of stones. Another set of footsteps approached.

"Did you find her?" said a rough, male voice.

"No. You?" replied his companion.

"No, but I thought I saw something a moment ago. I could have sworn I saw someone moving along the street, but now I see no one. If it's her, she must be hiding. Let's check every alley."

Alais twisted her skirts in worry beneath her cloak. *Please don't let them find me.*

She didn't dare move until they passed. She could only hope they wouldn't think to examine the construction site. Hardly daring to breathe, she grasped for a stone she could use for a weapon if needed.

"Come out, my lady. We know you're here somewhere." The voice sent chills down her spine. She curled into a ball, hoping she looked like a covered pile of building materials.

Steps came closer. Her hand became a fist around the rock she held. Victor would know what to do if he was here. But he wasn't. She was alone with nothing but her own wits to get her out of this. Well, she would show these two idiots she was more than just a decorative second daughter. They would pay for underestimating her.

"Come over here," one of the men said. "I bet she's hiding in here somewhere." Two sets of steps came closer. And closer. "What's that bit of fabric over there by the rocks? You don't think it's—"

Alais jumped up and began pelting her pursuers with rocks. One rock hit home, knocking back the closest one, who grasped his face. She got him in the nose.

"Easy there, girly. We mean you no harm," the man said in an oily voice, oozing with threat. "Just come with us and we'll keep you nice and safe for Sir Robert."

"Never!"

She kept throwing and hit the man in the chest and then the shoulder.

"You little bitch. That hurt," he hissed.

She threw again and caught him in the eye, and he reeled back.

Taking advantage of their momentary distraction, she ran. At first, she could hear them staggering after her, but then the sound of their footsteps disappeared into the night. She looked up and, outlined against the stars, were the turrets of Lady Helisende's castle.

Running up to the closed castle gates, she pounded with all her might.

"Who goes there?" asked a sleepy-looking guard emerging from the guard house.

Throwing back her cloak, Alais announced herself with all the hauteur she could summon. "I am Lady Alais, daughter of Lord de Vere, wife of Sir Victor of Guestling, Lady Helisende's nephew. I was attacked, and I seek shelter within the castle."

The guard looked her up and down and laughed. "And I'm King Louis of France. David, there's a doxy here for you. Says she's a real lady here to see the countess."

Another guard emerged, this one bigger and more muscular than the first. Taller too. Alais took a step back and pulled her cloak back around her. The man walked over to Alais and grinned lasciviously.

"Well, hello. What have we here? Such a pretty young thing you are. Much prettier than Rose's usual selection. You must be new."

He grabbed her chin and tipped it up. Alais shrank back from his touch.

"I am Lady Alais. I am married to the countess' nephew, and if you touch me again, the countess herself will make you pay. Now let me in."

"I'd be happy to let you come upstairs with me, *my lady*. I like a little company to keep things interesting on the night watch."

He grabbed her and squeezed her bottom. She stomped on his toe with all her might, and he yelped, hopping back.

She ran as fast as she could back out into the night, ignoring the angry epithets the guard shouted after her. If she couldn't get in at night, she would have to try again during the day. Perhaps then someone would recognize her from the month she'd spent imprisoned as a guest at Lady Helisende's behest.

What she needed was a safe place to spend the night so that she could try again in the morning. For hours, she searched the streets, and every time she thought she had a hiding spot, she heard voices and fled. At last, she descended through an archway and found herself in an enormous, stone underground warehouse. Who built it and when, she couldn't guess, but she had never been more grateful for this strange, arched construction. No one was down there but rats. Silence and darkness curled around her as she leaned against grain sacks, and at last, she drifted off to sleep.

A SHAFT OF dawn light filtered in from some unseen opening, and Alais blinked her eyes open. Where in heaven's name was she? Why did she ache all over? Taking in her surroundings, everything came flooding back—the escape, the night of being chased, her encounter with the guards at the castle.

She jumped up and brushed herself off, determined to get to the castle before most of the city was out and about. Cautiously looking around as she exited the warehouse, she wasn't far from the castle. She pulled her hood as far over her head as it would go and made her way back to the castle gates. To her relief, they were open this time, and she could see that the guards had changed.

Once again throwing back her hood and hoping her appearance wasn't too frightful, she approached the guards. One of them had a familiar face, so she walked up to him.

"Lady Alais?" he said as she approached. Relief washed over her.

"Yes, I am Lady Alais, daughter of Martin de Vere, Baron of Winchelsea, and now wife of Sir Victor of Guestling, Lady Helisende's nephew."

The guard bowed. "My name is Luke. I guarded your door when you were a guest of my lady's last year. You look as if you are in some distress."

"I am. I was attacked and separated from my husband. I escaped and am seeking refuge with Lady Helisende until my husband can be found."

Luke nodded. "Come with me. The countess will want to see you."

She followed him into the familiar castle that she had sworn she would never enter again after her imprisonment last year. The countess had treated her and her mother and sister well enough during their stay, and Alais was now married to Victor, which changed things. Still, she couldn't help feeling like a fly landing on a spider's sticky web.

Leading her through the grand entrance hall, Luke deposited her in a small receiving room. "I'll notify her ladyship of your presence and return," he said, leaving her to ponder her situation. Whatever Lady Helisende did couldn't be worse than being in

Robert's clutches, could it?

Several minutes later, Luke came to collect her. "Her ladyship is eating breakfast. She wishes for you to join her."

Alais nodded and followed. Walking down these halls brought back unpleasant memories, but she stuffed them away. There was no room for weakness before the countess. Squaring her shoulders, she walked into the enormous dining hall with as much dignity as she could summon.

Dressed in a severe gown of deep blue with rich gold embroidery at the cuffs and neckline, Lady Helisende looked her up and down with a predatory smile. Streaks of white shone in her golden hair. "What have we here? I thought I had seen the last of you, but here you are, a damsel in distress. Have a seat. Eat. Then tell me what brings you to my doorstep."

Alais sat down at the grand table to the side of Lady Helisende where a place had been set for her. The room was filled with empty trestle tables, and every sound echoed in the cavernous hall. Several small braziers had been placed around the table, but despite their meager heat, Alais couldn't help but shiver.

She looked down at the silver plate she'd been given, filled with fruit and pastries. Though she was famished, she didn't dare eat before answering her host.

"I married your nephew, Victor, three days ago," Alais began.

"So I heard. I knew you two would make a good match."

Alais let that pass without comment. When she was last at the castle, the countess had been relentless with her hinting about a nephew who needed a wife. "Two days ago, Victor's cousin, Robert, kidnapped me. He said he was going to kill Victor and marry me. I escaped last night and found my way to you this morning. I beg you to send me back to Lord Giles at Guestling."

"Now, now. Let's not be hasty. It's rather providential that you're here. Surely my castle can offer better protection than that sandcastle at Guestling."

Lady Helisende took a bite of a crunchy pasty.

Of course, Alais wasn't going to escape so easily. She stifled an inward sigh as she waited to hear what the countess had in mind.

"I'm rather regretting letting go of Victor. The Watch hasn't been nearly so disciplined since he left. Perhaps, I can come to an arrangement with your brother-in-law in exchange for your safe return."

It was as she suspected. By coming here, she'd become a pawn in the countess' game. Still, it was better than being imprisoned at Robert's house.

"As for Robert, he's stirred up mischief for the last time in Hastings. This isn't the first time he's given me trouble, though he's never gone so far. I'll see to it that he leaves Hastings for good. Thank God he's no relation of mine. Victor's mother was my sister, you see. And Lord Giles's sister was Robert's mother. Lord Giles has been a good and loyal retainer, and I have put up with much from Robert for his sake, but that is at an end. James," Lady Helisende said, gesturing to a servant. "Send the Watch to Sir Robert's house. If he is there, apprehend him, and bring him here. If he is not, set a guard. If he returns, I want to know."

"Yes, my lady," said James as he bowed and hurried out.

"And as for you," Lady Helisende said, turning back to Alais, "you may as well get comfortable because you'll be here for a nice long stay."

Alais swallowed hard. She had done what she could to escape Robert's clutches, but escaping the countess would require someone else to come to her rescue. All she could do was pray for Victor's safety and hope that she hadn't created too much of a political storm for Daniel.

CHAPTER TWENTY-FOUR

VICTOR ARRIVED AT the countess' castle looking decidedly the worse for wear. His shirt was missing a sleeve. His injured shoulder was bound. His fine cotte was slashed open in several places. But Victor didn't care. He had no time to make himself presentable. Alais was alone on the streets of Hastings with Robert's thugs chasing after her.

He hurried up to one of the guards at the gate. "Luke, isn't it? I must see her ladyship at once. Is she within?"

"My-my lord, what happened to—"

"No time. I must see my aunt immediately."

Luke bowed and stepped aside. "Of course, Sir Victor. I must warn you she is entertaining a guest."

Victor strode past. "I don't care if she's entertaining the Queen Eleanor. My quest is urgent."

As he entered, a servant came running up. "Sir Victor! We were not expecting you. What—"

"I need to see my aunt immediately."

Something in his grim demeanor must have scared the servant, who mumbled, "Right away," and went running.

Victor jogged to keep up as the servant guided him to the formal hall where his aunt conducted her daily business.

The room was cavernous with high, arched ceilings that disappeared into shadow. Tapestries with military scenes hung on the walls, illuminated by a few small braziers that failed to warm the space. His aunt sat in her accustomed spot in an ornately carved, tall wooden chair that was practically a throne. In a much humbler chair beside her sat a woman. Was it—?

Could it be—?

"Victor," Alais cried out and jumped up to run to him. He caught her in his arms and clasped her close, desperate to kiss her but knowing this was neither the time nor the place. Instead, he had to content himself with feeling her heart beating against his chest and holding her as tightly as he could without hurting her. "I was so frightened that Robert would succeed in his plan. I'm so glad to see you alive, though I'll never forgive him for hurting you." She took in his wounds and frowned.

"And I'll never forgive him for hurting you," he said, taking note of the bruise and cut on her forehead. Red-hot fury filled him at the sight. He wanted to tear Robert limb from limb for daring to touch her. And what else might Robert have done? Blood thundered in his ears, and it was all he could do to keep himself from tearing off in a rage to find his cousin now he knew Alais was safe. But Alais came first. And he knew she was far from safe in his aunt's clutches.

"Touching," said his aunt, watching them with a sharp eye. "Such a tender reunion."

Without relinquishing Alais, he turned to face his aunt. "My lady, I must return to Winchelsea with Alais without delay."

"Now, now. No need for haste. You are both injured and in need of care. Stay with me and recuperate. It is good to have you back, Victor. I've missed you."

She's missed my sword.

"My lady, I must return Alais to her family, and it was at your command that I swore fealty to the Earl of Winchelsea. We must return. We cannot stay."

His aunt smiled, her eyes sparkling with calculation. "But when your wife showed up on my doorstep this morning, I sent messengers to the Earl of Winchelsea. He is likely on his way as we speak. So, you see there is no need to go anywhere. Stay. We have much to discuss."

Victor took a deep breath to calm himself. "First, I would like a word with my wife in private. And I need to send a message to the men who are with me."

"Ah yes. The Templars. You never should have involved them, my dear. You should simply have come to me. But since you did, I'll have word sent to them that you have found Lady Alais, and she is safe. They are free to return to Westfield. I have sent a guard to Sir Robert's house to arrest the members of his household. If Sir Robert values his neck, he will not return to Hastings."

Victor nodded. He would rather have thanked the knights from Westfield in person, but it was more important for him to speak with Alais. "And a moment alone with my wife?"

She made a dismissive gesture with her hand. "Go if you must. But don't take long. I wish to speak to you before the earl arrives."

Grabbing Alais's hand, he led her from the hall and pulled her into a small meeting room with an ornately carved table and chairs and little else.

As the door closed, she flew into his arms. He crushed her to him, bending her backward with a kiss. Her lips filled him with fire as did her frenzied caresses. When he let her up for breath, he spun her around and kissed her again.

"Tell me what happened to you," he said, relinquishing her at last. "I was so afraid Robert had tied you up and locked you in some dark cellar. How did you escape from him?"

She took a deep, tremulous breath and answered, recounting what had happened since he last saw her and leaving nothing out. With every word she spoke, his fury with Robert deepened, as did his determination to find his cousin and end his sorry life. After she finished her tale, she squeezed her eyes shut. "I know what Robert must have told you. I promise you he didn't."

Thank God!

She looked up at him, eyes glistening and luminous with unshed tears. "I swear to you I didn't betray you. Nothing happened between us, no matter what he said. I know you must suspect the worst, and I have no way to prove to you that I'm telling the truth, but I beg you to believe me."

Victor tightened his arms around her and rocked back and forth. "I believe you, and I'm so sorry this happened. You were so brave. But please know that I would love you no matter what."

She exhaled and leaned into his embrace. A tear leaked out and trailed down her cheek. She burrowed her face into his chest. "I'm yours and yours alone, Victor."

As her loving words sank in, relief and joy flooded him. It still defied belief that she had chosen him, but he could no longer doubt that her affections were his.

"I know you are, no matter what may have happened. I want to be the only man to make your body sing. He couldn't do that without your consent, and I know he didn't have that. Even if his lies were true, I would still love you, though, for your sake, I'm deeply relieved nothing happened. You're mine and I'm yours, Alais. No matter what."

He wanted to take all the pain away, undo all that had transpired since that terrible evening at Guestling, but all he could do was hold her as she sobbed and love her with all his heart.

He was going to destroy Robert for hurting her. Wherever Robert had fled, he was going to hunt him down.

As her sobs subsided, she wiped her eyes. "What happened to you? He told me he was going to kill you. I was so worried." She touched his bandaged shoulder ever so gently. "How badly did he hurt you?"

"I'll be fine. It's just a flesh wound."

She laid a soft kiss on the bandage, and he thought his heart might burst. He was the luckiest man in England to have such a loving wife.

"I went after you as soon as I found the empty room and his note. He attacked me with a band of brigands on the way to

Hastings. I fought them back, and Robert ran. I chased him north all the way to the woods just south of Westfield when I lost him in the fog."

"Do you know where he was headed?" A vengeful fire lit her eyes as she spoke. Thank heavens she was angry rather than afraid. Just another thing he admired about Alais. She had spirit and fire.

"Not for certain, but he has some ties in Canterbury. I have reason to suspect he went there."

"What happened next?"

He smiled. "I let him go and came for you." He recounted the fight at Robert's house and his search for her after learning of her escape. "I've never been more scared in my life than when we found you were gone. The thought of you alone on the streets of Hastings…"

Fierce pride lit her eyes. "I survived without getting caught, as you can see."

He claimed her lips in a fast and passionate kiss. "I will never underestimate you again, though I have to say I never thought you would willingly come here."

She bit her lip. "It was the lesser of the two evils. Better to be caught up in Lady Helisende's political maneuvering than be imprisoned by Sir Robert. And now that I'm family, she *has* to treat me better, doesn't she?"

Looking her in the eye, he said, "Do not underestimate my aunt. She is a far more dangerous enemy than Robert, but I share your hope that she does not view you as an enemy. Even family, though, she treats like pawns on a chess board. She will try to use you to achieve her own ends."

Alais nodded thoughtfully. "I expected that. I knew it would stir up trouble for Daniel if I came here, but our marriage creates the groundwork for an alliance, however tenuous. Perhaps it is for the best if Daniel and Lady Helisende reach a more mutually beneficial understanding than their current agreement allows."

Victor would never cease to be amazed by the woman he

loved. "You are more clever and more insightful than anyone gives you credit for. No one ever bothers to look past your playful personality to see the sharp intelligence beneath, do they?"

She beamed and shook her head.

"Speaking of my aunt," he continued, "we should get back to her. I am anxious to learn what she hopes to gain from keeping you here, so that we can find a way to extricate you."

She nodded, and he kissed her forehead. Taking her hand, he led her back to the hall where Lady Helisende waited.

When they entered, they found her deep in conversation with Sir Thomas, the commander of her knights. His hair was grayer than the last time Victor saw him. The man looked like a sea cliff, all sharp angles and rough edges.

Sir Thomas caught sight of Victor and cleared his throat. Lady Helisende looked up and, seeing the two of them, smiled with undisguised avarice. "How lucky for us, Sir Thomas, that as the Earl of Winchelsea approaches, we have his commander under our roof," she said. "And his sister-in-law too. Last time the earl visited, he had the might of Hawkhurst at his back, not to mention the mercenary army he hired to defend Winchelsea. Now, though, we catch him at a disadvantage. Our soldiers are the equal of his, and he has no one to lead them. I'm so glad I sent you to Winchelsea, Victor. You've gained the earl's trust more quickly than I could have imagined, and now here you are, back with your favorite auntie. Come here and make yourself useful. Tell us how many men he has and how they are positioned."

Victor's jaw dropped. She expected him to betray his liege lord after sending him away? Did she think he had no honor at all? Alais's grip tightened on his arm. Her eyes widened in alarm.

"My lady, I cannot tell you that. I swore an oath to the earl at your behest. You told me to promise I was his man even if it meant using my sword against you."

Lady Helisende waved her hand dismissively. "Of *course*, I told you to do that. He'd never have trusted you otherwise. But would you truly choose loyalty to an oath over loyalty to your own flesh and blood?

Come now, Victor. I've known you since you were a babe. I've given you every opportunity to show your worth and grow beyond a mere Castellan's son. I made you the man you are. Do you dare turn your back on me now?"

The true magnitude of their peril came into sharp focus. His aunt didn't just want concessions on an agreement. She wanted him. She wanted all of Winchelsea if she could get it. And damn it all, what she said was true. He did owe everything to her. Even his match to Alais would never have happened if she had not sent him to Winchelsea.

For years, he'd served her without question. She was his liege lady and his benefactor, not to mention the closest thing he had to a mother. While he liked to think he'd achieved what he had through his own talent and merit, if he was honest with himself, he could see her hand in nearly everything he had done of any import. Did he dare defy her when she'd made him the man he was?

Alais's grip and questioning eyes brought him back to himself. His aunt may have made him, but his sense of honor had made him the knight he was. No matter what loyalty he owed her, he could not betray his honor for her sake. He could not break a solemn oath. Nor could he stand to betray Alais by siding against her family. He had to find a way out of this predicament that left his promise to Daniel intact.

"I owe you much, my lady, but my honor is my own. I will not betray Lord Daniel."

Sir Thomas's hand went to his sword, but Victor was quicker. He had no idea how he was going to fight his way out of his aunt's castle, especially with his injuries, but he had to find a way.

CHAPTER TWENTY-FIVE

"WAIT," ALAIS YELLED. Sir Thomas and Victor froze, swords drawn. Everyone turned to stare at her.

She had their attention now. What was she going to say?

They couldn't fight their way out of the castle, no matter how talented Victor might be with a sword, so a solution had to be negotiated. "My lady, what do you want from Lord Daniel?"

Lady Helisende's smile sent chills down her back. Thomas and Victor stood at the ready, but neither moved. "Smart woman you married, Victor. She's saving your neck, you know," the countess said. "My dear, never trust a man to do a woman's job. You see how emotional and hot-headed they are? Fools, the both of them." She motioned for Thomas to lower his sword, which he did reluctantly. "Now, let's talk."

"Yes, let's," Alais said, putting a hand over Victor's sword hand and giving him a reassuring look. Slowly, he lowered his sword. Thinking back to all the dinner conversations she overheard between Daniel and her father, she said, "Daniel and his cousins have Hastings surrounded on three sides. Canterbury is seeking to expand its territory. While Hastings's port dwarfs Winchelsea's, our power at sea exceeds yours when combined with our cousin's in Pevensey. You cannot hope to attack Winchelsea without invoking the combined wrath of Pevensey and Hawkhurst, and you would drive us into the arms of

Canterbury to bring you down if you attempted it. So, my lady, what is it that you hope to gain, since you cannot win Winchelsea without bringing about your own doom?"

Lady Helisende chuckled coldly and clapped slowly and deliberately. "Not bad. Not bad at all. Your brother-in-law couldn't have said it better. I am besieged by enemies, and I must take advantage of every opportunity to gain protection for Hastings. Your presence here gives me leverage, and I intend to use it."

"To what end?"

"Don't rush me, little girl," Lady Helisende snapped. "Your family may hold the political advantage outside these walls, but at present, you are the one surrounded by peril. Don't forget it."

Victor grasped his sword.

"Don't," both women said at the same time. Alais paired her command with a restraining hand on his arm.

"I would like some amendments to the agreement with Winchelsea. When Lord Daniel stole Winchelsea out from under me—"

"He didn't steal Winchelsea. He defended us when *you* refused."

Lady Helisende was the only one at fault for her own loss of territory.

"Winchelsea was mine, and I want it back."

"Never."

A long silence stretched as the two women stared each other down.

"Perhaps not today," Lady Helisende said at last in icy tones. "As you pointed out, I am at a strategic disadvantage. I might win the battle for Winchelsea but lose the war once Pevensey and Hawkhurst got involved."

"Then what is it you want today?"

Lady Helisende stood and paced.

"When we last negotiated, our goal was peace and nothing more. But Hastings has suffered from not having a closer alliance with its nearest neighbor and relations with Hawkhurst and

Pevensey have soured since last year's hostilities. I would rather ally with my neighbors, however much I mistrust you, than with Canterbury."

Alais could hardly believe her ears. "You want an *alliance* after threatening to invade?"

"As you pointed out, I cannot defeat you. Therefore, I must join you. What choice do I have? Hastings's independence and integrity must be preserved at all costs, and the Archbishop of Canterbury doesn't just want an agreement, he wants land. It has taken me years to consolidate my hold over Hastings, and I'll be damned if I'm going to let the Church carve it into pieces."

Alais narrowed her eyes. "This is a strange way to negotiate an alliance. Daniel is a reasonable man. Why not simply reach out?"

Lady Helisende clutched the arm of her chair until her knuckles shone white. "Do you think I haven't tried? Lord Daniel was content with the agreement we negotiated and hasn't even responded to my attempts to propose changes. But with you here, he'll come riding to the rescue. He'll *have* to talk to me."

Now that Alais thought about it, she wasn't surprised that Daniel ignored Lady Helisende's requests. Winchelsea had little to gain from amending the agreement.

"If Daniel agrees to renegotiate the agreement, you'll let us go?"

Lady Helisende shrugged. "For now. Though I might have a future need for you. After all, even a disloyal Victor has his uses, and now that you've married into the family, I expect regular visits. Whatever the reasons were for your hasty nuptials, your marriage nonetheless creates a new political alliance, one I mean to take full advantage of."

Alais shivered. "Let us go now as a good faith gesture, and we will tell Daniel what you want and make sure he comes to negotiate. And we will agree to regular visits, within reason. If you keep us here, you risk incurring Daniel's wrath. He is unlikely to agree to anything if he feels coerced."

Tapping her fingers together, Lady Helisende said, "You will spend six months of every year in Hastings. Lady Alais goes with Sir Thomas to find Lord Daniel. Victor stays."

Six months?

"One month, and we both go," Victor interjected.

Lady Helisende's attention whipped from her to Victor. "Four months, and only one of you goes. You choose which one. I can't lose all of my leverage after all."

"Two months, and we stay in Guestling, not Hastings," Victor countered.

"Three months, and I don't care where you sleep at night, so long as you spend your days here—both of you."

Victor nodded slowly. "Three months of Lord Daniel's choosing, and he can call me back at any time should he have need of me. *And* our agreement is predicated on Lord Daniel's approval. He is my liege lord, and I do as he bids."

Lady Helisende looked at him long and hard then pursed her lips. "I suppose I can live with that."

"And you will never attempt to hold either of us against our will again," Alais added. "Or *any* members of our family, currently living or future members. Furthermore, this agreement only remains in force while all three of us live. It does not pass to future generations. We must have your solemn oath if we are to return here."

With a chuckle, Lady Helisende said, "Smart girl, your wife. I knew you two would make a good match. Didn't I say so before you left for Winchelsea, Victor?"

Alais looked at Victor. She'd remembered all the hints Lady Helisende had dropped about her nephew when she was imprisoned the year before, but she didn't know Victor had been the recipient of similar hints. It made his initial reluctance to court her even more of a mystery, though perhaps he was as wary of his aunt's motives as she was. Either way, it cost her something to admit to herself that Lady Helisende had been right.

"What would you prefer, my love?" Victor murmured for her

ears alone. "Would you rather go to your brother-in-law or stay?"

There was no question. "I think you should stay, and I should go to Daniel. You're wounded and need care. Also, I think he'll take it better if your aunt detains you than if she detains me."

"Agreed."

"Have you decided which of you will go to Lord Daniel?" the countess demanded.

"I will," Alais answered. "We should leave immediately to be sure I reach him before he arrives."

Victor kissed her forehead. "I'll see you again very soon, my love," he murmured into her hair.

"I know," Alais whispered.

"Let us depart," Thomas said gruffly.

She followed the grizzled commander out, taking one last, longing look at Victor. It made her heart ache to be parted again so soon after being reunited. But it was temporary, she assured herself. With luck, she would see him again before sunset and possibly much sooner than that. After all, Winchelsea was a mere three leagues away.

Thomas seemed like a man with about as much humor as a rock, Alais thought sadly as she mounted the horse Sir Thomas directed her to. Her charm would go nowhere with him.

"My lady, are you ready?" he asked in gruff tones.

"I am."

Without another word, he mounted and rode out through the castle gates, keeping a brisk pace. She followed closely.

It was a lovely, clear, crisp autumn day with the sun shining and a pleasant bite in the air. The blue of the Channel flashed and sparkled beside them as they rode northeast along the ancient Roman road that connected Hastings to Winchelsea. The horses' hooves clopped on the massive paving stones between the grooves worn by centuries of carts traveling to and fro.

It was not the natural state of things for Hastings and Winchelsea to be at odds, as this road proved. Travelers and commerce had flowed back and forth unimpeded for time immemorial. Perhaps it was for the best that Daniel and Lady Helisende were going to talk, even if the reason for it was troubling.

Less than halfway to Winchelsea, Alais spied a carriage with a contingent of knights accompanying it in the distance. *Daniel.* Who else could it be? She quickened her pace, passing Sir Thomas, who swiftly caught up.

"You think that's Lord Daniel?" Thomas asked, his voice full of disdain.

"I'm sure of it. I can see his coat of arms on the pennant."

"Then we must be wary."

"We must make haste. The sooner I reach him, the better it will be for all concerned."

She trotted forward, ignoring Sir Thomas's grumbling behind her.

The carriage and knights halted as she approached. Carenza came bursting out of the carriage and running toward her. Alais dismounted just in time for a crushing hug from her sister. "I was so worried about you," Carenza gushed. "First, we got Victor's note saying you'd been kidnapped by Robert. Then we got Lady Helisende's message that you were with her. We didn't know what to think. And look at you. You're hurt!" She brushed Alais's hair away from the bruise and cut on her forehead.

"I'll be fine. Let me join you in the carriage. Victor is still in Hastings with his aunt. They are awaiting your arrival."

A glare of mutual distaste passed between Sir Thomas and Carenza. Alais had forgotten that they'd become acquainted during last year's hostilities.

Alais climbed into the carriage with Carenza to find Daniel looking like a thundercloud. "Alais, I'm glad to see you safe. Mostly safe. You're injured," he said, clenching his fists. "Did that harpy dare hurt you?"

Alais recounted her tale of misadventures to Carenza and Daniel, who listened in horror as she spoke.

"I'm sorry for ever suspecting you would willingly let that

snake of a man touch you," Carenza said when she finished. "I'm so glad you married Victor."

It wasn't enough to undo all of the hurt from that terrible night when Carenza turned against her, but it was a start. Apologies from Carenza were as rare as unicorns. "I'm glad I married Victor too. He was injured trying to rescue me. He calls it a flesh wound, but it looks like it bled a lot. I'm anxious to get back to him and see that he's properly cared for."

"And what should I expect from Lady Helisende?" Daniel asked.

Alais explained what she and Victor had negotiated. "She seeks an alliance to fend off the long hand of Canterbury. Before you dismiss it, I ask you to consider. It would be beneficial to Winchelsea as well if Hastings joined with you and your cousins to resist Archbishop Richard's designs. I know you don't like her, but there is something to be gained from negotiating."

Daniel and Carenza both stared at her as if she'd sprouted wings. "Since when do you know anything about politics?" Carenza demanded.

"I've always taken an interest, but no one cares what a second daughter thinks so I never said anything."

New respect spread across Carenza's face. She narrowed her eyes. "I won't underestimate you again anytime soon."

A compliment from Carenza! Alais could hardly believe it. That was even rarer than a unicorn.

"The countess was right about one thing," Carenza continued. "Your marriage to Victor forms a political alliance, even if it was unplanned. We may not have paid proper heed to a second daughter, but you are now at the center of a vital and fraught political relationship. You'll need all that knowledge you were hiding as you navigate the years ahead."

The carriage ground to a halt, and a servant opened the door. They were back in Lady Helisende's domain. Squaring her shoulders, Alais stepped down, summoning all the dignity and hauteur she possessed. She walked with Daniel and Carenza into the castle and back to the large hall where she'd left her husband and the countess.

Victor was there, thank God. He wore a fresh change of clothes, and his shoulder wound was hidden beneath his cotte. She wanted to run to him and pounce on him, showing him just how grateful she was to have such a husband. Instead, she forced herself to walk to him and demurely take his hand.

"Greetings, Lord Daniel and Lady Carenza. I'm so glad you've come," said Lady Helisende, standing.

"I do not care for the manner in which I was summoned," said Daniel. "I tire of your attempts to use hostages to gain my attention. If you ever try such a thing again, you will find the soldiers of Winchelsea, Hawkhurst, and Pevensey on your doorstep. Fortunately for you, my sister-in-law has convinced me that there are matters of mutual interest that we should discuss. Shall we get down to business?"

"With pleasure," Lady Helisende responded. "The rest of you are dismissed." Thomas bowed and left. Alais and Victor looked at each other and then back at Lady Helisende. "Yes, too. Surely newlyweds can find some way to while away the hours while we negotiate."

Victor grinned and led Alais out, guiding her through long, winding corridors until he opened a door to a bedroom. "My lady?" he said, pulling her inside.

CHAPTER TWENTY-SIX

"**B**ED. NOW," SHE murmured in his ear.

He clutched her hard and moaned softly so that only she could hear. "I am at your command, my lady."

Folding her into his embrace, he kissed her hungrily, and she responded with desperation to his touch. She needed him like she needed air to breathe. He picked her up, and she wrapped her legs around him as he carried her to the bed.

As he tugged the laces of her dress loose, she fumbled at the fastenings of his cotte, tearing it free. She pulled his shirt over his head, careful to be gentle with his bound shoulder, and feasted on his neck and shoulders as he pushed her dress down to reveal her breasts.

With a desperate moan, he pulled her against him and kissed her. She dug her nails into his back. No matter how close he was, he wasn't close enough. She needed more of him, all of him. Her fingers found their way to the ties of his breeches and yanked them loose. She shoved his breeches down and grasped the hard, hot flesh below.

"Oh God, Alais. I've never needed anyone like I need you right now."

"I need you too. Take me now. Please."

He pulled off her dress and slid off his boots and breeches in a fluid movement. Reaching to touch her between the legs, he dipped a finger between her folds and brushed the bundle of nerves there, sending lightening all through her body. With a guttural groan, he sank into the molten core of her, heat and sensation exploding all through her body as he filled her. It was too much and not enough. Frantic beneath him, she was desperate for something she couldn't name. A craving for connection and love overpowered her. She needed to feel, not just hear, his absolution for what Robert claimed to have done.

As he moved within her, all conscious thought disappeared. There was only light and sensation. It felt as if she had burst through the physical boundaries of her body. She was radiant as she shattered into a thousand pieces. The force of the ecstasy pouring through her left her transcendent, broken, and raw.

As her consciousness returned to her body, he convulsed. He cried out in his final throes, then rolled to his side, gasping for breath. She turned to face him, wrapping a leg around his hip, and snuggled into his arms.

Blinking, he raised his head and met her gaze with his own. He whispered, "I love you, Alais."

"You do?" Her heart broke into a thousand tiny pieces, knowing he said it despite Robert's lies. "I love you too."

He clutched her hard against him and kissed the top of her head.

"I've loved you nearly as long as I've known you," he continued. "I thought I was in trouble that first night when you left me speechless at dinner. I knew I was lost when you bewitched Socorro. I should have told you sooner. I should have told you on our wedding night. I love you so much I can hardly stand it. Don't ever leave me again."

"I didn't leave by choice."

"I know," he said softly, kissing her forehead.

An ugly, hiccupping sob escaped from her as she tried to contain the overflowing mess of her emotions. After all the fear of the past week, she found herself in the arms of a man who cared more about her joy than her purity, who worried more about her peace of mind than the succession.

He pulled her close. "I plan to show you every way I can how deeply I love you." She felt his flesh stiffen against her. "Including right now, if you'll have me."

"Now, and always." She kissed him.

Barely moving, their bodies joined, and they rocked together in an unhurried dance. His touch was so tender and gentle that it brought on even more tears. He caressed and kissed them away, murmuring words of love and reassurance until a tremor rocked her with aching bliss. She shook in his arms until he groaned and strained in hers, and they were still.

She dozed for a bit in the comfort and warmth of his embrace, exhausted from the lack of sleep the night before.

When Alais woke up in Victor's arms, it was late afternoon. He was still asleep. Neither of them had had a proper night's sleep in days. She eased herself out of his arms, trying not to wake him, when he reached for her.

"Stay. Please."

She let herself be drawn back into his embrace, his chest rising and falling against her back.

"I was about to ask a servant for some food. I'm famished."

"*Mm.*" He squeezed her close and kissed her neck. "Sadly, that's a good idea. I haven't eaten since you were kidnapped. I suppose I must let you out of bed." He relinquished her reluctantly, trailing his finger down her back as she got up.

She dressed and ducked out of the room to make a request of the first servant she encountered returning as quickly as she could. Soon there was a knock on the door, and when Alais opened it, she saw a small but sturdy girl standing there with a full tray holding a heaping platter of bread, cheeses, and cured meats, along with a pitcher of wine and two goblets. The girl moved into the room to set it down on a small table with chairs in the corner of the room. Once the servant girl had left, Victor pulled on his breeches to join Alais.

"So what are we going to do about Robert?" she asked, tearing off some bread and piling on meat and cheese.

"We?"

She took a sip of wine. "Yes, we. You don't think I'm going to let you go after Robert alone, do you? He's wronged me more than anyone."

Victor shook his head. "I would have thought after all you've been through you would want to stay as far away from him as possible."

"I want to see him pay for his crimes. I want to be present when he's brought to justice. Do you know where he is?" She popped a bite into her mouth.

"Probably Canterbury, possibly at an inn called the Black Rooster."

Taking another sip of wine, she mused, "Canterbury, eh?

Tricky going to Canterbury without attracting the attention of the archbishop."

Victor raised an eyebrow. "Not just tricky. Impossible. I've had dealings with him before on behalf of my aunt. He knows everything that happens in Canterbury. Nothing escapes his notice. If we go to Canterbury—"

"*When* we go to Canterbury…"

"*When* we go to Canterbury, we will need to do so with his full knowledge and approval, staying in his palace and coordinating with his men. I think it would be best if we went with Daniel. The two of them haven't met yet, and a formal visit from the earl would provide the perfect cover for us to take care of some personal business on the side. We'll have to figure out some way to lure Robert out from hiding. He'll expect retribution and won't be easy to find."

Alais chewed her lip in thought. "Robert has a weakness for me. What if I tried to lure him out?"

"How?"

Victor looked horrified by the idea, but at least he didn't dismiss it out of hand.

"A day of shopping, perhaps, with minimal guard."

His frown deepened.

"You can have as many men as you want tucked away out of sight, but I have to look vulnerable." She gave him a stern look.

Taking a deep sip of wine, he said, *"I'll* take you shopping. Robert wants me dead as badly as he wants you in his bed. The lure of both of us should prove difficult to resist. We can stop for refreshment at the inn where he's purported to be. That should draw him out if nothing else does. But I want your promise you'll run to safety the moment there's any danger."

She nodded. While she longed to take down Robert herself, she lacked the fighting skills to do so. "I trust you to defend my honor. And I know you'll put an end to him."

"You won't object if I kill him?"

"No."

Victor closed his eyes and took a deep breath. "Thank you. Because he deserves to die for what he did to you."

She studied her husband, a hunk of bread spread with soft goat cheese suspended halfway to her mouth. "You're so handsome when you're feeling vengeful."

He gave her a mischievous half-smile as he took a sip of wine. "I am, am I?"

His impish gaze set her on fire. How could she not have seen how ridiculously attractive he was from the first? Good God, he was delicious. She ran her foot along the side of his shin.

"Oh, that appeals to you, does it?" he asked, catching her ankle, and running his hands up her calf. "Maybe I should pursue vengeance more often."

She bit her lip to stifle a sudden, inexplicable urge to take a bite out of him.

"Come here," he said, giving her leg a gentle tug.

She put down her bread and cheese and complied. He ran his hand beneath her skirts, his fingers finding her burning center.

"Dear God, you are so gloriously insatiable," he said as he rendered her incoherent, "which is excellent news because so am I." Her knees gave way beneath her, and he maneuvered her into his lap where he continued his unrelenting torture. He pushed up her skirts and loosened his breeches, and just as she was on the brink, he entered her. Rocking together, they trembled with the force of their release.

They leaned against each other, panting, when they were done. "You realize we're going to starve to death if we can't even make it through a meal without coupling," he complained helplessly.

"I need you more than food. At least, today I do," she sighed against him.

"When we get back from Canterbury, I'm asking Daniel for an extended leave from my duties with nothing to do but tend to you and your pleasure. I'm going to make love to you until we're too sore and exhausted to go on, like that man in the cat song, though I suspect one hundred and eighty times won't be nearly enough for me with you."

"We should eat quickly before we lose control again."

Alais returned to her seat on the opposite side of the table, avoiding eye contact until she'd eaten her fill. She needed food, but she was ravenous for him. If she let herself so much as look at him, she knew she'd choose his touch over her sustenance.

As soon as they were done, they went back to bed, curling up together, breathing each other in, touching, and caressing. The rest of the day was passed in murmurs and cuddles between fits of torrid passion.

As the sun began to set, there was a knock at the door. "Alais, it's Carenza. It's time to go back to Winchelsea."

"We'll meet you downstairs," Alais called out, trying to make her voice sound normal despite what Victor's tongue was currently doing to her. She pulled a pillow over her face and bit down to stifle the cry that wracked her as she came yet again under Victor's tender ministrations. "I must look frightful," she said, tugging her fingers through the tangle her hair had become.

"You look spectacular."

"They'll all know what we were doing."

Victor shrugged. "We're newlyweds." He smiled, pulling on his clothes, and splashing water on his face. "It's probably for the best that we're being forced to take a break. We need to recover." He helped her with the ties on her dress.

"So that we can start all over again after we get to Winchelsea?" She gave him an innocent grin. He backed her against a wall and kissed her furiously.

"Yes."

"You taste like my peach."

"I like to eat dessert before dinner." He handed her a comb from the dressing table.

She dragged it through her tangles with difficulty. "There," she said, tucking in the last of her hair. "Do I look presentable?"

"You look delectable. I can't wait to take it all off again."

Without a word, she grabbed his hand and dragged him out the door.

CHAPTER TWENTY-SEVEN

AS ALAIS RODE through the southern gate of Winchelsea, she was greeted by the familiar sights and sounds of Fish Street. Workmen bellowed. Sailors swore and gambled. Ships creaked against their moorings. The briny scent of fish guts and ocean breezes tickled her nose. She wanted to climb down from her horse and kiss the slimy, filthy cobblestones.

Home! There had been moments over the last few days when she'd feared she'd never see it again. But here she was, safe and sound, with her husband by her side. Nothing had changed. While her world turned upside down, Winchelsea had gone on without her as if nothing had happened.

They turned onto Castle Street, and the castle came into view. Tears prickled in the corners of her eyes, and she tried to blink them away. She glanced at Victor. He was watching her carefully.

"Are you all right, my love?" he asked in a low voice, just barely audible over the clatter of hooves.

She smiled reassuringly. "I'm fine. It's good to be home."

Together, they rode through the castle gates and relinquished Snow and Socorro to the grooms. Victor immediately came to her side, taking her hand and folding it into the crook of his arm. She leaned against him, enjoying the ripple of his muscles beneath her fingers.

"Did we look at each other like that when we were newly married?" Carenza asked Daniel behind her.

"You still do," her mother chimed in with a chuckle. "I'm very glad to see my girls so happily settled."

Alais tamped down a burst of irritation. Her mother had tried to force her to marry Robert, and now she pretended to care for her happiness? But then, she *had* apologized.

Taking a deep breath, Alais reminded herself that her mother no longer had any meaningful power over her. She was a married woman and, as such, belonged to her husband's family now.

Though Winchelsea hadn't changed a whit, Alais was not the same. She knew her own strength in a new way, and she was bolstered by Victor's love and adoration. Perhaps it didn't matter anymore what her family thought of her.

With this new knowledge in mind, Alais said, "I'm glad you're happy for us, Mother. We're both very lucky that fate steered us away from the terrible marriages that might have been."

"Let's not speak of those horrible men." Her mother crossed herself.

Carenza had nearly been forced to marry a murderer, and Robert wasn't much better. But if her mother wanted to pretend she hadn't had a hand in either of those disasters, Alais wasn't going to bother to argue. Her own peace of mind would be better served by accepting her mother as she was, with all her flaws, and letting it go.

"Now I just need to find a good husband for Iselda," her mother announced as they walked through the portcullis and into the entrance hall.

"God help Iselda," Carenza whispered in Alais's ear.

"We'll help too," Alais whispered back. "We can't let Mother force her into a bad match."

"Agreed."

"What was that?" her mother asked, peering at them.

"Nothing," Alais and Carenza said in unison.

Her mother's eyes narrowed.

"My dear," said her father, catching her mother's arm and pulling her away, "we should let them rest and recover. There's something I wanted to consult with you about." He winked at his daughters as he led their mother off toward the solar.

Grateful for the reprieve, Alais leaned over to Victor. "Let's head upstairs."

Carenza and Daniel gave each other knowing glances.

"We should visit the nursery and see how little Charles is doing," Carenza said, pulling Daniel along.

Alone again, they climbed the grand stone staircase holding hands and headed toward her room. *Their* room now. She would have to ask him if he wanted to redecorate. Tapestries of ladies on palfreys might be a touch feminine for his tastes.

The heavy wooden door closed behind them, and Victor immediately pulled her into his arms, touching his lips to hers and sending a little thrill through every part of her.

When he broke the kiss, he said, "Much as I would love to pick up where we left off, I should let you have some time to yourself. I'm sure you want to bathe and put on fresh clothes for dinner. And I should see the healer about my shoulder."

Sadly, he was right. Though she still craved him, she *was* rather sore, and a bath would be heaven after everything that had happened. "Such a shame," she murmured into his neck, giving it a lick, then nibbling on his ear.

She was rewarded with an animal noise, rumbling deep in his chest.

"I suppose I will have to let you go until dinner," he said, pulling her closer so that she could feel his growing arousal.

"Wicked man." She nipped at his neck and grazed her nails down his back.

"Devilish temptress." He squeezed her buttocks so that she was pressed against the hot length of him, leaving her panting. "Until later, my love." Giving her one last squeeze, he released her.

With heavily lidded eyes, she smiled at him. Yes, soon enough they would be frolicking in bed once again. Now for a bath.

He poured himself a glass of water and composed himself before heading to the door, giving her one last, searing look. Then he was gone.

What a delicious man she'd married. She fanned herself with her hand.

Moments later, there was a quiet knock on the door.

"My lady? It's me, Dora."

"Dora! Come in, come in!"

As the old woman ambled into the room, Alais pulled her into a hug. "It's so wonderful to see you!"

"And you, my lady. We were all so worried when we heard what that nasty man did to you. Thank the Blessed Mother you're home where you belong." Dora took a step back and looked her over. "You look like you need a chance to freshen up. Let me have a bath drawn for you."

After stepping out into the hall to give instructions to another servant, Dora returned and tsked at her gown.

"This has seen better days," Dora said, examining it closely. "I'll see what the ladies downstairs can do to salvage it. Let's head to the bathing chamber."

Picking out a clean shift and gown, Dora led the way downstairs and along the hall to a small room at the back of the castle that housed the enormous barrel for bathing. There were hooks on the side of the room for hanging clothes and a small wooden stool with a clean cotton cloth for drying off. The tub was full of hot, steaming water, strewn with fresh herbs. Dora helped her take off her dress then left her in privacy, and for the first time since she was captured, she was able to take full stock of the state of her body.

Her wrists and ankles had marks from where she was tied up. Her forehead was still swollen and tender where Sir Robert had hit it to knock her out. She must look a fright but thank the Lord he didn't do worse.

Lower down, she had a sweeter ache from her afternoon in bed with her husband. He had almost succeeded in chasing away her lingering horror at her abduction. But now that she was alone again, unwelcome thoughts and memories returned to haunt her.

She climbed into the hot water and let it leach away her aches and the lingering chill in her bones, as well as the feelings of filth and disgust that enveloped her at the thought of Robert's touch, thick as a second skin. Her mind kept bringing her back to her mother berating her for not marrying Sir Robert. She shied away from it, trying to think of anything else, but something in her kept circling back to it, worrying at the wound.

Victor. She was married to Victor, who loved her and trusted her. It was clear in everything he did. His love was a balm for her battered soul. He loved her despite her sins, perhaps even because of them. The pleasure they shared was beyond anything she'd ever imagined, and he celebrated her rather than condemned her for it. She was lucky beyond all measure to have found such a husband.

And she was filled with his seed. Perhaps even now, her womb was quickening. She smiled at the thought. What adorable little babies they would make together. But was she ready to be a mother?

She thought of her own mother, pulled away from her family several years younger than Alais was now to marry a stranger. She'd met her husband for the first time on their wedding day. How fortunate her mother was to be married to a man as kind and generous as her father. If only that experience had mellowed her and made her more sympathetic. But her mother was who she was, and Alais would never change that.

The only thing Alais could do was commit to being a better mother herself. She ran her hand over her flat stomach and smiled. With Victor by her side, she could do anything, even raise children, unready though she might feel.

She dunked her head under the water and then massaged

scented oils through her hair, working through the knots with her fingers. At last, she climbed out of the tub and dried off with a cloth. She felt better, cleaner, readier to face what was to come. Sir Robert would pay for his crimes. She would see to it if it was the last thing she did.

Dora knocked on the door and helped her dress, then led her upstairs to do her hair. By the time she headed down to dinner, she felt almost like her old self. Her heart skipped a beat on seeing Victor, clean and shaved, wearing a fresh set of clothes. His gaze held all the smoldering promise she could hope for as he took her hand and settled her into her chair beside him. She would almost have forgotten the state of her forehead if Iselda hadn't gasped and offered to make her a poultice on seeing her.

"I'll be fine, but thank you," Alais said, giving her little sister a reassuring look.

As they settled into their meal, the men talked of nothing but plans for the visit to Canterbury and how to capture Sir Robert. To her dismay, Alais was ignored once again. Everything was back to the way it had been. She was the invisible middle child once more.

When Carenza chimed in, they all listened to her, but then, she was Carenza. Her sister had always had an air of authority that made her impossible to ignore, even as a child.

"We can spare ten men for the traveling party and Winchelsea," Carenza said in a voice that brooked no dissent. "I won't leave Winchelsea undefended while we're away."

"I think—" Alais began, hoping for once they would listen.

"Ten men should be sufficient," Daniel said at the same moment, drowning her out. "Any more and we'll alarm the archbishop."

No one noticed her, or so she thought until Victor took her hand beneath the table and cleared his throat.

"Alais, what do you think of the plan?" he asked, loud and clear.

Everyone paused and turned to her.

"Do you need me to explain it again?" Carenza offered. "I know you weren't listening."

Victor squeezed her hand harder and said, "Yes, she was. She's always listening. I'd wager she knows as much about the plan as you do."

Oh, Alais loved this man so much. He'd noticed!

"It's true," Alais said, laying her eating dagger beside her trencher. "I've always listened. You've just never taken notice. I agree that ten men should be sufficient. We should include a few archers in the mix in case they are needed. I recommend we take eight knights from Winchelsea and two men from the Watch. Their skills at finding and apprehending criminals will come in handy as we lure Sir Robert out."

Daniel nodded slowly. "I was thinking the same."

"As for the archbishop," she continued, "I think you should consider a hefty donation to the Church with a promise of ongoing contributions, in exchange for a halt to his ambitions to expand within our territory. His spending is extravagant, and he wants his coffers full more than he wants another parcel of land to tend."

"I've heard that too," said her father, looking at her with new respect.

"I recommend that we send a knight ahead to announce our visit to the archbishop and then spread word of it as far and wide as possible within the city of Canterbury. We want Sir Robert to take the bait when we come to town. A member of the Watch should accompany the knight to spy on Sir Robert and learn as much as possible before we arrive."

"Good thinking," said Carenza, giving her a puzzled smile. "Who are you, and what have you done with my sister, Alais? I always thought you were too preoccupied with dresses and troubadours to pay any mind to these sorts of things."

"I am the same sister you've always had," Alais said with a laugh. "You just never appreciated me properly. I'm more than a breathtakingly gorgeous face, you know." She winked at Carenza.

"Ah, there's the Alais I know. Even with a purple lump on your forehead, your vanity knows no bounds." Carenza rolled her eyes, chuckling.

"Sisters," Daniel said to Victor, shaking his head.

"*Mm-hmm*," Victor answered with that irresistible sideways grin of his.

"So what else do you have to say about our plan for Canterbury?" Daniel asked, turning to Alais.

"I'm so glad you asked," she said, grinning from ear to ear.

CHAPTER TWENTY-EIGHT

I T TOOK TWO weeks of planning and another five days of travel to reach Canterbury, but they were there at last. Victor was relieved to pass through the tall, crenelated towers of the archbishop's palace.

Daniel sent messengers ahead informing Archbishop Richard of their visit, so they were expected. Sir Elias came striding out in a velvet and fur cloak to greet them in the courtyard as servants led away their horses and guided their knights away to living quarters. He gave Victor a long, piercing look, then turned to Daniel.

"My Lord, it's a pleasure to see you again," he said with a bow. "The archbishop asked me to welcome you to Canterbury and bring you to join him for dinner as soon as you are settled in. Follow me."

He led them into an entrance hall with an impossibly high ceiling and a grand staircase leading up to four stories of gallery landings. Banners hung from the galleries with the archbishop's symbol, a white Y filled with black crosses on a field of blue with yellow accents. Servants were dressed in the same light blue shade as the banners. It was a forbidding space, lit by torches that failed to spread their light to the far reaches of the hall. Sir Elias led them up two flights of stairs to rooms on the third floor, inviting them to join him in the entrance hall as soon as they were ready.

Victor and Alais had a room that overlooked the front courtyard. The narrow, arched window allowed them to watch as people came and went through the enormous palace gates. The room itself was comfortable with a roaring fire in the hearth and luxurious, carved wood furnishings. The bed was covered in a rich blue brocade coverlet with matching curtains and canopy.

Once they were settled in, Sir Elias led them down to a vast dining hall filled with courtiers and holy men. Archbishop Richard was at the head table and stood when Sir Elias led the three of them to their seats by his side.

Sir Elias introduced them. "My lord, I am pleased to present the Earl Daniel Rossignol, Countess Carenza Rossignol, Sir Victor de Guestling, and Lady Alais de Guestling."

Daniel and Victor bowed deeply, and Carenza and Alais followed suit with low curtsies.

"Welcome to Canterbury," Archbishop Richard intoned in a deep voice with a slight nod of acknowledgment, gesturing for them to be seated. His dark hair was streaked with gray and cut into a chin-length bob. His salt and pepper beard was trimmed into a neat point. He wore white vestments that were richly embroidered and draped to the floor. "I was sorry to hear about the death of your uncle. Lord Raymond de Broase was a troublesome man but a good friend to the Church." The archbishop gave a brief smile, but it didn't reach his sharp, calculating eyes.

Victor held his breath. A year and a half ago, Lord Raymond de Broase had tried to invade Winchelsea and kill Daniel. Fortunately, Daniel had defeated his uncle. It didn't bode well that the archbishop chose to start the conversation with condolences.

"My lord," said Daniel, "you honor us with your hospitality. I am grateful for your warm welcome, and I look forward to discussing a number of matters of mutual interest. I hope that in time you will consider me a good friend to the Church as well."

"Daniel," the count said, inviting them with a gesture to be seated. "I have been impressed with your handling of relations with Lady Helisende and your cousin in Hawkhurst. You seem to have negotiated favorable agreements for yourself, taking land away from both without provoking them to fight back. It was clever of you to give Hawkhurst back to your cousin. Some saw it as a sign of weakness, but I think it shows foresight. You gained an ally in young Raymond where you might have had an enemy. The de Broase territories were hard enough to hold together without adding Winchelsea to the mix. If you had taken Hawkhurst, you wouldn't have lasted long. As it is, you are in a strong position."

Daniel smiled and nodded his head, accepting the compliment without commenting on it. *Wise decision*, Victor thought.

"Tell me, Victor," the count said loudly, giving him an irritated look. "How is your aunt getting along with the other Cinque Ports?"

Thank heavens he and Daniel had prepared for this question. "My aunt has always had friendly relations with the other Cinque Ports. Her daughter just married the Baron of Hythe. But my aunt has always maintained her independence. She is a friend to all, but bows to none. She has always respected the power of Canterbury. I know that she wishes nothing more than peace and friendship with all her neighbors."

"And what do you think of Helisende, Daniel? Does she offer you friendship?"

"My lord," Daniel said with a placid smile, "the countess has shown herself to be an intelligent and canny leader, and we have allied our families through marriage as well as by agreement. Our mutual respect has allowed us to keep peace in the region, and we stand united with Hastings as well as my cousins in Hawkhurst and Pevensey when it comes to mutual defense and trade. It is a most fruitful relationship."

Victor watched Carenza exhale in relief. A small, amused smirk crossed the count's face as he noticed Carenza squeezing

Daniel's hand.

"Tell me, Lady Alais," the count said, turning and smiling like a cat pouncing on a mouse. Victor went rigid and squeezed Alais's hand harder than he ought. "What do you think of Helisende? I understand you were her…guest…around the time Lord Raymond de Broase died."

Alais smiled and took the question in stride. "The countess has long been an ally of Winchelsea. Now that I am married to Sir Victor, she is family. I am honored to play a part in strengthening such a longstanding alliance."

The archbishop pursed his lips in disappointment. He certainly wasn't expecting her poise and diplomacy. *What an amazing woman I've married!*

"If I may, my lord," Daniel interjected. "There was a small matter I wanted to bring to your attention—a bit of business we must take care of in Canterbury. Sir Victor's cousin Sir Robert committed a crime and must be brought to justice. We have reason to believe he is here."

"He is, and he's become quite a nuisance." Victor shouldn't have been surprised, but he never ceased to be amazed by the archbishop's attention to detail. "I would be delighted if you could rid me of him. The wives of several of my vassals have complained of his unwanted attentions, and he owes money to nearly every lord in town. I believe he is entangled with a money lender I am trying to apprehend named Matthew."

Matthew? Of course, Robert would be involved with a lowlife like Matthew. Perhaps there would be an opportunity to take care of both at the same time.

"Rid me of Sir Robert," the count continued, "and I will consider it a favor. Rid me of Matthew as well, and I will be most grateful indeed."

"Sir Victor has a plan," said Daniel, "and we'd like permission to coordinate with your men."

"I grant you permission to do so," the archbishop said with a wave of his hand. "Sir Elias, make the necessary arrangements."

"Yes, my lord."

"Thank you, my lord," said Daniel. "Now, I understand you were negotiating with Hawkhurst about grain shipments."

From that point forward, Archbishop Richard's focus was entirely on Daniel, and Victor could relax and eat at last.

He looked down at his plate. There was some lumpy pink stuff and some charred brown stuff and a bright yellow something. The expensive spices and sauces made the food all but unrecognizable, and his appetite suddenly left him. What he wouldn't give for a bit of Marie's cooking! He managed to move some of it around on his plate but didn't take a bite.

"Eat," said Alais under her breath. "Even if you don't want to, you need something in your stomach, and we have to play our part as gracious guests."

Victor forced himself to pick at the food while Alais made polite small talk with a priest from London. It was a relief when the meal finally ended, and Sir Elias led him off to coordinate the capture of Robert, and possibly Matthew. Not that Victor had any intent of capturing Robert alive after all he'd done, but there was no need to announce that to the archbishop's men.

After dinner, Alais and Carenza retired with the countess. The archbishop and Daniel were still engaged in deep conversation. Sir Elias tapped Victor's shoulder and beckoned for him to come.

"I believe you wished to speak with the head of the Watch. Come. I will show you to him."

"Thank you." Victor followed, anxious to develop a plan for Robert's baiting and capture.

Sir Elias led him down labyrinthian hallways until they exited the palace. They crossed a wide cobblestone street to enter a low, stone building. The walls were lined with hooks from which hung weapons of every description from clubs to broadswords. A roughhewn table and benches sat in the middle of the room.

"This is Dagobert," said Sir Elias, gesturing toward a burly, black-bearded man in a simple, rough, woolen cotte. "He leads the Watch. Dagobert, this is Sir Victor de Guestling, a guest of the archbishop. He needs your assistance apprehending some-one."

"It is good to meet you, Dagobert," Victor said with a nod.

"And you, my lord," Dagobert answered with a bow. "How can I be of assistance?"

"My cousin, Sir Robert, made an attempt on my life and kidnapped my wife. I have reason to believe he's here in Canterbury, possibly at an inn called the Black Rooster."

Dagobert looked to Sir Elias. "The archbishop is aware of Sir Robert," said Sir Elias. "He has caused some difficulties here in Canterbury. The archbishop wishes to aid Sir Victor's efforts to seek him out and bring him to justice."

Nodding, Dagobert said, "As you wish, my lord. Sir Victor, how did you propose to apprehend this Sir Robert? Should we go to the Black Rooster and arrest him?"

"No, he has armed men in his pay. If we are forced to go to the Black Rooster, this will end in unnecessary bloodshed. Better if we could lure him out. I propose taking my wife shopping in the neighborhood of the inn. Sir Robert hates me and wants her. I suspect he won't be able to resist the bait of both of us walking about unguarded and will attempt to attack us as we shop. I would like to agree with you on a route to take, and I would like your men, as well as those that I've brought, to wait out of sight and apprehend him when he comes out. If all else fails, we storm the Black Rooster."

Victor wanted to avoid the Black Rooster at all costs. Robert would have the advantage there. He could hold out with a small number of men against a much bigger force, and the risk to life and limb of taking him on in his chosen warren was so much greater. And then there was Alais. Victor didn't want her to join him in the inn. She wouldn't like it, but he would have to insist. If it came to that, she would stay with guards well away from the action.

"Let me get a map of the city," said Sir Elias, leaving and

returning several minutes later with scrolls in hand.

For the next two hours, they sat together and laid out their plan.

CHAPTER TWENTY-NINE

ALAIS OPENED AN eye and squinted at the window to see the light of dawn peeking in. Victor shifted in bed beside her. Nearly every day since being reunited, they had started their day making tender love. She hoped today would be no exception. Her body hungered for him with a ferocity she never thought possible. If she'd thought the marriage bed would tame her appetites, she was wrong. Very wrong.

His hand, resting on her breast, began to move, and she felt hot breath and lazy kisses on her neck and shoulder. His arousal pressed against her bottom in the most delicious way, and she squirmed against him, wanting more. He laughed sleepily, pinching her nipple, and letting his hand drift down.

"Eager this morning, aren't you, wife?" His hand found its destination. "Oh, and so wet for me. God's wounds."

He strained against her as his fingers parted her folds and found that secret spot that sent lightning bolts through her. And with that, she lost the ability to form conscious thoughts. Everything was reduced to a wave of blissful sensation.

Was she making too much noise? Perhaps. And she didn't care. All that mattered was the man turning her and settling himself between her legs. A moment later, he was inside her, and she lost her mind. Everything was heat and longing and belonging. She was his. His. His.

Each thrust brought her closer to the edge. Soon everything was lost in a burst of heat and light. She felt his spasm within her. They collapsed together, a tangle of arms and legs.

"I love starting my day this way," she said, enjoying the feel of his chest beneath her hands.

"Are you ready for today?" He tucked a stray hair behind her ear.

"You mean for our shopping expedition?"

"Yes. You don't have to do this, you know." He must have said it at least ten times last night. If he thought he was going to talk her out of this, he was sorely mistaken.

"I *do* have to do this. I couldn't stand to stay behind while you faced him. He's wronged me as much as he's wronged you."

He kissed her forehead. "I know. And I think you're very brave."

"You say that as if it didn't require bravery on your part."

Smiling and pulling her close, he said, "It doesn't. Not like it does for you. I'm a fighter. I know I'm at least his equal with a sword, if not better. You, however, are defenseless."

She pulled back and looked at him. Really?

He thought she was defenseless after everything she'd been through? "Not entirely. After all, I did manage to escape his clutches once all on my own, and I didn't even have a weapon that time. This time, I'll have a knife."

Victor laughed. "See what I mean? Brave. When you were in peril beyond any you'd faced in your life, you fought back with every means at your disposal, ignoring how the odds were against you. You're the bravest woman I've ever met." He kissed her cheek. "And the most intelligent."

He kissed her neck. "And the most beautiful." He kissed her shoulder.

"Mmm. You had better stop or we won't make it out of here on time to meet the Watch."

He nipped at her shoulder. "Let them wait."

"Now you're being ridiculous," she said, pushing away with a playful grin. She got out of bed and went over to her trunk, well aware of his reverent eyes caressing her body. As she pulled on her shift, he made a little noise of disappointment.

"We need to finish this business with Robert so that I can have the uninterrupted time with you that I think we both deserve after all that's happened," he said, getting out of bed and pulling on his breeches.

Soon they were dressed and downstairs, eating a hasty breakfast before going out to meet the Watch.

Victor took her to a low stone building across a courtyard. When she entered, she saw twenty men arrayed around a long trestle table. The walls were hung with weapons. What was that wicked-looking curved one for, she wondered. It was exciting to see the Watch at work. This was a world she was rarely allowed to enter, being strictly the domain of men. About half of the men were familiar to her—knights that had traveled with them from Winchelsea. The other half were strangers, and they all wore the insignia of the archbishop.

A tall, burly man with a thick black beard stood at the head of the table. When they came in, he bowed and mumbled, "My lord, my lady," and gestured for them to be seated.

"Gentlemen," the man said in a voice that carried the length of the room. "My name is Dagobert. I oversee the Watch here in Canterbury. Sir Victor and I planned today's operation last night, and I will be taking the lead as we carry it out." He nodded to Victor.

"Men of Winchelsea," Victor said, "You will follow Dagobert's orders as if they were my own." Some of the men shifted, but none of them said a word.

Dagobert pinned a map of the city to the wall with a dagger. "We are attempting to lure out a known criminal by the name of Sir Robert. Sir Victor, can you provide a description?"

"He's the same height and build as me and looks enough like me to be my brother, but with curly hair. His eyes are a lighter shade of blue than mine."

The men of Winchelsea, at least, knew very well what Sir Robert looked like. His performance in the recent tournament was memorable.

"To lure him out, Sir Victor and Lady Alais will go on a shopping expedition here," Dagobert said, pointing at the map. "We have reason to believe Sir Robert may attempt an attack on them if he thinks them unprotected and unwary. We will remain out of sight stationed here, here, and here," he said, pointing again. "If at any point you see a disturbance or hear either of them yell Sir Robert's name, you are to intervene and capture the man. If we are unsuccessful at luring him out, we will enter the Black Rooster Inn and take him. Expect armed resistance if we do so. Sir Robert is known to employ armed men, and the inn is also headquarters for a criminal named Matthew who we have been unsuccessful at quelling to date. If you have an opportunity to take Matthew or any of his men, you are encouraged to do so."

At that moment, Sir Elias swept in the door, and all heads turned. "Yes, please put an end to this Matthew. He has plagued Canterbury and other cities long enough. I will be joining today's mission to see to it that we are successful." There were murmurs of surprise at this announcement from the Canterbury men. Apparently, the archbishop's right-hand man didn't often bother himself with the Watch.

"We are honored, my lord," said Dagobert with a bow. Turning back to the men, he continued, "To avoid arousing suspicion, we will stagger when the groups go out. You will all wear plain woolen cloaks to hide your insignia and allow you to blend in with the citizens of Canterbury. If you are wearing armor, please remove it. A stout leather jerkin should suffice for this work.

To maintain the illusion that we are simple men going about their business, group one will be playing dice. Group two will be pretending to repair a broken cart. Group three will be haggling over horses. Any questions?

No? Good. Group one leaves in ten minutes. Let's divide you up."

Dagobert went among the men, tapping them on the shoulder and directing them into groupings. "I will lead group one," he said. "Jacques will lead group two. Sir Elias will lead group three."

Alais watched as one by one the groups departed. She felt butterflies in her stomach as the moment approached for her to depart with Victor. This was one of the most dangerous things she'd ever done in her life. Why couldn't she just stay at the archbishop's palace in safety like any normal woman in her position would?

But then she felt the comforting pressure of the dagger tied to her leg. It gave her courage. She could do this. Especially because Victor would be by her side every step.

I want revenge on Robert for all he's done to me and to Victor. How dare he try to kill the man I love! I can and will face him one last time.

"Are you ready?" Victor asked at last.

"I'm ready."

In the courtyard, they mounted and rode at a leisurely pace to the beginning of their route. Tying up their horses and paying an enterprising youth to watch over them, they headed to their first stop—a milliner's. It was larger and grander than any she'd seen, even in Hastings. For a moment, she forgot her peril and marveled at the array of hats and headpieces in every possible color and design. There were gorgeous gorgets, beautiful barbettes, and cauls with jeweled nets to hold one's hair in place. There were horned, heart-shaped, and cone-shaped headdresses in every imaginable fabric. There were scarves and wimples in every shade and shape.

She gave Victor a questioning look, and he smiled. "Choose whatever you like, my love." The shopkeeper looked her and Victor up and down and rubbed his hands together in glee. Alais allowed herself to be swept away as the shopkeeper proudly displayed his wares. She almost forgot the danger she was in as she tried on one headdress after another. By the time she was done, the merchant had three large bundles to deliver to the archbishop's palace, and the man positively glowed as Victor counted out the coins.

"Was it too much?" she asked tentatively as they strolled up the street to their next stop. "I forgot I'm not supposed to be enjoying myself."

Victor shook his head. "You know I love to spoil you. Besides, what would I do with your dowry if not spend it on you? I already had more than I could ever need for myself. If hats make you happy, then hats you shall have. I confess I can't afford three large bundles at this next store, though," he said, nodding to a jeweler. "But sometimes the best things come in small packages."

In the jewelry store, Victor took the lead, asking the jeweler to show them his finest pieces and having Alais try on one after another. She could hardly believe how sumptuous and extravagant these pieces were. She felt like a queen as she tried them on.

"I like the rubies," Victor said after she'd tried on half a dozen necklaces that would not have looked amiss on Queen Eleanor herself. "You always look stunning in red."

"Oh, Victor. That was my favorite too!"

"We'll take the ruby necklace and the matching earrings and bracelet," Victor said to the jeweler who smiled so widely it looked like his face might split in half.

As they left the shop, Alais had a prickly feeling on the back of her neck as if she was being watched. She tightened her grip on Victor's arm. "I saw him too," he murmured so that only she could hear. "Let's get you safely in the dress shop, and I'll deal with him."

Her stomach was in knots as they stepped into a large fabric and dress shop with a wide array of gowns in various styles and colors on display. Some of the designs were quite innovative and lovely, unlike anything Alais had seen. "Buy whatever pleases your fancy, my love," Victor said loudly in front of the overjoyed shopkeeper, handing Alais his purse. "I have some business to attend to." He kissed her on the forehead and was gone. Alais had a moment of panic before she composed herself. She didn't like to be separated from him, especially knowing he was going into danger. But this was what they'd agreed to. She would be brave and follow the plan.

Gathering herself, she looked at the shopkeeper. "This is a very interesting design over here," she said, gesturing. "Would it be possible for me to try it on to see how the style suits me?"

Smiling, the shopkeeper said, "Of course, my lady. It may not be exactly your size, but we can tailor anything to your exact specifications, and, of course, we can make it in any fabric you desire. Here. I have a little room back here where you can change."

Alais followed the shopkeeper back into the depths of the shop to a curtained-off area. The shopkeeper handed her the dress and went away. As she was tightening the ties at the side of the gown, a strong arm grabbed her from behind, and a hand clapped over her mouth. For a moment, she froze in terror.

"Left you all alone and undefended again, has he?" Sir Robert murmured in her ear.

Alais screamed with all her might and bit his hand.

"Stop that," he hissed, and she felt the sharp bite of a cold blade at her neck. "You're coming with me."

CHAPTER THIRTY

A LAIS'S SCREAM STOPPED Victor in his tracks. Of course, Robert would go after Alais the moment Victor left her alone. He should have seen this coming.

Charging back into the shop, sword drawn. "Where is she?" he demanded. The terrified shopkeeper pointed to the back. Running, he yelled, "Robert!"

He arrived in time to see a swinging back door and a carriage moving off at some haste. He couldn't keep up with a horse for long, but he could try. Running after the carriage, he followed it through the winding streets of Canterbury until it came to a stop in front of the Black Rooster Inn. In the distance, he saw Robert disappearing inside with Alais at knifepoint.

He heard running feet behind him and turned to see Dagobert and his men following. "Robert is in the inn," Victor yelled to them. Dagobert nodded and sent two of his men off to alert the other groups. "He has Alais. I'm going after him."

It took Victor's eye a moment to adjust as he burst through the door. In the dim light of the common room, he saw a dozen men, all of them armed. Upon seeing him with a drawn sword, the serving wench immediately fled to the back, and the barkeep picked up a bludgeon.

Out of sight, there was a scream. *Alais*. Victor launched himself toward the doorway at the back, determined to get to her. As expected, every man in the room raised his sword. Ordinarily, he would relish the challenge, but he had no time.

The first man came at him. Victor knocked his sword away and went crashing into the second. *No time.* He sliced the man across the chest, leaving a dripping red line. *Have to get to Alais.*

Three men closed behind him. He stabbed backward. A grunt told him he hit home. *She's in his clutches.*

The iron stench of blood mixed with the scents of sweat and ale that pervaded the inn.

Spinning, he hacked at one man and then the other. They were like so much wood he had to chop through to get to his wife. They fell like trees.

Alais needs me.

He heard a commotion behind him and knew it must be Dagobert and his men.

Two men stood between him and the door. He chopped. He cut. Two more men fell to the floor bleeding. He reached the door at last.

"Alais, I'm coming," he yelled, plunging through the door headlong into another man. Victor hardly saw him. Rage pulsed through him. Desperation. His hand acted on instinct, taking down the man before him. *No time.*

He heard a thump and a muffled scream coming from below.

A cellar?

Ripping open the door of the first room he saw, he found nothing. The second, nothing. The third had three armed men and a trap door. One man moved to block Victor while the other two dropped down through the trap door.

Their swords clashed and clashed again. This one had some skill. It would have been fun to find out how much if he weren't in such a desperate rush. But as he swung and slashed, only a piece of his mind was on the fight. The rest was with Alais. That monster had her. Again. And he'd allowed it. He should never have let Alais come along on this dangerous mission. What had he been thinking?

"There's a door down here. He's taking me away," Alais screamed.

No! He can't take you!

The man he'd been fighting lay bleeding and groaning at his feet. Victor ran for the cellar door and dropped down. The pressed dirt floor muffled his landing.

In the wavering light of two torches, he saw Robert by a door, huddled over something. A lock, perhaps? There were four men besides Robert, one holding Alais, two with torches, and one with sword drawn, facing toward him.

"Victor, is that you?" Alais yelled. The man holding her hit her over the head with the hilt of his sword, and she slumped sideways, then to the floor.

Victor saw red. There was a roaring in his ears. He barreled toward the man who had hit Alais, ready to rip, cut, kill.

Robert turned around and their eyes met. "Finish him," Robert ordered, then turned back to the door, grumbling, "Damned rusty lock."

Victor crashed against Robert's men like an ocean wave. He was everywhere, moving so quickly they didn't know which way was up. One of them tripped and fell to the ground. Victor stabbed. The man would never get up again.

Smashing into the man who'd hit Alais, he knocked him back. This one kept his feet and raised his sword again lightning quick, striking back. He cut Victor across his right forearm but not deeply. The pain only served to amplify Victor's battle rage.

With swift movements, Victor backed the man into a pile of crates. No matter how the man tried to block, Victor found a way through his defenses. The man began to panic and swing wildly. Victor slashed, then thrust. The man slumped to the floor. The bastard was dead. Good riddance.

Blood dripped from Victor's blade as he stalked toward his cousin. "It's time to end this, Robert. Turn around and fight, you coward."

The men with torches held their swords but did not advance.

Robert turned.

With an exaggerated sigh, he said, "Never trust a henchman to do your dirty work." He drew his sword and stepped over Alais. Over his shoulder, he ordered, "Keep trying to open that door. It's our only way out."

As his cousin stepped forward, Victor felt his stomach clench. Everything depended on his beating Robert once and for all. But Robert was not an easy foe. They were evenly matched. Victor took a deep breath in and a deep breath out, calming his mind and body. He couldn't afford to let his fury cloud his mind. He needed clarity to fight with the speed and deadly precision required to not only best Robert but end his life.

Robert was cornered and all the deadlier for it. Victor looked with loathing upon his one-time companion and playmate. As children, they were practically brothers. But Robert had destroyed any vestiges of brotherly feeling Victor might have had when he kidnapped Alais, not to mention his various attempts on Victor's life. The man was broken, beyond redemption. He had to be stopped.

I'm fighting the beast that destroyed Robert as much as I'm fighting the man who stole Alais.

Robert attacked, testing, trying to lure Victor within his reach. Victor shut him down with swift strokes.

"Maybe it's for the best my men failed," Robert said, circling. "This is how it should be. You and me. No one to interfere." He struck. Victor struck back. They continued to circle.

"This is how it must end," Victor agreed. "But it should never have come to this. You're my family, my blood. Why do you hate me so?"

Victor twisted and stabbed. Robert dodged and slashed. Dancing to the side, Victor narrowly avoided his blade.

"Why do I hate you? How could I not? You always had everything, and I had nothing. Your father loved you. Mine hated me. You were the countess' precious nephew. I was barely a noble. You had Guestling. I had a broken-down flour mill. And then there was you…"

With a wild yell, Robert launched himself at Victor, who dodged to the side in the nick of time.

"You were so good." Robert slashed.

"And smart." He thrust.

"And handsome." He cut.

"And talented." He swung his blade, missing Victor's neck by an inch. "It was disgusting."

Victor countered each stroke with precision, watching for any hole in his cousin's defenses.

"And even now after I ruined your perfect face," Robert continued, "you're the one Lady Alais prefers. You're Lord Daniel's commander. And you're *still* the fucking heir to Guestling."

Robert attacked again, and Victor struggled to keep his calm in the face of it. *No, I have to keep my wits about me. I need precision, accuracy. It's the only way to save Alais.*

"Why do you want Guestling so much? It's a tiny market village, not much more productive than your mill."

Spotting a hole in Robert's defense, Victor struck. Robert blocked just in time. "I don't want Guestling. I *need* it. I'm in debt up to my ears, and Matthew's going to kill me if I don't pay him off. I needed Lady Alais's dowry too, but it's too late for that. Though perhaps there's some way I can get my hands on it once you're dead."

"God's blood, Robert. Why couldn't you just ask for help? Father and I would have been more than willing before all of this."

His words seemed to enrage his cousin beyond anything else he'd said so far. Robert attacked with deadly fury and succeeded in giving Victor a deep cut along his ribs.

"I'm not your fucking charity case," Robert yelled, kicking Victor in the side where he'd wounded him.

Victor stumbled, barely catching himself. He was in trouble.

Just at that moment, one of the men with torches yelled, "Sir Robert, I got the door open."

Robert looked away for a split second. It was the opening Victor needed. Lunging forward, he stabbed, catching his cousin in the side.

Robert's eyes went wide, and he roared in pain, stumbling. One of his men caught him and pulled him toward the door. The other dropped his torch and grabbed Alais, dragging her. Victor was losing them.

There was a mad scramble by the door, and Victor threw himself forward. Then Robert gave an unearthly scream and collapsed to the ground.

The two men disappeared into the neighboring cellar.

Alais stood, shaking, with a dagger dripping blood on her gown. "It's finished," she said, dropping the dagger as if it burned her.

There Robert lay in a growing pool of blood, the monster dead at last, only the limp body of his dead cousin left.

Victor threw his arms around Alais. "You're safe, my love. You're safe."

She trembled in his arms. "I didn't want to kill him, but I had no choice. I woke up, and they were dragging me away. But I could finally reach my knife."

"He gave you no choice." He hugged her closely to him. "I'm so sorry he took you again. I never should have let you out of my sight."

Another tremor shook her head to toe.

"Let's get you out of this dark cellar, shall we?" he said, grabbing the torch off the ground.

She nodded, leaning heavily on him. She was in shock and no wonder. He needed to get her back to the castle.

As he turned to leave, he took one last look at his cousin. In death, the monster that twisted him was gone. All he saw was the shell of his childhood companion. He reached to gently close his eyes and said a silent prayer for the soul of the deceased. It was over.

Carefully guiding Alais, he helped her up the ladder. When he arrived in the common room, an unexpected sight greeted him. Dagobert was locked in fierce combat with Sir Elias with Dagobert's men surrounding the pair, swords drawn.

"What is this?" he asked one of Dagobert's men, who was standing nearby.

"Turns out Sir Elias is Matthew. Several of his men recognized him when he came in today with the Watch, and they betrayed him to us, begging us to spare their lives."

Sir Elias? Facts rearranged themselves in his head. It made sense. He was in Winchelsea for the tournament when the merchant was killed. He had taken deadly aim at Victor during the tournament, presumably hoping to take him down so that Robert could inherit and pay his debts.

Why did he turn on Robert now? Because Robert had foolishly drawn the attention of the rulers of Winchelsea, Hastings, and Canterbury. He likely deemed it too dangerous to let Robert live.

Victor eased Alais into a chair and drew his sword. He had a score to settle with Matthew. Dagobert's men parted for him, and Dagobert smiled as he joined the fight.

"It's over, Sir Elias. You know I'm the better sword. Surrender now," Victor said, joining Dagobert in an attack.

Sir Elias spat on the floor as he attempted to block the rain of blows. "I'd rather die in combat than at the end of a gibbet."

"We don't always get what we want," Victor said as he spun behind Matthew and slashed at the backs of his knees, slicing through flesh and sinew. Matthew collapsed on the floor like a puppet whose strings had been cut. Dagobert quickly disarmed him, and one of his men tied him up.

"I've been hunting Matthew for two years," said Dagobert. "And to think all that time he was hidden in plain sight. The archbishop will be pleased to see justice served at last."

Victor sheathed his sword and went back to Alais. "Now it is truly finished. We can go back to Winchelsea with no deadly threats hanging over our heads."

Helping her up, he pulled her into an embrace and kissed her hair. "Do you feel well enough to ride?"

"I think so."

"Then let's go get our horses and head back to the castle."

CHAPTER THIRTY-ONE

Alais clutched her ermine stole as she and Victor returned home from Christmas mass. A cold wind howled, but she didn't care. The Christmas feast was one of her favorite events of the year, and she could hardly wait to show off the new velvet gown she'd commissioned in Canterbury.

But Victor was fidgeting. Something was off. What could have him so worked up on Christmas Day?

"You aren't worried about next month's visit to your aunt, are you?" she asked, putting a soothing hand on his shoulder.

"What?" He looked genuinely bewildered. "Of course not. Why do you ask?"

"It's just that you've been restless all morning. Something is on your mind. Is it something to do with the negotiations with the archbishop's representative? I thought you said those were going well."

His brow furrowed. "They are."

"Then what's eating at you? There's definitely something."

"Has anyone ever told you that you are altogether too perceptive?"

Alais's heart fluttered at his words. It was so delicious to get compliments that had nothing to do with her looks.

"Only you."

He smiled his adorable, endearing half-smile.

"You still haven't answered my question," she said, squeezing his arm.

"All shall be revealed very shortly," he said, waggling his eyebrows and giving her a cryptic smile.

What was he up to?

As they entered the castle gates, Victor pulled her aside just as she was about to go in the front doors.

Mark from the stables came running up.

"Is everything ready as I asked?" Victor asked.

"It is, my lord."

Victor heaved a sigh of relief and turned to her.

"I have a gift for you, my love. Come with me."

A gift? That was what this was all about?

"Victor, I already have more silks and jewels than I know what to do with." Really, it was too much. He didn't need to spoil her like this.

"This is better than silks and jewels," he said with a sly grin.

"Better?" What had he done? It was with a mix of excitement and trepidation that she followed him as he led her into the stables.

"Definitely better," he said coming to a halt in front of the stall next to Socorro. "Meet Ventus."

Alais gasped as she looked at the gorgeous and powerful chestnut horse before her. The same size as Socorro, Ventus stamped and whickered as if ready for a race. He held himself like a prince among horses, proud and powerful. Victor placed an apple in her hand.

"Your very own charger, my love. The knight I bought him from was very tardy handing him over, but fortunately, he came through."

"Ventus," Alais cooed, "we are going to be great friends."

Ventus eagerly devoured the apple and nudged Alais's hand for more. Alais laughed. "He's absolutely beautiful. You're right. This is better than silks and jewels."

She pulled Victor toward her by the collar and brushed her

lips against his. He responded immediately, moaning against her lips, and running his hands up her back. His tongue traced the seam of her lips, and she opened to him. Familiar warmth rippled through her body and pooled in her center. He pressed her up against the side of the stall and deepened his kiss as she raked her nails down his back.

"Keep this up, and I may pounce on you in the hay," Victor said when she finally released him.

"I like the sound of that, but first…" She drew a finger along his jaw, down his neck, and then down his front. "We race."

Victor smiled broadly. "I thought you'd say that."

He turned. "William," he yelled, "come saddle Ventus and Socorro. Lady Alais and I are going for a ride."

Soon the horses were ready, and Victor stood beside Ventus, offering his hands to help her up. As she straightened her leg, he took a playful nip at her bottom, which was level with his face. "Victor," she admonished, but William was looking the other way.

"Tonight, I'm going to make you my Christmas feast," he said in a low voice only she could hear. The prickling warmth of a blush spread across her face.

"If you aren't too full of pudding," she teased, enjoying the view as he turned toward Socorro and mounted. Good Lord, the man had lovely legs.

Soon they were wending their way down Castle Street, picking their way carefully along the icy cobblestones. They passed pilgrims fresh glowing with zeal from Christmas mass, townsfolk in their holiday best, and mummers acting out the Christmas story.

As they turned on Fish Street by the docks, it was quiet for once, the raucous noise quelled temporarily for the holiday. Riding out through the eastern gate, they wended their way down to the beach.

"No Dora to chaperone us this time," Victor said.

Alais laughed. "I almost wish we'd brought her for old time's sake."

"You torture that poor woman enough without bringing her out on a freezing winter's day."

"Too true. I hope she's up at the castle sipping a tisane and eating pastries."

Ventus pawed restlessly at the sand.

"Patience, Ventus," she said, petting his neck. "You'll get to run all you want in just a moment. Are you ready?"

Socorro glared at her as though she'd insulted his pride.

"Do you know… I think Socorro might be jealous?" Victor asked.

"Oh, Socorro. You'll always be my sweet boy."

Socorro tossed his head and looked away.

"I told you she'd break your heart, my friend. Let's win this race so you can regain your pride."

"Ready…Go!"

Alais tore along the beach on Ventus's back, not even bothering to check where her opponent was. This was how it must feel to fly, she thought as she and her steed floated down the beach, the wind tearing at her hair. She couldn't contain her joy and yelped with glee.

When she passed the rock at the end of the beach, she didn't stop. She wheeled around and charged back. Only after completing the full loop did she rein in Ventus and come to a halt.

Victor arrived on Socorro moments later.

"I won," she crowed.

He laughed. "You cheated. You didn't tell me we were racing there and back. I thought we were stopping at the rock."

"I know. I just couldn't bring myself to stop. He flies, Victor. Where in Christendom did this horse come from?"

"Not in Christendom, I'm afraid. He originally comes from Arabia. It cost me dear, but I've never seen a finer steed. No offense, Socorro," he said, giving his horse a reassuring pat.

"I love him."

"And here I thought you loved me."

"I love you more than all the horses in the world, more than the moon and stars, more than Christmas and my birthday, more than anything or anyone, really."

He was everything to her, this beautiful, brave man with his warrior's face and fierce heart. There was nothing he wouldn't do to see her safe and happy, and she knew it. The same was true of her. She would face any danger, sacrifice everything to see him happy and at peace.

"And I love you with everything I am. Every day, I wake up thinking my heart will surely burst with it. You are a danger to my health and sanity, and I wouldn't have it any other way. I love you more than I ever thought possible, and I will do so until the day I die and then on into eternity."

Ventus stamped impatiently, and Socorro tossed his head.

"I think the horses are annoyed by our maudlin nonsense," Victor said, the fierce love in his eyes belying his amused tone. "Race again?

Full loop this time?"

"Of course!"

"Ready and…*Go!*"

They raced for another hour until her ears ached with the cold and her hair was such a tangle, she didn't think Dora would ever be able to tame it.

"We should head back," she said regretfully, pulling her stole tighter around her. "We need time to get ready for the feast."

"You're cold. You should have told me. Of course, we can head back."

She must have looked quite a sight as she rode up Castle Street with Victor by her side, but she didn't care. Revelers were everywhere, making merry and partaking freely of the wine and ale the castle provided one and all for the feast day as they climbed up the hill to the castle.

After relinquishing their steeds to the stable hands, they sauntered into the castle hand in hand with all the guilty delight of children who have been up to mischief. Carenza caught sight of them as they hurried to their room.

"Where have you two been? I've been looking for you." She looked them up and down, observing the state of Alais's hair and Victor's too-wide grin. "Never mind. I don't think I want the answer to that question. Just hurry up and get ready for the feast. Don't make us wait for you."

As soon as they were in their room, Victor pressed her against the wall kissing down her neck, and her whole body went up in flame.

"We don't have time," she complained, not really wanting him to stop. "You heard Carenza."

"Let them wait. I need you." His knee pressed between her legs, and she gasped.

"After the feast," she said with more conviction than she felt.

"I'm not sure I can wait that long. Can you?" he asked, nibbling her ear in the most delicious way.

Someone knocked on the door. "Alais, are you almost ready?" her mother asked through the door.

"Soon Mother," she called back.

With a sigh, Victor released her. "After the feast," he said with a look full of promise.

Victor dressed quickly and went downstairs to avoid temptation, or so he said. With Dora's help, Alais put on her new, red-velvet dress with a brocade panel in front and long bell sleeves that dripped to her shins. Dora *tsk*-ed at the state of her hair but soon had it pinned up in elegant side buns beneath a crespin whose gold net was studded with pearls. A wisp of sheer white silk draped down the back from the circlet. Last, Alais donned the ruby necklace, earrings, and bracelet Victor had bought her in Canterbury. She was ready.

When she made her entrance in the grand dining hall, she was the last member of the family to arrive. Jugglers and musicians entertained at least half the town, gathered beneath their roof to celebrate the feast day. The hall was decorated with festive tapestries, and braziers and candelabras gave it a merry light. Evergreens decorated the trestle tables, and the floor was strewn with fresh rushes and herbs.

She heard murmurs and gasps as she entered, and with some petty delight, she saw her outfit was even grander than Carenza's. But then Carenza had always had a rather severe sense of fashion. Why she wore that awful pearl rosary with the tiny carved skull all the time, she would never understand.

What mattered most, though, as she made her entrance was the look of wonder and adoration on Victor's face. He looked like he was enthralled by a holy vision and nearly dropped his silver wine goblet. As she took her place beside him at the table, he whispered, "You are a queen among women. I am honored beyond words to be at your side."

Daniel stood, and the hall hushed. He looked commanding in his midnight blue velvet cotte with slashed sleeves and billowing folds flaring from the waist. He gave a brief speech in honor of the holiday, commenting on the new ties with Hastings and Canterbury, and invited her father, Lord de Vere, to bless the feast. Her father led them in the Lord's Prayer as they all bowed their heads. When he finished, he spread his arms with a smile and said, "Let us feast!"

An entire roasted boar was carried by four servers and placed in the middle of the table. An army of servants appeared with a seemingly endless procession of platters and tureens for their table and then for the rest of the hall. There was venison, mutton, and sweetmeats. Hot, crusty loaves of bread and cheeses were laid on every table. There was pottage and roasted root vegetables. Mulled wine, mead, and ale flowed freely.

Alais took a sample of everything, unable to resist the decadent aromas.

"How is the venison today?" Victor asked, leaning in.

She took a bite. "Quite good, actually. The cooks didn't overcook it for once."

"Excellent, then I'll have some," he said, reaching for the platter.

"I'd skip the mutton, though. It's rather tough."

He grinned. "Thank you for saving me from mediocre mutton, my lady. I am in your debt."

They ate until they could eat no more, and then the plum pudding arrived. Victor winked at her as he served her a slice, despite her groan. As usual, she had overindulged. Nonetheless, she ate the rich dessert and even nibbled on a gingerbread cookie. She thought the ties on the sides of her gown might burst if she took another bite.

That's when the first troubadour stepped up onto the low wooden stage at the side of the room. Alais sipped mulled wine and leaned against Victor, who wrapped an arm around her as they listened to the plaintive tune about a beautiful lady locked away in a castle and a lover who lived merely to look upon her face from afar and no more. Another troubadour took the stage and sang a fiery song about going to war and laying siege to his cruel lady love.

Daniel and Carenza got up and sang a merry Christmas carol. By the end, everyone in the hall was singing along. A few were even dancing. Daniel gestured for the other troubadours to join them on stage with their lutes, and they each took turns leading a verse in a reprise. Before long, they'd run out of real verses, and the performers were improvising increasingly ridiculous parody verses.

Victor stood up and held out his hand. "A dance, my lady?"

She stood and accepted his hand, and soon they were whirling to the music, which had somehow devolved into increasingly ribald country songs. Daniel and Carenza surrendered the stage, leaving four troubadours to hold court, and everyone got drunker and sillier.

When she had danced until she could hardly stand, Victor whispered in her ear, "Do you think we can go now?"

Alais looked around. Her parents were dancing. Carenza was leaning back casually in Daniel's arms, obviously tipsy. Iselda had already excused herself and gone to bed.

"Yes, I think we can."

"At last."

He pulled her upstairs to their room and showed her that Christmas had hardly begun.

EPILOGUE

Alais wore her new burgundy silk dress with the wide V-neck showing off the swell of her breasts, and the draping bell sleeves that reached the bottom of her skirt. It was made from fabric purchased in Hastings, and it made her feel like a queen. On her head, she wore a matching hat that curved up on the sides like horns and had a delicate veil draping down in back. Her hair was tucked demurely beneath a sheer veil that hung down the back, down to her shoulders. Around her neck was the double-stranded pearl necklace with an enormous ruby medallion that had belonged to Victor's mother.

Dora sighed as she stood back to look at her work. "You look magnificent, my lady. Sir Victor won't be able to take his eyes off you."

Alais laughed. "Sir Victor couldn't take his eyes off me if I was wearing a lumpy brown sack." She examined herself in the mirror. "But I do quite enjoy stunning him into speechlessness. It's getting harder these days, you know. He says he's started to get used to me. But I bet this dress will do the trick."

"You should go down to the great hall, my lady. They'll all be waiting for you."

"Thank you. I don't know what I'd do without you." She gave Dora a quick hug.

"Oh, go on with you." Dora shooed her away with one hand

and dabbed her eyes with a hankie with the other.

As Alais walked down the beloved halls of the castle and down the grand staircase to the great hall, she found herself pondering the changes the last year had brought. Birthdays always made her pensive, though she would never admit it to anyone else. How different her life was now than it was a year ago! She still lived in the castle in Winchelsea with her family, but she felt like a different person. It wasn't only that she was married now. She'd changed inside. It was as if she used to float along on the surface of life, and now there was so much more. She used to live for attention, starved for affection, and now she felt...content? Could that be? And useful too. Who would have expected that?

She walked into the great hall to see the people she cared about most in the world seated around the table. First, she looked at Victor who, she was delighted to see, dropped his wine goblet on seeing her. She gave him a look full of smoldering promise, biting her lip. By God, he was delectable. He came and offered his arm to take her to her seat.

"Where were you all morning?" he murmured in her ear as they walked, or really processed. Yes, they were a two-person procession, she decided.

"I went down to the Bird's Nest." A woman named Jane, who bore a striking resemblance to her, had started a home for women seeking to leave prostitution and abusive homes, and Alais had taken a charitable interest in seeing that it was well-provisioned. When Victor confessed his familiarity with Jane, she couldn't stop laughing for half a day. He was so worried about what she'd think, but it only served as further proof he'd been infatuated with her from the start, even when he thought his suit was hopeless.

"It's amazing what she's done with the place. You'd never know it used to be a brothel. The Sisters from the Abbey are supporting our efforts as well now. It's incredible what she's accomplished in such a short time."

"What you've *both* been able to accomplish," he whispered in her ear as he pulled out her chair so that she could sit. "I know how hard you worked." Louder, so that the rest of the table could hear, he said, "You are a truly amazing woman, Alais, and I am the luckiest man alive."

Giles, who came over from Guestling for the festivities, yelled "Hear! Hear!" in her father's ear. Her parents raised their glasses in agreement.

"Maybe the second luckiest," Daniel quipped, kissing Carenza's hand.

"We shall have to agree to disagree," Victor answered with a laugh.

"You're both wrong," her father said, shaking his head with a smile. "Because not only do I have the best wife in the world but the best daughters." At that, everyone cheered and raised a glass. "And my sons-in-law aren't bad either," he added with a conciliatory grin.

"Not that it's a competition," Giles interjected, "but I have the best son, the best daughter-in-law, and..." he looked around the table for dramatic effect, narrowing his eyes, "the best cook." Everyone burst into laughter at that.

"Marie is here, by the way," he told Alais in a loud whisper that everyone could hear. "I brought her along. I thought you might like some proper cooking on your birthday."

"Lord Giles," Carenza interjected. "I believe I can outdo even you. You see, I have the best husband, the best parents, the best sisters, the best son, and..." she paused, "the best troubadour."

"You?" Daniel asked with an innocent smile.

"Hush your nonsense! You know I meant you," she snapped back in mock outrage.

"Oh, Carenza," Alais said, shaking her head. "I can beat you. I have the best husband, who also happens to be the best swordsman. I have the best parents, the best sisters, the best father-in-law, and..." she smiled regally, "it's my birthday."

Iselda stood up with her cup, looking awkward, with a nervous smile across her face. Everyone went silent and turned attentively, wondering what she could possibly say after all of that. "I love you all." They all watched her expectantly, waiting for her to continue. "That's all," she said, blushing furiously and sitting down as the whole family burst into raucous shouts and applause.

The feasting began, starting with Marie's sublime pottage, followed by snapper in red wine sauce, stuffed capons, suckling pig, and a peach tart for dessert.

"A peach tart?" Alais murmured to Victor, raising an eyebrow.

"Don't you like it?"

"It's delicious. It's just…"

"You're thinking of the song."

She nodded.

He smiled.

"Can one ever have enough peach tart? I, myself, find it quite delicious. I wonder how much peach tart I could eat in one sitting before my tongue got tired." He reached out to squeeze her thigh beneath the table, sending a shiver up her spine.

"But I've eaten so much. I need some time to digest before the…um…tart eating begins."

"Of course. No need to rush," he said with a lascivious grin that promised a long and lugubrious night ahead.

As the meal wound to a close, Alais's parents, Giles, and Iselda all excused themselves and headed off to bed. Daniel sent for more wine and for his friend Gerard, the troubadour, who joined them with his lute. He sang a few old favorites as they all sat and drank wine and laughed together. As the evening progressed, they all got drunker, and he moved on to some of the more risqué songs he knew, including one by Guillaume IX, Count of Poitiers, and Duke of Aquitaine, about two horses that made Alais giggle.

"Do you know the one he wrote about the cat and the man from Auvergne?" Alais asked with a devilish smile.

Gerard froze, looking around at the others with wide, worried eyes.

Victor burst out laughing. "Don't panic, Gerard. She's heard it before."

"And I am the birthday girl," she added with an ingratiating grin.

Gerard looked at Daniel, who chuckled and shrugged, and then at Carenza, who looked conflicted, but then sighed and said, "She's an adult. She's married. I suppose it's past time I stopped trying to protect her innocence and defend her virtue. She's her own woman."

Alais stared at her. Carenza was treating her like an adult? Carenza was passing up an opportunity to scold and moralize? What was the world coming to?

"Besides," Carenza added, "I like the song about the cat too."

Alais gasped. "You do?"

"What do you think I am, a nun?"

At that, Alais burst into drunken giggles.

Gerard launched into an admirable performance of the cat song, almost as good as Victor's friend, Richard. But instead of doing the ladies' voices in falsetto, he invited Carenza to sing. To Alais's enduring shock and wonder, Carenza knew every word.

"I'm not nearly the prude you think me, Alais," Carenza said when they'd all recovered enough from their laughter to speak again.

"Oh?" After years of listening to Carenza's moralizing, Alais couldn't help being deeply skeptical.

"Here. I'll prove it. I propose a little competition. Let's see who can come up with the filthiest verse."

Daniel pulled his head back, and his eyes widened. He looked down at his goblet. "I can't tell whether I'm too drunk for this or not drunk enough."

She waved her hand at him in the universal sign for don't-you-worry. "It'll be fun. We'll each take a turn. I'll start. Gerard, would you do the honors on the lute?

"Some years ago I wished to be a nun,
But I confess I didn't have much fun
Until one night I stole a secret kiss
And learned that lips and tongues could lead to bliss.
But there are other places tongues can reach.
I lose my mind when my love eats my peach."

"Your turn, Daniel," she said, giving him an innocent smile.

"Good God," Daniel groaned, shaking his head, and emptying his goblet. "Just please, please never breathe a word of this to anyone, especially your parents." Alais and Carenza both stared at him as if he'd lost his mind. "Fine," he grumbled and cleared his throat.

"Pity the man who falls for a de Vere.
You'll lose your wits and sanity I fear,
For lustful thoughts will haunt you all day long
And make you dream of things priests say are wrong.
I want to tease her 'til she's overcome
Then make love to her 'til my cock goes numb."

A look passed between him and Carenza that could have set fire to the castle's stone walls. Alais couldn't help blushing as she watched them. Gerard cleared his throat loudly to remind Carenza and Daniel of their audience.

"Gerard, are you blushing?" Daniel asked. His friend looked abashed and cleared his throat again. "I think you should go next."

Fingers skittering from the lute as he missed a strum, Gerard gulped. It took him a moment to regain his rhythm and his courage. At last, he closed his eyes and launched into his verse.

"My lovely wife may not be a de Vere,
But I'm a maudlin fool when she is near.
I like a lady with an ample breast,

And nothing can compare with my love's chest.
I love to lick and pinch her lovely tits
Until my teasing sends her into fits."

"Victor, show us what you've got," Gerard challenged, laughing with relief now that his turn was done.

Turning to Alais, his eyes full of ardor and mischief, Victor began.

"My love, I want you every waking hour
And when I sleep, I'm still under your power.
I grow hard each time I see you pass
And see the swell of your exquisite ass.
Your back is just as lovely as your front,
But nothing can compare to your sweet—"

"Nope," Carenza interrupted, her face bright red. "Too far. She's still my sister, after all."

"If my verse is too filthy to let me finish, does that mean I win?" he asked, taking a sip of wine.

"It depends."

"On what?"

"Our final contestant," Carenza said, fixing Alais with a pointed glance.

Oh God. It's my turn. She'd never been able to compete with Carenza in verse, but there was no way she was going to back down.

"I think perhaps it's time to go to bed
and put in action all that you have said.
This birthday is the best I've ever had.
I never knew Carenza was so bad.
You've given me ideas for tonight.
Let's head to bed and fuck 'til morning's light."

"So who won?" she asked, giddy from her performance and definitely quite drunk.

"Who cares?" Victor said, grabbing her hand and pulling her to her feet. "It's time to go upstairs."

And then they did, and it was a very good birthday indeed.

About the Author

Leslie Vollard has a longstanding passion for the Middle Ages. Her obsession with all things medieval dates back to college when she dug through archives at the Bibliothèque Nationale in Paris to study the 12th century troubadour, Arnaut Daniel. In her work, she brings courtly love, chivalry, and the troubadour tradition to life. Romance reigns supreme in her steamy novels about how love conquers all.

Leslie lives in Long Island with her delightfully nerdy husband and two cats. She loves gardening, baking, and reading love poems in dead languages.